FROZEN TIDE

FROZEN TIDE

Ren Knopf

ARBOR
AB
BOOKS

Frozen Tide
Copyright © 2007 Ren Knopf
Published by Arbor Books Inc.

This is a work of fiction. Names, characters, places, and incidents either are the product of the author's imagination or are used fictitiously, and any resemblance to actual persons, living or dead, business establishments, events, or locales is entirely coincidental.

For further information please contact:

Book design by:
Arbor Books, Inc.
www.arborbooks.com

Printed in the United States

Frozen Tide
Ren Knopf

1. Title 2. Author 3. Fiction

Library of Congress Control Number: 2007923080

ISBN 10: 0-9790469-8-X
ISBN 13: 978-0-9790469-8-8

Dedicated to The Maverick Club, with special thanks to Mike Knopf and Mark Messina.

Chapter One

"Rogue wave!"

Nate Reid buried his face into a pair of icy, wet gloves and turned with the wind to let a freezing wall of water slap his back and shove him across the sheet of ice that covered the deck of the *Westender*. The instant the sea retreated Nate turned in its face. Amidst 25 mile-per-hour winds and a thick curtain of sleet, he could barely see the other deckhands, let alone the buoy on crab pot 33.

A searchlight blasted an opaque beam through the night sky and bobbed off buoy 33 on the open sea just yards from the edge of the 130-foot crab ship. Nate stared down the beam, refusing to blink amidst the veil of sleet that tore at his pupils. He dug his feet into the frozen deck below, forcing his legs to move forward on the slick floor against angry winds that fought to push him backwards.

Nate's shins felt like splintering old two-by-fours, but he pressed against them, lurching forward. His knees burned and his teeth clamped into a maniacal grin, biting down amidst each cold punch the wind threw at him. He kept his eyes on the beam.

"Come on, thirty-three's coming in!" a disembodied voice shouted. A gloved hand appeared from the darkness.

Deck boss Ian Coleson grabbed Nate's wrist and yanked him

into the railing of the ship. Before Nate could blink, a 700-pound steel cage swung into view directly over his head. The giant crab pot crawled with massive spiny spiders and Nate saw dollar signs in each one. He immediately snapped into motion.

Nate attacked the cage with a predatory pounce and with Ian's help, pulled it toward the deck. He forced his aching shoulders to swing the heavy pot into position in spite of their painful spasms. With an abrupt jab, he helped Ian slam the cage on board, knocking a bounty of Opilio crabs from their steel trap.

Hundreds of crabs slid across a metal countertop onboard and deckhands raced to the harvest, plucking and measuring the creatures, tossing the smaller animals back into the black, arctic night and feeding the larger ones to the boat's colossal holding tank.

Nate's eyes glowed pink and glossed with sleep, but they still searched for every male crab that measured more than six inches in length. He counted them off and then threw his face toward the sea again to scan its choppy waves for the next buoy.

"Thirty-four!" he shouted to the deckhands.

"I'm on it." Ian raced to his side, grabbing the heavy grappling hook used to snag the pot.

The *Westender* pitched, enduring each violent wave that swelled beneath it, and Nate disciplined himself to keep his stare forward, at the buoy. He watched Ian toss the hook toward the next crab pot with his body pressed against a slight metal railing encased in a thick layer of white ice. But the wind stole Ian's rope, and Nate tried to remain patient. Then he took his eyes off the buoy.

While Nate waited for the crane to reveal the steel cage, his eyes began to drift deep into the distance in search of the buoy that must have been swallowed by the sea. A muted voice echoed in his mind, begging him to land his gaze on something—anything, but sleep made his eyes scan the invisible blackness of the sea, and his body give in to the numbness of the frozen rain around him. Soon he began to sway with the feral rocking of the waves.

"Nate, heads up! Look out!" Ian's voice barely reached him when a 30-foot wave built of what looked like tar and ice, roared toward him, erasing everything from his view. Stunned and disoriented, Nate threw his body toward the deck. He crashed into the steel crab pot and felt it tear through his immersion suit directly into the skin on his elbow. He tried to jump to his feet, but a second wave crashed overhead and swept him and the pot from the ship.

The wind swung the giant contraption like a child's toy, high off the deck and back toward the water. Nate shut his eyes and clung to the pot, feeling naked and blind as he swayed over the cruel sea. A gale whipped the cage with another violent tug and Nate could no longer hear the familiar whirr of the ship's engines. He forced his head down against the frozen metal and opened his eyes to reveal a black hole of endless ocean, just waiting to swallow him.

He looked in the distance at the *Westender* and pushed his head up, toward the amber rope that secured the crab pot to the ship's crane. Nate followed the yellow line as it disappeared into the darkness, and noticed the slack on the line increase until the rope wobbled and twisted wildly in the night sky. With just a barely audible crack as its warning, the bristly rope sentenced him to the wicked waters of the Bering Sea.

The instant Nate's body plunged into the sea, his greedy lungs gasped, filling with icy water. Nate wheezed and pulled his torso above sea level. He heaved the sea from his burning lungs and tried to keep his head above water. And his eyes finally opened into the bright searchlight from the *Westender's* bow.

Nate adjusted his vision through the piercing light until he could make out two figures bustling on deck. He tried to focus on the silhouettes, but his entire body began to shudder. His arms and legs floundered and his teeth chattered so hard that they felt like they would fall to pieces.

Barely coherent, Nate watched a blurry ring buoy descend upon him. Without thinking, he threw his arms up high to let the lifeline descend across his palms. The rope landed directly on his hands, yet he did not feel it; his mind could not convince his numb fingers to close around it.

Nate's outstretched arms caused him to plunge like dead weight under the water and his legs had begun to warm into its frigid hold. His eyes could see the ring above him, bobbing and fishing for his body. He kicked his legs and pumped his arms, but went nowhere. Then a final moment of clarity told him that only his mind had done the swimming and his limbs had long ceased to move. The *Westender* began to disappear from sight as Nate watched himself sink deeper into the Bering Sea.

"Nathan!" Sarah shrieked into the darkness and her body jumped from underneath a warm sea of heavy, wool blankets. She tumbled off the bed and slammed onto the hard wooden floor two feet beneath.

Shocked at the sensation of her knees banging into knotty oak, Sarah padded the floor with her hands and tried to regain consciousness. Poised on all fours, she took loud, deep breaths. A cramp in her diaphragm and a dry, stiff throat told her that she had hyperventilated through the same dream again.

Sarah tore the blankets from her torso and kicked her legs against the sheets that entangled them. Once free, she thrust the blankets aside and huffed heavy puffs of breath that ordered her long, ash-blonde hair from her face. She took a careful stand in the dark and watched the red and green stars clear from her eyes until they settled on the ghostly silhouettes of her furniture and belongings.

The autumn breeze outside gave a coy howl and she felt a

cold dry gust creep directly through her bedroom wall. It coaxed her skin into goose bumps, making her hug her toned shoulders with dry fingers that crackled along the soft skin. After rubbing her arms vigorously, she pulled a blanket from the floor and wore it as a cape, then counted thirteen steps to the opposite side of her bedroom. Her foot had barely grazed the rough base of her unfinished bureau when she glided her fingers across its surface, feeling for the smooth shellac of her desk, and finally the warmth of her computer.

Sarah throttled her wireless mouse with her right hand while waving her left hand behind her in search of a chair. Her enrobed body balanced in an awkward position when her computer awoke, stabbing her eyes with a bright screen that was momentarily impossible to see.

A royal-blue website came into focus, reading, "Alaska Departments of Fish and Game Homepage." Sarah clicked her way toward the latest news on the crab fishing season and crossed her fingers while her other hand scrolled for the date the season would end. Her fingers fell limp when she read, "Crab season still in effect until further notice. Last time checked on this computer: 03:49 a.m." The clock on her computer screen blinked 4:26 a.m.

"No use pretending to sleep anymore," she admitted to the empty room.

Under the glow of her computer, Sarah stepped around her bulky oak dresser and braced herself for the frigid breeze that threatened to assault her the second she opened her bedroom door.

"Just get it over with." She gripped her rusted doorknob and thrust the door open, accepting the full brunt of the icy blast.

In spite of a vigilant case of the shivers, she crept down the hallway guided by a halo of light that emanated off her computer monitor. The only upstairs window rested just outside her bedroom, and it revealed nothing of Dutch Harbor in the darkness of an early Alaskan morning. Nevertheless, Sarah brushed a thin coating of frost from inside the glass and leaned into the casement to see the gentle orange glow of the streetlight in front of the volunteer fire department. Even they were still asleep.

Sarah hoisted her heavy blanket over her shoulders and lifted the bottom, exposing her feet to the rush of air that wafted through the rickety floorboards where she stood. She took a sharp preparatory breath and then stampeded down the hallway to the tavern below. Although she weighed slightly less than 120 pounds, the skeletal wooden staircase creaked and complained at the weight, biting her feet with its icy steps in retaliation.

"Son of a bitch!" Sarah plopped to the ground clutching her right toe after smashing it into a full beer keg that rested at the bottom of the staircase. "I'm too old for this creeping-around-your-bar shit, Jack."

Sarah hobbled twenty-six steps to the center of the tavern with her arms stretched outward like a zombie. She grabbed for the cold copper railing of the bar's countertop and followed it into the darkness until she reached its end. Then she punched her left hand down, striking the light switch exactly where she predicted it stood, illuminating the only light dim enough not to shock her dilated pupils.

A rope of neon light let out a deafening buzz in the desolate bar and broadcast the name, "The Wheelhouse."

"We're opening early today, Jack," she said to the sign as she took a seat at the bar. "Twelve years taking care of your watering hole while you're out fishing should earn me a glass of morning brandy, Captain—lucky for you, I don't drink."

Sarah reached around the bar and pulled out a tin drum of Bloody Mary mix, yanked a glass from over her head, and poured herself a tall virgin cocktail. Before taking the first sip, she turned to face the framed photo she had awoken to in the middle of every night—since the beginning of the red king crab season on October 15.

"Cheers, Captain." She lifted her glass to the photo of Captain Jonathan "Jack" Samuelsson standing proudly beside the *Westender*, his 130-foot house aft fishing vessel.

Six men lined up next to Jack, comprising the first crew ever to work Jack's first and only ship. Although the captain had aged twenty years from the forty-year-old man he was in the photo, he still wore the same crazy, cocked smile on a face full of thick stubble. At just more than five and a half feet tall, he almost matched Sarah's height, but he stood on a strong, stocky frame behind a shell of tough, bronze skin that protected him from the Alaskan winds.

In the picture, Jack's crew was made up of four deckhands, two of whom moved to their own vessels in the passing years, one who didn't have the guts to return for another season, and one hard worker whose fishing career would come to an untimely end ten years after the photo was taken. The ship's first engineer would meet the same unfortunate fate. The final fisherman in the picture looked like a baby standing among giants. Greenhorn Ian Coleson was only eighteen years old when he took his first winter voyage into the Bering Sea.

"God bless you and the *Adrienne Anne*—traitor." Sarah gulped a mouthful of bloody mix and stared through the picture into Ian's naïve green eyes.

Minutes passed and Sarah's tired gaze dragged underneath the photo to meet a collection of loose pictures taken within the past five years. Jack had barely aged on the wall-side gallery but her baby brother, Nate, had grown from an infant to a man. Sarah noticed that at age 19, Nate bore a striking resemblance to Ian, wide-eyed and carefree, with an expression of naïve excitement across his face.

By 5:30 a.m., the morning sun gave a muted effort to light the neglected horizon of Dutch Harbor, but Sarah couldn't help but repeatedly flash back to her earlier nightmare. Two hours later, amidst the outdoor bustling of morning traffic, she lowered her eyelids and surrendered to a prayer for her baby brother on his first journey as a greenhorn aboard the *Westender* in the ruthless Bering Sea.

Chapter Two

"Hey, Bait Boy, lift your head out of that chum bucket for a minute and get over here!"

"What now, Josh?" Nate tried not to break his concentration after he had finally gotten into the rhythm of chopping stale cod.

"You're kinda' friendly with the Captain, eh?"

"Yeah, so?"

"So the other deck hands and I think he might be out of his gourd. Think you can put down those fish guts for a minute and go talk to him?"

"Oh sure, I stop my grunt work and the pots go un-baited. Then I piss-off the guys again and you're throwing raw cod in my bunk. I get four hours of sleep a week, asshole. And I'd like it in clean bunk."

"Believe me, nothing you can do today will get those guys any more pissed than they already are at Captain Jack up there—they're ready to chop him up and use him for bait."

"You're the deck boss, you go talk to him," Nate said.

"Believe me, I have. And if I go up to that wheelhouse one more time bitching that we're heading damn close to fished-out waters, he'll throw me overboard."

"So you want me to go bitch for you?"

"You've got that cute, newbie look about you. Now how could he be mad at that face?"

Josh grabbed Nate's face and shook it hard enough that it caused him to wobble off balance. He waited for Nate to right himself before continuing. "It's not just for me, Greenhorn. It's for all of us out here. We'd love to just follow Jack's lead, but we're risking our necks out on that frozen deck pulling pots for no damn catch. Our last pot brought in thirty-three crabs after a day's soak and almost all of them were golden crab, so we had to toss 'em back. Braxton and Rodriguez haven't slept in three days, working their asses off trying to get their hands on some profit. The Game Department's gonna call the season and we'll all go home empty-handed if we don't get the hell out of this wasteland. Come on, Nate, just talk to the guy."

"Alright fine, your wussy-ness, whatever you say."

Nate shook his hands free of slimy bait and trudged up the slick metal staircase to the wheelhouse, overemphasizing each ache that tore through his exhausted muscles while Josh and the other deck hands watched.

Upon entering Jack's sanctuary, he was awarded with a disappointing waft of diesel heat that fed the enclosed cockpit of the vessel.

"Good morning, Nathan," Jack said without taking his eyes off the horizon.

"How'd you know it was me?"

"You smell like a bait boy, even out here. Take a seat."

Nate remained standing. "The guys think you're, well, Josh said the others wanted me to tell you that the guys are a little…"

"Off like a Band-Aid, Nate, what's on your mind?"

"The guys think you're friggin' nuts, Jack."

"Well now, tell me how they really feel." He crunched down on the same soggy cigar that rested in his mouth since the beginning of their journey, two weeks earlier.

"They don't know why you're steering us straight into waters that are already dry, I mean, fished-out. Honestly, I don't get it either. The crab tank's barely half full and we haven't pulled up a decent catch all day. We're losing money. And I thought you said this year was, 'The Year.'"

"I say that every year, kid. In fact, your sister's just about ready to kill me if I mention it again." Jack chewed on his cigar. "But this really is the year, I can feel it. The crabs know it too, that's why they're playing hard-to-get. I've been following those ugly little crawly bastards for the past few seasons now. I've also been watching that weather site Sarah showed me last year, and the red king crab's been migrating. That fished-out wasteland those guys are whining about is reseeded. We're heading north for the catch of our lives.

And dammit, if I don't collect enough cash to get the hell out of Dutch Harbor this year, I'll...well, I'll stop scaring your sister with my yearly promise to leave my bar in Alaska for a pretty girl on a tropical island."

"So there is something up that cigar-burned sleeve of yours, huh old man?" Nate took a seat.

"Yeah, of course there is. The *Westender* and I have been plowing through this bitch of sea for close to twenty years—and I toughed it out for more than a decade before as a deckhand. So I wouldn't leave the guys high and dry—I'm not nuts, kid."

"So you'd just pack up and leave all this for Hawaii?"

"Well, I got a reputation to protect, don't I? If I don't live up to my word one of these years, I'm just a rambling old fisherman."

"And you'd leave without a goodbye? What about the *Westender*? You couldn't leave it to Josh, he'd just run her into the bottom of the sea. And Sarah wouldn't run your bar without you—she doesn't even drink."

"It's a pipe dream, kid, don't overthink it." He checked his GPS and looked into the horizon.

"You are a brave man. When I told Sarah I was even thinking

11

of using my pay this year to check out the California coast, she nearly annihilated me with—that look. She's dead set on my saving that dough for college. I swear she thinks she's my friggin' mom."

"Well, it's not a bad idea."

"Neither is cashing it in for a surfboard and some sun for a change. Sarah's just pissed because she's pushing 30 and still stuck in your bar downloading her education from Bumfuck Online University. She's probably back home getting e-ordained at this very moment."

"You know, having a minister in a family of crab fisherman ain't so bad, Greenhorn." Jack leaned forward in his seat and tapped at the screen on his GPS. "Now get your scrawny butt on deck and tell the boys to wake the hell up and get those crab pots ready. We're gonna hit pay dirt in T-minus right damn now."

Nate flew out of the wheelhouse, jumped three stairs, and stuck an impressive landing on the icy deck that got the attention of deck hands Rodriguez and Braxton. He relayed Jack's message and the men mustered up enough of a second wind to call the other two deck hands to duty and begin the arduous task of chucking crab pots into the sea at their captain's command. The ship held 150 steel cages onboard and the crew threw them at what they had dubbed "ground-zero"—the most uninhabited area of the Bering Sea.

After the last of the baited pots sank out of sight, the men seeped below deck and crawled into cramped quarters to catch what little sleep they could while they waited for their prey to unwittingly creep into the 49 square-foot cages. While they slept, a message flew across the airwaves from the Alaska Fish and Game Department directly to Jack's radio in the helm of the *Westender*. The season would end in two days.

"Wake the hell up! It's crunch time!" Jack's voice boomed belowdecks, waking his crew from a dead sleep.

Nate was the first to hit the galley and grab for the can of instant coffee.

"No time, kid, we've got to lift those pots and drop some more," Jack said.

"But they've only been in a few minutes."

"A few minutes? Sleep's got the best of you, rookie. It's been five hours." Jack grabbed the coffee can and dumped a handful of grounds into a nearby dirty mug. He added tepid water and stirred the concoction with his index finger. "Drink up and get out there baiting. And for the love of God, get your immersion suit back on—you want to freeze to death out there?"

Nate hobbled on deck halfway between his immersion suit and sleep, only to find four deck hands already sliding across the ship to their first pot, which dangled from the *Westender's* giant crane.

"Hey, newbie, get your ass over to that cod pronto. We'll need more pots after we pull these up." Josh said.

"What?" Nate rubbed a fresh coat of icy spray from his eyes to reveal crab pot 126 nearly bursting at the seams with an awesome bounty of gigantic king crabs.

"I take back everything I said about Jack Samuelsson." Rodriguez shoved Nate forward with two tough slaps to the back.

"One-zero-four—A hundred four!" Josh called through the ship's intercom, reporting the number of usable king crabs in pot 126.

"Over a hundred in a pot that's only soaked for five hours—is he serious?"

"Believe it, Greenhorn," Rodriguez said.

"And bait those damned traps, you slow son of a bitch." Josh tried to sound stern, but the goofy grin on his face betrayed him.

Jack sailed the *Westender* through the night, ordering his men to drop pots at strategic locations along the way. With each pot that came out of the water, his men became increasingly excited, wired at the thought of topping off the boat's 300,000-pound capacity crab tank with profitable bounty in just hours.

By 6 o'clock a.m., a reluctant sun in Alaska's January glazed the morning horizon to reveal a crew of fishermen taking their first break from a frantic pace. The ship's engines growled as the boat started to change direction.

"Hey Jack, don't quit on us now—We can't be over our limit. Hell, we'll store the crabs in the damn galley if we have to," Josh said.

"You can use my bunk, if it helps," Nate added.

"Sorry to spoil the party, guys, but it looks like we've just about reached our boundaries." Jack pointed to the silhouette of an expansive oil tanker toward the north.

"What the hell is that thing?" Nate said.

"Meet Odin Energy, gentlemen."

"You mean 'The Man'. I hate those guys."

"Me too, kid. But that damn tanker will end up saving everyone some money if they find an alternative fuel source out there—something better than fish oil, at least."

"They'd better hurry the hell up, 'cause as far as I'm concerned, they're just constipating our catch," Rodriguez said.

"How much space to we have to give that tanker? We've got at least a dozen pots ready to go and I for one don't want to waste my finely-chopped cod guts."

"If we get too close, Odin will call the Coast Guard and we'll waste our last few hours buried in paperwork." Jack gave his stubble a long scratch and hung his head as if he could see through the boat's deck, directly into the crab tank below. "I suppose it wouldn't hurt to fish around the perimeter of the rig, but I can't guarantee a better catch than what we've already got. That tanker's been squatting out there for a while. The crabs are probably worse as we get closer, but the law does say they can only keep us a couple miles away until the season is over."

"At that tiny distance, why bother zoning at all?" Rodriguez said.

"Nobody expected a fishing rig out this far." Jack paused, then said, "What the hell, let's drop those damn pots and let's quit wasting Nate's fish guts."

Jack ran up to the wheelhouse with the gait of a man half his age and coaxed his ship to ease back toward Odin's perimeter.

"Keep it slow, Jack, no hurry," Nate whispered to himself, watching the daunting tanker grow as they approached it.

The *Westender* reached its boundary in no time and the other deck hands had joined Nate to gape at the giant vessel.

"I'm no science brainy-brain, but—that's a research vessel?" Rodriguez broke the silence.

"I'm a shit-ton smarter than you, partner, and it doesn't look like a geeky science lab to me either," Braxton said.

"That's 'The Man' for ya. 'The Man's' gotta do everything big time cuz he's got no…"

"You guys heard Jack, start dropping some crab pots. Brax and Eber, swing pot one into place and get ready for my signal— and Nate, shut up about 'The Man.'"

The expansive steel cage slid into the water prompted by a shove from the two deck hands. The second a splash confirmed its descent, they spun around to continue working, but were stopped in their tracks by Josh, who signaled to them while peering so far overboard, it looked like he would jump.

"Hold up, I lost the buoy!" Josh screamed over roaring engines and crashing waves.

"Now who's slowing us down?" Rodriguez said.

"Can anyone see the buoy? For Christ's sake, we just dropped it."

"I think it sunk, boss." Braxton joined the others. "Think we got a bum buoy?"

"Guys, leave it. The next pot's ready to go."

"You don't just leave a ghost pot, rookie. They trap and kill crabs—you might as well just dump cash into the ocean and leave it." Josh said.

The four men stood over the sunken pot for several minutes until they heard the telltale signs that Jack was slowing the boat.

"What's the distraction now?" Jack left the wheelhouse and strode toward the others.

"Something funny's going on, Captain. We lost the buoy on the first pot—it just went under."

"It's a bum buoy, Josh. It'd be a waste of time to fish for it. I'll push up a little and you guys prep pot two."

The men hurried into position and poised pot two to plunge into the water while Jack headed aft to the wheelhouse. Nate's eyes bobbed from the crab pot to the tanker, and back down to where their ghost pot had sunken. Then he stared into the area where the next pot would land.

"Jack, wait!" Nick shouted. "You have to see this!"

The men steadied the crab pot on the deck and Jack followed Nate's finger toward the gurgling body of water beneath.

"Looks like the sea's carbonated." Braxton said.

Jack helped the five men push the pot aside and peered over the edge of the boat to gape at what looked like a sea turned to cola. They were soon joined by engineer Mark Watson, who had spent most of the trip keeping the ship's largest crane in working order.

"Now it looks like the sea's got rabies," Josh said.

"Watson, is something leaking?" Rodriguez said.

"You got me stumped. But whatever's happening, it's getting worse."

"I'd call it a cold fog, but I don't feel any ice spray." Jack inhaled, searching for the freezing spray that would stand his nose hairs at attention, but succeeded in triggering a violent coughing fit instead. When the fit was over, he stared into his cupped hands.

"Oh, Jesus, it can't be..." Jack looked up at the crew. "Get the hell off the deck! Go below!"

Nate jumped at Jack's booming voice, catching his wild eyes for a moment before he raced aft like a man on fire. The deck hands abandoned their crab pot and stampeded across the deck to get below. Meanwhile Nate's eyes transfixed on the line attached to the ghost pot. Even though it was several yards away, he saw it jerk violently before it sunk out of site. The boat pitched a fit simultaneously under increasing air bubbles that shot to the surface like a geyser. The air grew dense and began to stab Nate's lungs with each breath.

"Nate, come on!" Josh called to him from a few steps away.

Nate turned to follow the others, catching sight of their bright orange immersion suits heading below deck at a painfully slow pace. He began to understand their gait as he also found the walk to the stairs impossible, using lungs that refused to take air. Black blotches crept into Nate's peripheral vision. Then everything went black.

Chapter Three

"Sarah, wake up," a voice whispered.

Sarah buried her head further into her crossed arms and leaned over the railing into the counter of the bar, making sure she covered her ears. Warm breath replaced the fresh air that seeped around her arms until breathing became arduous and she had to awaken.

"What do you want?" Sarah spoke into the bar without lifting her head.

"Is that all the welcome I get after two weeks working the most hazardous job on the planet?"

"Ian?" Sarah lifted her head and squinted into the sunlight.

"Have a nice nap?"

Sarah's eyes nestled in Ian's childlike smile and she instinctively threw her arms around him in a crushing hug.

"Wow, hold me any closer and people will think we're back together."

"Don't read into it, you jerk. I'm just happy you're alive and in one piece."

"Yeah, I wish I could say the same for the *Adrienne Anne*. We took her in a couple days early after we lost our crane again. Then we had some engine trouble and our fuel pump started getting cranky. But all in all, it was a pretty good season, considering. Okay, I admit it, I had to duck out for the big weigh-in at the fishery yesterday and grab some sleep. I'll cry over my miniscule paycheck later."

"Nobody else is back yet then?"

"The *Westender*'s not back, if that's what you mean. But the other boats have been trickling in since this morning. The Grand Aleutian Hotel is already filling up with Japanese buyers, so they'll be chomping at the bit by the time Jack and the boys make it in—fashionably late, of course."

Ian stretched over the bar to swipe a stale cup of coffee. "Jesus, Sarah, have you stayed up every night this season?"

"No, of course not. Losing sleep is your job. I just got up this morning to get the bar ready. From what you're telling me, we're gonna need more booze for the locals if our rich Asian guests are sucking up all the good stuff downtown."

"Uh huh, is that why I see half-empty bottles behind the bar and about eight Bloody Mary-stained glasses in the sink?"

"I was just about to…"

"I know you Sarah. I bet if I go upstairs to your loft, it'll be covered in fishing maps, weather charts, and…let's see…the Alaska Department of Fish and Game bulletins?"

"He's my brother, Ian. And Jack's closer than family too. And unlike some people, I'd rather risk a messy room and some sleepless nights than turn my back on the people I care about."

"Don't get me wrong, I think it's great that you keep track of the season like you do. Of course, if you really wanted to put your money where your mouth is, you'd quit calling the kettle black and get your ass back out there with the rest of us."

"Don't go there, Ian." Sarah stepped back, holding his gaze with glossy brown eyes. Suddenly aware of her appearance, she tucked her T-shirt into her jeans and whisked her hair into a knot on the back of her head that began to immediately unwind into a fury of blonde locks.

"I'm sorry, Sarah. I didn't mean to..."

"Whatever, Ian. Welcome home." She repositioned her hair and turned toward Jack's office at the far corner of the tavern.

"From what I heard, the *Westender* was doing better than all of us put together."

Sarah stopped with her back toward Ian.

"Brian radioed Jack from the *Adrienne Anne* a few days ago. He said Jack was having the catch of his life, following a new crab migration pattern—a theory he got from an Internet-addicted bar maid who cross-referenced fishing routes with weather patterns and added plate tectonics and global warming to the mix." He waited. "You're a fisherman, Sarah, admit it."

Sarah stood speechless in the center of the tavern. She felt a thick knot of hair spring free and bound across her shoulder blades. By the time she turned to face Ian through her mane, the large wooden door of The Wheelhouse was creaking behind him.

Chapter Four

"*Westender*, this is Odin research vessel, *Asgard*. You must move your ship from this area immediately."

The *Westender* replied with silence.

"*Westender*, you must move your ship, or we will have to take action. Repeat—move your vessel immediately."

"There's still no answer," The *Asgard's* Chief Mate, Brenda Anderson, reported to Captain Peter Ivanov.

"Then something's wrong out there. The fishing season is over as of yesterday and that boat's damn far from the Aleutian Islands."

"We were told nobody would fish anywhere near here. Should we call the Coast Guard?"

"No." Ivanov stared at the distant ship with icy blue eyes. "Kell Odin ordered any obstruction to be dealt with efficiently and quietly, without inquiry and bureaucracy from the Coast Guard. This research is delicate—and who knows what that fishing vessel has destroyed, sitting out there like that. We'll get our own security team up here immediately and take care of this matter ourselves."

"Should we contact Mr. Odin about this as well?"

"That's definitely a negative. He's meeting with the other oil gods in Juneau for the next few days about the governor's

Natural Gas Pipeline Contract. It won't look good if he leaves the summit and we're counting on that conference for more funding."

"So he's coming back here pretty soon to report on that meeting?"

"Yes, Anderson. Why do you think I want security up here now?"

"Aye, Sir. Security is online and awaiting your orders."

Ivanov snatched the radio and barked succinct orders to Kell Odin's handpicked security team. The team comprised four experts donated from the Chinese People's Liberation Army Navy and their American leader, a turncoat from the US Navy's Special Boat Team.

Upon receiving their captain's orders, the security team boarded one of Odin's rigid inflatable boats and raced to the *Westender*.

"Captain, we've run into a problem," the team leader, Erik Bergen reported minutes after leaving the *Asgard*.

"You haven't even boarded that fishing vessel yet. What could possibly have gone wrong?" Ivanov choked the radio.

"We had to back up a bit, Sir. We have what looks like a leak here."

"The boat is leaking?"

"No, Sir. The sea is."

"What?" Ivanov shared a look of confusion with Brenda Anderson. "Explain your situation."

"It's a gas leak of some sorts. It seems toxic and pretty suffocating. We're awaiting your orders on boarding the *Westender*."

"As long as you have oxygen, I want you on that ship. I'll get Research and Engineering down to that so-called leak. Whatever's going on in the water is none of your concern, understand?"

"Yes sir. We have oxygen—we're circling and boarding the ship on the port side."

22

"Sir, what do you think security was talking about? Do you think the boat had some kind of gas leak?"

"I have no idea, Anderson, and we're both being paid not to care. We have a team of expert engineers and scientists, not to mention Kell's Gestapo at our beck and call. Let them handle the dirty work."

"We're onboard the fishing vessel, Captain." Security reported back within minutes.

"What do you see?"

"There's definitely something wrong here, Sir. The crew seems incapacitated and the boat has been set adrift for some time now. Our team is searching the area and they've so far reported one crab pot dropped on deck and evidence of at least one more in the water close to the boat's position now. It has no marker on it. Judging from damage to the deck and the ship's equipment, it looks like this thing's been tossed around."

"Don't waste any more time investigating what happened on the boat. Just get it out of here. It has to be completely gone before Odin returns for his meeting."

"Are you suggesting demolition, Sir?"

"For the love of God, don't demolish it. It's a fishing boat, for Christ's sake. It's full of civilians." Ivanov paused to run both hands through his balding head of black oily hair, shedding its strands into his clammy palms. "Take it back to port."

"Sir?"

"Find out where that boat came from—probably Dutch Harbor—and get it back there. Buyers are swarming the fisheries down there and they're counting on the bounties those vessels bring in. If this boat doesn't show up with the rest of them, there will be a search party after it, and that's our necks."

"And the crew?"

"Take the *Westender* back by yourself. Send the rest of Security back here."

"I meant the crew of the *Westender*. What do you want me to do with them, Sir?"

Ivanov took the radio away from his face and hung it down by his side. He looked toward Brenda and gave a subtle nod, feeling his heart momentarily pump harder. He took a rattling breath and executed his orders.

At 2:15 a.m., three days after the Alaskan king crab season had ended and one day after the last fishing vessel had docked, the *Westender* quietly sailed into Dutch Harbor. Robert Kennedy worked the fishery alone at that hour and he was the first man to see the ship in the glow of the almost full moon.

Kennedy straightened himself and tried to fake consciousness as the boat approached the dock. It shimmied into a peculiar position for unloading and he punched the intercom, alerting the fishery that the final catch had come in. The large fishing boat cast a spray of orange light on the dock and accentuated the cloud of breath escaping Kennedy's nose and mouth into the frigid night air. He rubbed his hands together and stomped life into his legs while the boat's driver took his time emerging from the wheelhouse.

A tall man finally hopped onto the dock and crept toward him with his head hunched down as if he was mesmerized by his own boots. Kennedy turned his gaze toward the man's footwear as well, and momentarily lost himself in the crackling sound of the boots on raw timber. He began memorizing each step and blaming his exhausted ears for not recognizing their rhythm as the typical beat of fishing boots on the cold dock. As the steps grew closer, Kennedy finally righted himself and searched for the stranger's eyes.

"*Westender*, it's about time. They told me to stay on the lookout for you guys. Where've you been?"

"We had some trouble." The man spoke downward into his chest.

"I guessed that. Most of the migrant workers have gone home for the season, so you'll have to be patient while we unload your crab tank." Kennedy held his clipboard into the closest light on dock and flipped through the pages. "*Westender*...here it is. You're Captain Jonathan Samuelsson then?"

The fisherman fired an index finger at the third name on the *Westender*'s roster.

"Oh, Cliff Braxton. Sorry, I just assumed since you were the one bringing the boat in, you were the captain. Hey, where is the rest of the crew, anyway?"

"Unalaska. We had a long trip and the guys wanted to sleep it off. I drew the short straw."

"Well, like I said, it's late. We've got a fishery full of zombies and newbies, like me, so bear with us. I hope you weren't expecting a quick getaway." Kennedy paused, catching the sailor's glassy stare. "Oh, I didn't mean to insinuate you're not a hard worker..."

"Insinuate. And you don't have to be too careful about unloading. Most of our catch probably bit the dust when we got knocked around and drifted off course. In fact, I'd rather not stay for the tally."

"Embarrassed, huh? Hey, a paycheck's a paycheck is my theory, even if it does come with heavy fines for over-fishing. But I don't know how you migrant workers see it. You probably just want to get the hell out of Alaska—that's common. I just need you to sign a few things while we clean out your ship. Then you can wrap up here and shove off to Unalaska with your crew."

Chapter Five

Sarah stared into the solid maple finishing of the antique boat steering wheel that framed the tavern's only clock. By 11:30 a.m. she had finished oiling the dry wood on the bar's counter for the third time after cleaning and hanging the glasses in descending order above the three different serving stations. For the third day since the *Adrienne Anne's* return, she ordered herself to stay away from early breakfasts made of Bloody Mary mix, but she still hadn't been able to sleep at night.

Entranced with the grooves in the maple frame, Sarah stood motionless with a cold wet rag in one hand and her other hand supporting her weight against the counter behind her. Every time the wind kicked the front door to the tavern, shifting it just centimeters from its frame, she jumped back into consciousness and peeked at the entrance with wide eyes.

"That's enough." Sarah snapped out of her pose and threw the rag at the counter. She marched to the door and grabbed the wrought iron slide lock that would put an end to the wind's mockery.

"Wait, don't lock us out! We'll only drink the cheap stuff, I promise." The unmistakable voice of Captain Brian Eriksson penetrated the door and his large palm slapped into its thick glass window.

"I'm so sorry. I thought you were the wind." Sarah opened the door and let Brian and Ian precede her into the tavern. "Can I get you guys a drink?"

"A drink? Even this old captain can't stomach alcohol before noon. Better make it a Bud. And where the hell is Jack hiding anyway?"

"Jack? What do you mean?"

"Don't tell me he hasn't come in to work yet. You figure a guy as tough as Jack would bounce back from the season and get his ass down to the bar. He's got three days of no drinks to make up for."

"Ian, the *Westender* isn't back yet. Jesus, you told me yourself Jack was running late." Sarah withheld two cold Budweiser's. "Maybe you don't need a drink after all."

"Ian's not nuts, kid. The *Westender* came back last night at 2 a.m. Now I'll take my Bud with a glass because I'm classy."

"Wait a minute, if the boat's back, where's the crew?"

"Well, it did come back pretty late, and from what I heard from Paul at the dock this morning, it was hurting. I'm no Jack Samuelsson, but if I brought the *Adrienne Anne* back late in that kind of shape, I'd want a day off too."

"Unlike you Brian, I totally understand Sarah's beef." Ian toasted his bottle to her. "She's got a lot of stocking up to do if The Wheelhouse is gonna open tonight. I'd be damn salty if I was here working my butt off and Jack didn't make it back before opening time at…seven?"

"Nine, Ian. We open at nine on the day everyone's back, just like every other year."

"Neither of you should have a beef with Jack. I've known the guy since both our boats were just piles of timber. In fact, he's probably at the dock right now cleaning his baby up.

You know, Sarah, it wouldn't hurt you to get a good nap in

before nine. You look more beat than my new bait guy this year." Brian shared a laugh with Ian. "Now we'll get out of your hair and let you relax a little."

The guys finished their drinks and swept the bottles into the sink along with two unused pint glasses. Brian gave a wink and Ian stared too long at Sarah before turning for the door.

"We'll be back at nine," Ian said. "And don't spend your whole day greasing that bar—the guys have enough trouble holding on to their drinks without your oil slick getting in the way."

The high pitched chirp of Sarah's phone tore her from a restful nap. Without any windows in her loft, her digital clock reported that she had mistakenly slept for nearly five hours. She reached over the clock that bore 8:15 p.m. into her eyeballs with its bright red lights and picked up her phone.

"It's about damn time!" she answered.

"Ms. Reid, this is Paul Dorsey from the fishery. We've been trying to reach Jack Samuelsson."

Sarah sat up feeling her face flush with embarrassment. "I'm so sorry Paul. I thought you were my brother. You got the upstairs line—did you try calling down to the bar?"

"No answer. Listen, I got the Coast Guard breathing down my neck here. Apparently the second shift guy let Jack dock his boat right in the shipping lane last night and we've got freighters coming to pick up their containers. You tell Jack he's got about ten minutes to get his ass down here before we impound his boat."

"Can you even impound a boat?" Sarah yawned. "Don't worry about it Paul, I'll find Jack."

Sarah put down the receiver of her old corded phone and immediately picked it back up to dial Ian's number.

"Dammit, Ian, pick up the phone!" She waited through six

rings until his answering machine picked up, then threw her phone back in its cradle. "You owe me again, Jack."

In the darkness, Sarah stepped out of bed and ran her hands across its foot in search of her scratchy wool sweater. She plucked the garment from a freezing pile of laundry and pulled it over her head amidst a dazzling display of static cling. She shuffled to the doorway and pulled a pair of mouton-fur mukluks over her feet, forcing the ends of her jeans inside.

After a lock check, Sarah hopped into her 1994 Ford Festiva and cajoled it to run. The fan belt on the car's heater let out a screech as she cranked up the heat and skidded onto the road. She pulled her hands into her wooly sleeves to avoid the biting cold left on her steering wheel. But just as the needle began to ascend from cold to warm and the heat began to kick in, she was already pulling in to the fishery.

"Sarah? I was expecting Jack." Paul spoke through the window of the car.

"You might see Elvis first." She turned off the engine and followed Paul to the dock.

"Well, here it is—the *Westender* in all its glory. Right out in the middle of the damn harbor."

"Don't get all pissy with me Paul, I didn't leave it here. Jesus, she looks like hell. What'd you guys do to her?"

"The night guy said she came in like this. In Jack's defense, he didn't dock her. Some deckhand took it back. His name's on the list here…Cliff Braxton ring a bell?"

"Braxton? Isn't he the one who looks like Geddy Lee?"

"You know him then?"

"No, not at all. He's a migrant guy Jack hired for the season. He might have worked on the Nor'easter last year."

"Well, since ol' Geddy isn't here to defend himself, let's just call this Jack's snafu and get this boat taken care of."

"I can move her for you, but Paul, has anyone seen Jack? I mean, did he even show up for the weigh-in?"

"I figure he must have, with a catch like that. My guess is he took the money and ran."

"I don't get it."

"Well first, the boat comes in three days late with some migrant guy at the helm. Then the guy leaves while they're cleaning out Jack's crab tank. He brought in the most enormous bounty of king crab I've even seen in one season and we're starting to piece together Jack's little plan. He hit the jackpot on that catch and by the looks of the boat, he decided to finally cut his losses and head for the tropics. I just wish he'd moved her first."

Sarah bypassed Paul and strode directly for the *Westender*, which wasn't docked very far from the receiving area. She slunk her hands back into the sleeves of her sweater and held on to the icy railing of the boat's port side as she carefully boarded. The boat swallowed her foot with her first step onto its deck and she nearly dropped on her face. Sarah looked back to see that the flooring in several areas had been torn. She tried to kick free from the gap in the floorboards and her foot was awarded back to her sans boot.

"What the hell happened, Jack?" She whispered to herself, rubbing the sore ankle that had plunged through the floor. She plucked the boot from the greedy deck and pulled it back on with a hefty tug, throwing her head back in pain as it ground over the knot in her ankle. Sitting on her butt looking up from the deck, she saw the crane loom overhead. It held the line and buoy of crab pot number two.

"Hey Sarah, keep sleeping on the job and we'll never get that bar open!"

Sarah craned her neck to see Ian's messy brown hair wisp in the wind. Although he was pushing forty, his face was illuminated by a boyish grin.

"Is that all you think about, you alkie? Give me some help up here." She shouted back.

Sarah kept her eyes on the deck and steadied herself against a tower of crab pots to ensure safe footing. Moments later, Ian bounded on the boat, catching himself just before he landed in the same gash that had captured Sarah's foot.

"Well, this old girl's looked better...I meant the boat, not you."

"I got that, Ian. I'm also getting a little more than worried. Paul said Jack got the catch of a lifetime and had a deckhand bring the boat back. And look at this ship. The deck is torn and full of junk crab carcasses and the crane looks like it lost pot two."

"Looks more like pot two hit the deck." Ian inspected the torn flooring. "That's why this thing is so torn up right here." He looked up at the crane. "See? The line got tangled and ripped off the crane and the pot crashed down on deck. The sea didn't tear this boat up, her own equipment did."

"Great, well that still doesn't clear anything up. If a pot hit the deck, why didn't the guys just haul it over to the rest of the pots? And since when does Jack bring home a broken crane? Watson's one of the best fix-it guys there is and he didn't bother to fix a tangle?"

"Hey, don't ask me. I've never been able to figure out Jack. But if I had to take a guess, going by my experience in the business, I'd say what happened here is the last straw. You said it yourself, Jack was having the catch of his life, then something mechanical must have gone wrong and he had a bear of a time getting the ship back. That'd be enough of a sign for me to retire after how many years?"

"At least 35 for Jack. Twenty on the *Westender*. You really think Jack just took the cash and left?"

"Honestly, I didn't think he had it in him. But he has been vowing for the past ten years that he's gonna call it quits any day now and leave us with nothing but a postcard from Hawaii. Maybe he did it."

"Come on, Ian, we both know that's just something Jack says."

"He's said it for the past ten years, Sarah. I'd think you'd believe it by now."

"The fact that he's said it every single year is why I don't believe it. He's got plenty of cash. If he really wanted to get out of here, he'd have gone to Hawaii years ago. But I know Jack too. He loves this ship and he loves this town, even though it gets cold here and some people get cold along with it."

"Sure you're still talking about Jack?"

"How did you know I was here, anyway?"

"My Caller ID said you tried to get me, so I went to the bar and checked the messages. I heard Dorsey calling for Jack. I checked your loft but you weren't around, and I noticed those wookie boots of yours were gone...."

"Stalker." Sarah flashed a quick grin before kneeling to the boat's deck.

"Don't." Ian grabbed her arm and eased her back on her feet, staring into her eyes until she looked back toward the floor. "Let me take the boat back, Sarah. You've done enough of Jack's dirty work for one day."

"You just want me to get back and open the bar."

"If a full bar doesn't bring Jack out of the woodwork, then at least we can finally celebrate his retirement in style."

Chapter Six

"Well, it looks like Ian's enjoying a nice Jack Daniels coma. You gave him the bottle on purpose, didn't you Sarah?"

"He said he'd get me to love whiskey by last call—and dammit Brian, he's right."

"Masterfully done. We could've used someone like you on the *Adrienne Anne* this season...I'm sorry but I didn't mean..."

"You can talk to me about fishing. I sort of expect it living on Dutch Harbor, running a bar called 'The Wheelhouse'."

"I just never know."

"I do have a question for you though."

"Shoot."

"You've known Jack longer than all of us. Did it strike you as one bit odd that he's not back yet? I mean, he left his boat—his baby—with a deckhand. And he never came back to prep her for the off season. He even got fined—and the boat looked like a bomb hit it."

Brian smiled. "Jack's lucky to have friends like you to worry about him. But the boat came back with a full crab tank and a warm-blooded deckhand. That tells me two things: they caught something out there, and they got back to port intact."

"So you think he just left us for Hawaii without a word?"

"If I was gonna leave this place after forty years of fishing and drinking, that's the only way I could do it. Jack's tough against the wind and the waves, but he's a softie when it comes to the people he cares about—and he's an idiot when it comes to saying goodbye. Don't tell him those last two things." He winked.

"What about my brother? I haven't heard from Nate either. In fact, I haven't heard from any of the crew."

"Who'd want to hear from Josh Redmon?" He laughed. "I'm sure the other guys made it back fine. I've only met Josh and that guy who looks like Geddy Lee, but migrants usually go home to their families after the season. As for Nate…didn't I hear you hounding him about college? No offense, but I wouldn't be surprised if he ducked out for a little R&R before facing his big sister and a four-year sentence at the University of Alaska."

"I wish I could be as optimistic as you are. Everyone partied tonight like there was something to celebrate, and I spent the whole time chugging nothing but water, with a knot in my stomach the size of a crab pot."

"That's just part of being Sarah."

"What do you mean that's just me? You think I'm neurotic?"

"I think you're a compassionate person, kid. I think you worry about everyone around you so you won't have to worry about yourself. You don't drink alcohol because you worry about your father…"

"That's legitimate. Alcoholism is hereditary." She picked up a rag from the bar and began to scrub the counter.

"You download college degree after degree because you're worried about your brother's education. And you're probably going to stay up planning next season's fishing routes for Jack after you play the worst-case scenario in your mind all night."

"You're acting like I'm an obsessive control freak or something." She stopped smudging the rag around the clean bar.

"Hey, if I ever went through what you guys did those years

ago, I'd worry too. And if I don't get a postcard from Hawaii soon, I will get a little salty. But you…you're not crazy and you're not a nag, Sarah. You're just…"

"Tired." She forced a smile. "You think you can get Ian home tonight?"

He looked at their lifeless friend strewn across four bar stools. "No problem, kid. But you have to promise to get some shuteye tonight. You're putting us crab guys to shame."

"Eight hours, Captain—I promise."

"I guess I wouldn't be me if I slept through the night," Sarah said to her empty loft. She threw her hands in front of her and made her way in the dark to her bedroom door. Since she hadn't bothered to change out of her jeans and sweater, the journey downstairs to the bar was no challenge at all.

Sarah flicked on the neon light and let her hands scrounge through the shelves underneath the bar until they felt Jack's rolodex through the thick coat of dust that covered it. She brought it into the light and began rifling through the alphabet until her fingers stopped at "Redmon," the only name she recognized from the *Westender's* roster. Sarah's hands reached for the phone, but her eyes settled on the boat-wheel clock that read 3:45 a.m.. She put the receiver back in its cradle, pulled the address from its resting place and stuffed it in her back pocket.

Feeling a familiar knot begin to grow again in her stomach, Sarah slumped backwards into the broad wooden beam that stood in the center of the bar. She tucked her hand in her back pocket, feeling the edges of the address card. Her eyes glossed over to the nearly empty can of Bloody Mary mix, but rested on the bottle of Absolut that would complete the cocktail.

"I can't do this for another night." She clutched thick locks of hair in each hand and pulled them over her face as she

35

slumped to the ground. She leaned to her side and pulled Josh Redmon's phone number from her pocket. With heavy breaths, she tore it into pieces and threw them to the sticky ground beneath her.

Sarah let her eyes search for the vodka bottle again, but as they swept over a case of Sam Adams lager, her mind screamed "Boston." She sprung to her feet and tore through the rolodex in search for Mark Watson, the engineer from Boston who just might be awake at 7:45 Eastern Standard Time. A knot tore her stomach nearly in two when, in the place of Watson's address, she found a pack of matches from Centerfolds strip club in North Oxford, Massachusetts.

The rolodex shattered like glass when it hit the wall twenty feet from where Sarah threw it. She grabbed the drum of cocktail mix and threw a rag over the vodka bottle on her way back up to her computer.

Sarah opened up her web browser and navigated directly to the School of Marine Biology on the University of Hawaii website. She logged in using a student account number from the previous semester.

"DUT5533, how can I help you?" A familiar screen-name appeared.

"Hi, Dr. Kiho. It's me, Sarah Reid. I want to follow up on some questions I asked a few weeks ago about the conditions of the Bering Sea this year."

"Hey, Sarah—I didn't realize my favorite online student was back. Are you signing up for part two of my class?"

"Sorry, Dr. Kiho, I just need to know if conditions were favorable around the migration area we discussed. You know, was the weather good and all that."

"No problem. I could give you a shipload of maritime charts and maps, and I could get you in touch with our

36

meteorology guys. But if you want a quick answer, I recommend satelliteearth.com. It's a few weeks behind real time, but it will give you an actual look at conditions in the area. How did the season go, anyway? Were we right about the catch?"

"The crabs were right where you predicted, but the boat came back looking like a bomb hit it. I just want to know what went down. Will that satellite site give me a good view of the sea's activity?"

"If anything big happened, the satellite will pick up on it. But if it doesn't work for you, feel free to log on and check back with me—I'm here every night running some tests of my own."

"Thanks Dr. Kiho!" She logged off.

Sarah opened a window to www.satelliteearth.com and entered her location. A grainy, black and white picture loaded up within seconds, and she could see her town enrobed in a thick coat of early autumn snow from the previous month, before king crab season had started. She set her account to automatically refresh with each updated photo and let her mouse-hand guide her through an aerial look at Jack's expedition.

Her hand slowed as a large vessel occupied the entire screen. Sarah entered the ship's coordinates into her search engine and was awarded with the name, "Odin Energy." According to her online GPS, the tanker nestled itself on the outskirts of golden king crab territory, splitting the distance between the edge of Jack's itinerary and Russia's Kamchatka Peninsula.

Sarah's favorite web browser swallowed the key word "Odin" and spit out web sites on the position of women in Norway and Norse mythology. She rebutted with the key words "Odin Energy" and found a direct link to its homepage.

The words, "Odin Energy" spun onto the screen in a flash video of vivid color and Sarah skipped the introduction in favor of the corporation's virtual tour. After clicking through three useless screens, she finally caught sight of the Odin research tanker, *Asgard*, the same vessel that engulfed the satellite image on her screen.

Sarah tried not to skip words as she read, but the blinking of her computer monitor against the sleep in her eyes made Odin's mission statement difficult to decipher. From what she could understand, the *Asgard* was a tanker converted into a research ship that conducted studies on the safety of collecting methyl hydrates from the bottom of the Bering Sea. Funded by an exorbitant government grant as well as through private investors, Odin touted that it could put an end to the use of oil platforms that often ran into the paths of icebergs, risking the lives of crews called to move the behemoth structures.

"That looks more dangerous than crab fishing," Sarah said to the computer as her eyes bore into a picture of several men racing through wild storms to move a giant platform. Underneath the picture was a message by owner Kell Odin himself:

Methyl hydrates exist naturally underneath the sea and may be collected through a simple pipeline attached directly to the tankers we use to transport our oil today. In compressed gas or liquid form, methyl hydrates are plentiful and easy to move. Few obstacles keep us from a methane-fueled future, and even they are molehills compared to the treachery that await our competitors whose platforms are built on danger and uncertainty.

The page went on to explain Odin Energy's part in the Alaska Natural Gas Contract. Sarah read until she reached a menu at the bottom of the page. She clicked back to the window displaying the *Asgard* directly in Jack's fishing path, assuring herself that if something had happened to the *Westender* during its trip, the tanker was certainly equipped for a rescue, or it at least could have caught sight of the crab ship safely retrieving its catch and continuing its loop.

Sarah dragged her mouse to the site's menu and clicked on the highlighted words, "Contact Us." A text box popped up on her screen and her fingers began to type. She tested several salutations in the box and ran several versions of her message through her head. But as the sun began to rise at 5:45 a.m., Sarah lifted her fingers from the keyboard, speechless.

Chapter Seven

Peter Ivanov's shoulders stiffened when he heard the unmistakable CT7-8 turbo shaft engines of Kell Odin's S-92 helicopter approaching the *Asgard*. He called the remainder of his security team to greet Odin at the landing pad and cringed as the aircraft touched down on the supertanker.

"That beast was made to land on platforms, not my ship," Ivanov said to Brenda Anderson.

"Don't worry, Captain, I'm sure Bergen didn't say anything to Odin about that fishing boat."

"He better not have—his neck's on the line, too." He wiped his palms on his pants as he watched Odin step down from the helicopter preceded by his guard, Erik Bergen. "I don't know what's worse sometimes, getting caught by the Coast Guard or working under a guy like Kell Odin."

"Odin pays better."

Within minutes, Ivanov could hear Odin's shoes clicking up the metal stairway to the bridge of the *Asgard*. He barked orders at his crew to look busy and stay out of the way as Odin approached, and Brenda Anderson brought up the Alaska Natural Gas Summit on her computer.

"News is good, sir," she whispered into Ivanov's ear just as the door swung open.

Ivanov stood at attention when his boss entered and Bergen turned to leave.

"Wait here, Erik," Kell ordered his guard.

"So, you bring good news from the summit, Sir?" Ivanov said.

"The vote was unanimous. The major oil corporations will receive their share of revenue for the project, Alaskans will have more jobs, and the Alaskan pipeline will expand down the northern slope of the United States to serve the mainland."

"And what about our project? Several of your senior scientists have been anxiously awaiting your arrival. They want to know if they still have jobs."

"I intend to meet with the senior scientists to announce formally that their jobs are secure. Our project received full funding, thanks to the Alaskan government who primed our investors at the summit." Odin seemed taller than five-foot-ten when he stood at attention and spoke with the voice of a politician. "After all, we are the foremost corporation researching the means of extracting methyl hydrates safely from the bottom of the sea—an endeavor that will expand Alaska's energy contribution to the world, in the long-run."

"The Governor is no skeptic, I see."

"Skeptic, Anderson? Who could be skeptical about a little research project while Exxon is spending millions of government moneys to move Hibernia from the path of the North Atlantic iceberg migration? The state and our private investors come out like Mother Theresa funding a mission like ours. And no other research group has even come close to the kind of progress we've made."

"And if the DNR Commissioner decides to pop onboard for a tour?" Ivanov said.

"I welcome the Department of Natural Resources with open

arms. A guided tour of our facility would only reinforce his support for our endeavor."

"Even if he brings his own PhD's to investigate?"

"Science does not change depending on the individual using it, Peter. In fact, much of Odin Energy's new, government-friendly credo comes from a dissertation by self-proclaimed environmentalist, Dr. Kamuela Kihomi—a complete stranger to me. Now, back to our progress—I trust everything has run smoothly since my departure?" Odin looked toward the belly of the supertanker, which housed millions of dollars in equipment and researchers.

Ivanov shared a look with Bergen. "Everything seems fine, Sir. You know I don't dabble in the ways of science. But the sea has been relatively calm and I haven't heard any explosions down in the think tank."

"So everything's running so smoothly that you sent my head of security to accompany me for my flight here. Perhaps I should have a look around before I head back to the mainland." Odin's silver eyes pierced directly through Ivanov until the captain dropped his gaze to the floor. He did not look up until he heard the definitive sound of Odin's confident stride slip through the door, toward his downstairs laboratories.

"What happened in Alaska?" Ivanov grabbed a fistful of Bergen's shirt, but the guard remained at attention.

"I know how to follow orders," Bergen said through his teeth, removing the captain's hand.

"Then this is your debriefing. What happened?"

"I brought the boat back to its port, like you ordered. Then I boarded the chopper you sent and picked up Odin as planned. He assumed you sent me from the *Asgard* by helicopter to retrieve him for this afternoon's meeting."

"Back up to the port. How was the boat received? What about its crew?"

"Don't insult me, Ivanov. I dropped the crew off safely before bringing the ship back to port. I followed protocol to sign her in."

"They weren't suspicious about the catch onboard or the captain absent for his payment?"

"Please. You act like that operation is run by the Special Forces themselves. A hypothermic night man and a bunch of foreigners unloaded the catch. The captain collected his payment through a direct-deposit to the Amaknak Maritime Credit Union, account number 166535388, if you must know that as well. The ship's crew consisted of migrant workers, one of whom signed in the *Westender*, for all the port authority knows. It's all spic and span, Ivanov. I did my job."

"And you're sure no suspicions will arise?"

"I just follow orders. The rest is up to you."

Erik Bergen excused himself just as Kell Odin's footsteps began to sound up the stairs to the ship's bridge.

"Everything looks in working order, Peter." Odin strode from the door, stopping inches from Ivanov's face.

"Everything up here is fine, sir. We've had no mechanical difficulties, if that's what you mean." He leaned back on his heels, creating an immeasurable distance between himself and his boss.

Odin paused, breathing steady waves of hot breath across Ivanov's already perspiring face. His thin lips pursed together in a shrewd grin. "Page Alena Saenko. I want her division to check the temperatures surrounding the extraction point at the bottom of the sea."

"Why, Sir? Did you notice anything was wrong with the sea?"

"Even a subtle change in temperature or stability down there could create a reaction large enough to sink this tanker with you on it, Ivanov. That's why we have all these scientists onboard, and that's why I would like to see Dr. Saenko—for reassurance that our project is moving along according to plan. Now please page her…that is, unless you would like to report anything."

"I've seen no problems here, Sir. I'll page her immediately."

"Good." Odin placed a heavy hand on each of the captain's shoulders. "I've procured enough funding from the summit to keep you employed for an extensive amount of time, Peter. I certainly hope you take your job very seriously. After all, I carefully hand-pick my employees and I would hate to see anything cut my project short."

Ivanov slowly turned from Odin's grasp and placed a clammy hand around the ship's intercom. His wide thumb left an oily fingerprint on the call button as he paged Dr. Alena Saenko, Odin's special projects manager.

Chapter Eight

The ceiling of the Amaknak Maritime Credit Union pitched into a high peak to create the illusion of expansiveness, but in reality, it just sucked the heat farther away from the floor where Sarah stood in line.

"You should really wear a coat, Miss," an older woman dressed in head-to-toe down said.

"This sweater's actually really warm." Sarah pulled the collar from her neck with her hands still hiding in its sleeves.

Inside her palm, she crumpled her supply list for Jack's bar. While the line barely moved, she added all of the costs from the list to approximate the withdrawal she would take from the bar's account. She subtracted the savings she would earn by switching to less expensive brands, and added her salary to the mix, leaving room for tips in order to save Jack a few pennies.

"Next!" a hulkish woman finally shouted to Sarah from the teller's desk.

She pulled her withdrawal slip from her back pocket and scribbled the figure $2,567, pulled it back, and rounded. "Twenty-six hundred should do it for now." Sarah smiled.

The woman snatched the paper and snuck it underneath the counter, typing feverishly on her hidden keyboard. "Sorry, you're overdrawn." She gave the slip back to Sarah. "Next."

"Wait but you can't just 'next' me. I've been waiting in that line for over an hour. What do mean I'm overdrawn?"

"You have no money in this account, ma'am." She shoved the slip at Sarah again.

"Well recheck it."

The woman dropped her eyes below the counter again. "Sorry, nothing. Next!"

"Oh come on, you didn't even look that time."

"Ma'am, I have other customers. Your account is overdrawn. Now unless you have other business here, I suggest you come back when you're ready to fill out one of these." She pushed a deposit slip toward Sarah, flashing a quick smile.

"Now wait a minute, Brunhilda. You're only open one day a week and there is no way in hell I'm living on scraps for the week just to go through this whole ordeal again. Jack docked two days ago with a full tank of red kings, do you know what that means? It means four dollars a pound for a total of 1.2 million dollars, give or take some dead ones. So I'm sorry if I'm having trouble believing the account is empty. Can you check another account of his? The name is Jack Samuelsson."

"Ma'am, I can't open another customer's account for you."

"I'm not asking for money from it. I just want to know where the money went."

The teller looked toward a lone security guard who began to make his way toward the counter.

"You're not scaring me, Butch. Steve and I went to high school together." She waved to the approaching guard. "Steve, tell this woman I know Jack. I just want to see why he hasn't deposited his payment from the season into his bar account."

"Sarah, I think you should leave," Steve said.

"Leave? Steve, you were at the bar last night sucking down drinks on the house from me. Now I just want to restock but this woman says I'm overdrawn. I haven't touched that account all month. Jack's a valued customer here, I'm just trying to help his business."

"Sarah, come on, before you make a scene." Steve placed a hand on her arm, nudging her away from the counter.

"If someone's looking suspicious around here, it's this credit union for hiding people's money with their hidden little computers and their gargantuan receptionists that…" She felt Steve's grip tighten around her arm. "Fine, I'll go."

"What the hell is wrong with you, Reid? You can't ask for other people's money in a bank. That's like saying 'bomb' in an airport." Steve marched her across the line of customers toward the only door in the building.

"Fine. I'm sorry for the scene, okay? But I've been up all night with—I'm just so damned tired."

"Well get some rest and send Jack to get his own money for the next couple days, okay?"

"There it is again." Sarah pulled her arm from his grasp as they walked into the brisk outdoor air. "I can't just get Jack to the bank because I haven't seen him. Nobody has. And I guess now his money's missing too. Doesn't anyone find anything wrong with this? For the love of God Steve, you're a cop—don't you see anything wrong with this?"

"I'm a security guard, Sarah. But since you ask, I don't find anything odd about a 60-year-old retiring and getting out of Alaska. Now granted, I don't work at the bar, I just drink there, but it makes sense to horde your dough if you're retiring and moving away. Really, who else would see anything wrong with Jack's money tied up in his own bank account but you?"

"You're right, and I'm completely crazy." She marched away from Steve. "I knew I should have signed Jack up for online banking."

Sarah pounded her foot against the gas pedal in her Ford Festiva, listening to the engine whine and refuse to shift gears. Her breath fumed from her nostrils in white clouds that settled as condensation on her car's windows while the windshield refused to defrost. She flicked on her windshield washer and cranked the wipers in order to whisk the liquid away before it could freeze into a more opaque coating.

The fishery soon came into view and Sarah felt her heart send a fiery pulse through her body and her stomach turned. She roared up the driveway and screeched to a halt, startling several workers. Oblivious to the sub-freezing weather, she jumped from the car wearing worn jeans and her wool sweater, and stormed toward Paul Dorsey.

"I need to talk to the night guy who signed in Jack's boat," she said, skipping salutations.

Paul paused, stunned. "Robert Kennedy? He was temporary labor. He's done for the season."

Sarah felt a prickly heat rush through her body and her breath nearly escaped her. She caught her breath and rushed past Paul toward the fishery's records office.

"Sarah, what do you think you're doing?" Paul chased her into the fishery and grabbed her by the wrist.

"Where's the money, Paul?" She tried to pull away.

"What the hell's going on here?" Ian called as he approached from the office. "Do you man-handle all your clients, Paul?"

"She's not my client and barging into a work area is a safety hazard, Ian."

"I'll take care of this Paul." Ian held a hand out, motioning for Sarah to step back outside. "Now what the hell's got you all steamed up?" He followed her to her car.

"Fed up is more like it, Ian. First, Jack had someone else bring his boat back. Then he docked it in the middle of a shipping lane. Nobody has heard from him or the deck hands since mid-season but I guess there's nothing wrong with that either. But the guy who saw the boat dock is gone too now? And where in God's name is Jack's damn money?

Come on, Ian. Please tell me you think this doesn't add up. Everyone in this town is starting to treat me like I'm crazy. Do you really believe Jack is in Hawaii and my brother is sunning it up with him?"

"Look, I know you worried about those guys all season, but you have to calm down. You can't just come barging in here…"

"He had a full tank of crab, didn't he? And isn't that a damn remarkable catch?"

"Yes, of course."

"Then why is his bank account completely empty? He left me no money for the bar."

"I don't get you, Sarah. You were partying with the rest of us the other night. We were all sure Jack took his money and retired with it. I'm sorry he didn't leave any cash behind. But did you really think his retirement plan included you and a bar in Alaska that he'll probably never work at again?"

"And Nate? What about him?"

"Greenhorns make next to nothing. Why would you expect a cut from Nate?"

"You dumbass, I mean how could Nate afford a trip to the tropics on his pay?"

"He's twenty. He has nothing to do with that money but spend it on sun, drinks and girls."

"So you really think there's nothing wrong with Jack and Nate abandoning us?"

"They didn't abandon me, Sarah. But if you want to be cynical, I guess you could go on thinking that a bunch of horrible things happened to them. As for me, until I find any evidence either way, I'm going to assume that Jack did what everyone expected him to. And you believed that until this money issue came up."

"Now you think I'm only upset because of the money? If anyone has dollar signs in his eyes, it's you and your move to the *Adrienne Anne.*"

"It always comes back to that, doesn't it Sarah? You think I'm supposed to feel guilty because I left Jack's crew almost ten years ago after he…"

"That's enough, Ian."

"Why? Because I'm not too chicken-shit to admit that the great Jack Samuelsson is a lunatic at the helm? He takes risks, Sarah. He risks his catch and he risks his crew. And I do believe something happened out there this season. I believe he dragged his crew through hell so he could make a buck and quit this job."

"Shut your damn mouth, Ian."

"No, Sarah. I'm sick of taking shit from you about my leaving Jack's crew for a better one—it was ten years ago, get over it. And I'm sick of you avoiding the fact that Jack Samuelsson steered us directly into that storm ten years ago and pushed that ship until it finally quit. And he left our guys to freeze to death in that sea. You deal with it by staying on land. I deal with it by getting back on the job. And Jack's obviously dealt with it by promising to retire every damn winter since the accident. And now that he has, I'm perfectly fine with that."

Sarah felt the cold breeze press freezing tears against her face, but she refused to wipe them aside. She stared into Ian's eyes and waited for his face to relax. He dropped his shoulders and a sigh began an impending apology, but Sarah turned back toward her car.

She slumped into the Festiva and drove home feeling her eyes burn and the wool of her sweater itch against the bare skin around her neck. She left her car in front of the tavern's entrance and slid out quietly. The door barely latched into place in response to Sarah's halfhearted shove.

Once inside, Sarah locked the door behind her, dimmed the lights and turned down the heat. She trudged to her loft and let out a frustrated sigh as she sat at her computer to face the satellite image of the Odin research vessel, *Asgard* on her screen.

Chapter Nine

"Dr. Kamuela Kihomi." Sam Kiho typed his full name into the login screen on his computer and waited for the screensaver to disappear. From the computer's desktop, he opened a results report from his chromatography data software to monitor the progress of his latest test.

Behind his seat in the Oahu laboratory on the campus of the Hawaiian Archipelago Laboratory Organization (HALO), Sam glanced at the high pressure liquid chromatograph. Earlier, he had collected and prepared core samples of sediment that rested on the top layers of the ocean floor. He had since sliced and dried the samples and injected them into the chromatograph, which forced them through a high-pressure purification column.

Although the computer recorded the test results for him, Sam stared into the screen, waiting to catch any evidence of polymers in the samples. He knew he had at least a 60 minute wait before he could transfer the purified solution into the mass spectrometer, which determined the molecular weights of the particles.

After 20 minutes of staring at the computer, Sam's gaze began to swim into the screen. Feeling the familiar signs of eye-strain, he shrugged off his lab coat and stretched his arms behind him in a pose that would put most athletes to shame. Under the fluorescent lights of the laboratory, his skin glowed in a golden tan from the morning he spent aboard HALO's research vessel where he collected samples from the island's Pacific coast. He took his dark brown eyes away from the screen to rest them on another perfect Hawaiian sunset captured through the tall arched window that embellished an otherwise stark workspace. He began to study the bright oranges of the setting sun's rays and the purple tinge where the horizon met the ocean, when the computer chimed for his attention.

"Dr. Kiho, are you busy?" A window popped onto his computer screen, obstructing the chromatography data.

Sam swiveled back toward the screen and his eyes adjusted while he typed. "Aloha, Sarah. I'm just waiting on a test to finish—what can I do for you?"

Sam could tell she typed several letters, deleted them, and paused. "Are you working on methyl hydrates research?"

"Not at the moment. Right now I'm looking for deposits of polymers that are being carried away by the ocean's current into deposit zones."

"Huh?" she replied.

"I'm studying the flow of trash, mostly plastics, to see if they're hurting the environment."

"Oh. Can I disrupt your garbage study then? I need to know about methyl hydrates as a fuel source."

"Methyl hydrates are my specialty. But that research is back in my lab on the university campus. You caught me at HALO. I can probably answer some questions offhand though."

"Thanks. First question: what exactly are methyl hydrates?"

Sam closed the other open windows on his screen and diverted his attention to Sarah. "Let's see…it starts with methane, which is emitted when sea life deceases and decomposes. If that methane rests a couple miles below sea level, where there's a lot of pressure, it gets compressed into a methyl hydrate. So, a methyl hydrate is methane mixed with sea water crushed together into a crystal structure—a concrete-type crust of ice, pretty much. Was that clear?"

"I get it so far…but how is this fuel?"

Sam paused to translate his response into English. "Methane is a natural gas that we can use for fuel. And one liter of methyl hydrate holds 168 liters of methane. So this stuff is naturally compacted fuel."

"Sounds like it can save us from an oil crisis. Why isn't anyone drilling for it now?"

"Methyl hydrates are under extreme pressure. If a drill disturbed that lattice of ice, it could expand to 160 times its size in an instant. It would release deadly gas and the sea could immediately swallow any boat within its range. The turbulence could send shockwaves through the ocean resulting in tsunamis that could obliterate the coastline."

"Oh, is that all?"

"Why are you asking about methyl hydrates anyway?"

"I downloaded satellite-earth like you said, and right in the middle of Jack's fishing route was a supertanker owned by Odin Energy. I went to the Odin website and they said the tanker was researching methyl hydrates." She paused. "That got me to wondering if they either saw Jack's boat or if their research could have disrupted his route somehow."

Sam opened a browser and searched for Odin's website. "Does the site say exactly what that tanker's doing up there? I've been studying methyl hydrates longer than they have, but I've never needed a supertanker for my research. Are you sure that tanker's not just for transport of the reserve natural gas in Alaska? They were part of the Natural Gas Contract, which means they might be transporting some of Alaska's reserve fuel to the mainland."

"The satellite picture I see is from last month—before the contract. And the tanker hasn't moved anywhere. Plus, their website says it's researching methyl hydrates—and they're doing something with carbon dioxide. Does that make any sense?"

Sam scanned the web site. "This site should win an award in double talk. Did you read that they're using CO2 or just researching it?"

"Does it matter?"

"Well, some scientists have offered carbon dioxide as an alternative to drilling. Basically, they propose using CO2 to warm the methyl hydrates enough to extract the methane. They basically want to pull the methane out and replace it with carbon dioxide, which we can stand to get rid of anyway."

"Sounds like a good idea."

"In theory, sure. But a sudden change in temperature, especially a warm change, can have the same effect as drilling into the crystal layer. The methyl hydrate could expand and..."

"It would be catastrophic, I got that."

"What exactly happened to your friend's ship?" Sam typed.

"It didn't get swallowed up by the sea. But it came back to port with a full tank of crab and no crew."

"That sounds more like the Bermuda Triangle than the Bering Sea. What did the authorities say?"

"They fined the ship for coming back late and over quota, but they didn't say anything about the missing crew. Supposedly a deckhand brought the ship back and everyone here thinks Jack took off to Hawaii—have you seen him?"

"I'll keep on the lookout...continue."

"My brother was on that ship and he hasn't even called. Jack made a killing and didn't put any money in the account for his business, and the ship was a mess."

"Define mess. Except for the mysterious crew disappearances, what happened to make you think there was an accident?"

"For starters, a crab pot had broken from the crane and

smashed on deck, but I couldn't find the pot anywhere. Another few pots were left in the sea and a remaining pot was full of junk crab carcasses."

"Which means what, exactly? I'm not a crab fisherman."

"Well, you never just drop pots in the sea and leave them there to kill crabs. You also don't let your pots get so twisted on the line that they jam up the crane and break it. And you always throw the smaller crab back—plus, you could get fined for catching the wrong type of crab. You don't pile dirty pots back on the stack because then they're all messed up when you need them."

"Sounds to me like the guys abandoned the boat mid-catch."

"Thank you! I thought the same thing, but everyone here is saying I'm nuts. Judging by their last call made to a fellow ship, the *Westender* was last spotted in the area where we predicted the new crop of crabs would migrate. That puts them right near Odin's supertanker. I don't mean to say they had an accident with the tanker, but…"

"You're right, something is definitely fishy there…sorry, no pun intended."

"Do you think I could contact Odin Energy? You know, ask them if they saw anything?"

"Unfortunately, getting a human on the phone at that corporation is next to impossible. It's akin to calling the president of the United States."

"What about contacting the *Asgard*? That's the tanker."

"I'm thinking no. Actually, I'm still stumped with the whole idea of the supertanker. Why on earth would Odin need a ship that big just for research? Methyl hydrate samples are small enough to hold in your hand, so you certainly don't need an oil tanker to transport them. Ironically, this ecological research of theirs seems like a gross waste of resources—unless he's doing some kind of sophisticated study that I haven't heard of yet."

"I'm glad you're a skeptic too, but what can I do if I can't contact Odin and I can't talk to anyone around here?"

"You've already done it, Sarah. I didn't get a grant in methyl hydrate research to just sit on the beach and watch the sunset. I'll have part of my team look into that stretch of the Bering Sea for you."

"And what about Odin? What if they did see something happen on the *Westender*?"

"If they didn't report it…well, that raises a huge red flag. Keep your distance for now. I'll see if I can talk to any of their researchers—scientist to scientist—about that tanker. Meanwhile, try to stay on the positive about your friends—take confidence that they're fine and we're the ones who need help!"

"Thanks. You know you make neuroses sound appealing. Good luck with your trash tests, Dr. Kiho!"

"Mahalo!" he logged off.

Sam left Odin's website on his computer screen as a reminder. His chromatograph finished on cue and he tried to focus on the test. He carefully injected the purified solution into the mass spectrometer to determine the presence of polyethylene in the samples.

After it had degraded into the ocean, the polyethylene looked like sand to the naked eye. But Sam's test had determined that the dangerous plastic rested on the ocean's floor, where it could harm sea life. He turned to his map of deposit zones, where the polyethylene deposits would collect as the ocean currents changed directions. Sam knew that if the zones rested in biologically sensitive areas, they could harm fish and disrupt the growth of the coral reef. He turned back to his computer to post the question, "Would bottom-dwelling fish be affected?" But before he could post, he caught site of Odin's webpage.

Sam tried to read the page objectively, but could not keep his mind from drifting back into Sarah's messages. He leaned into the computer screen as if to interrogate it, reading the website more closely until his mind felt scrambled.

"You sneaky double-talking bastard," he said out loud as a wide grin grew across his face. He had gotten to the line in Odin's site that posted word-for-word what Sam had written in his dissertation on marine ecology. Sam knew the line well—it comprised 200 characters of gibberish that he had tacked on to his first page in order to eliminate the awkward page break at the bottom of the PDF file.

Rather than letting Odin's idiocy enrage him, Sam saved his files and sent his computer into hibernation with a cool hand. He eased back into his lab coat and strode toward the exit, dimming the lights on his way out. The lab exited into an outdoor courtyard of thick green grass and leafy gingko trees. Sam listened for the calming ocean waves coming from the opposite side of the building and thanked Oahu for rejecting the Nene, a loud goose that cackled to him nightly while he grew up on Kauai.

Across his small arboretum, Sam caught the lights of the HALO research vessel creeping into the campus' largest laboratory. Walking closer to the dock, he could see a dark, barely visible silhouette meet the boat. It walked with the unmistakably blithe stride of his father, Dr. Iohunakana Kihomi. Most called him Dr. Kihomi, while they referred to Sam as Dr. Kiho.

"Dad," Sam called as he ascended the outdoor staircase that resembled a smaller version of Rome's Spanish Steps.

His father waved from the top of the staircase as the research boat sailed underneath, directly into the laboratory that surrounded the harbor like a tunnel.

"Dad, I need your advice on something." At exactly six feet tall, Sam greeted his father eye-to-eye with a gesture caught between a hug and a strong pat on the shoulder.

"What's up, Kami?"

"I got a call, well, an instant message from an online student from over at the university."

"Hah." Dr. Kihomi threw his head back with a robust laugh. "Did he give you a brain teaser you couldn't figure out again?"

"No, Dad." Sam felt himself blush and knew only his father could bring about that reaction. "She brought up a question about methyl hydrate research...and Odin Energy."

"Ah, Kell Odin. Kami, you and I have forgotten more about methyl hydrate research than Kell Odin could ever take the time to learn. So, what's the big question?" Dr. Kihomi motioned for Sam to follow him into the lab.

"It's more of a favor than a question." Sam said, matching his father's stride. "According to my student, and I believe her information is reliable, Odin's got a supertanker anchored in the middle of the Bering Sea, supposedly researching the extraction of methyl hydrates with carbon dioxide. You're thinking what I'm thinking, right?"

"That Odin's displaying that behemoth ship means he's obviously compensating for something he lacks." Dr. Kihomi laughed again.

"Cute, Dad. But I was wondering what the hell he thinks he's doing out there with a supertanker and probably a boatload of researchers. She said he hasn't moved for at least a month."

Dr. Kihomi stopped at the indoor bay before boarding the research vessel. "If I know Kell Odin, I'd guess that this is just another public relations stunt. He has just signed with the Natural Gas Contract which has gained him stock in all of Alaska's surplus natural fuel. They're expanding the pipeline to send Alaskan fuel across the mainland and I'm just guessing Odin wants first place in sharing those profits."

"You think the supertanker is just a billboard?" Sam stood eye-to-eye with his father again. "Why is his website full of press releases about methyl hydrate research?"

"PR, Kami. The first person to figure out the safe means to extract methyl hydrates wins the keys to world domination, financially. I don't doubt he wants in on that rat race. The problem is he's not smart enough. All the best scientists are right here." He winked. "I wouldn't worry about Odin's men stepping on your toes. Impatience will get the best of him and he'll chase the dollar into another venture soon enough. Then he'll leave saving the world to the people who actually care about it."

"I'm not worried about him finding a new fuel source before I do, I'm just worried about what he's doing up there. Someone with that much money and that few brains...I would hate to see the Bering Sea's version of the Exxon Valdez."

"You do have a valid point, Kami."

Sam paused, taking in the enormity of his father's facility. "Dad, you're the only guy I know with the credentials and the connections to take on Kell Odin."

"And you would like me to use my connections to get you on that supertanker of his, am I right?" Dr. Kihomi cast a proud smile.

"I'd love to see what the hell he's doing with all that space." Sam grinned, throwing a strong arm around his father's shoulders.

"Alaska's pretty cold this time of year, you know."

"And that means..."

"You'd better take a heavy coat when you go."

"Which is when?"

"I'll have a guided tour set up for you as early as next week," Dr. Kihomi said. "Just give me some time to make a few calls. Governor Orlowski owes me. And Odin wouldn't dare get in the way of a politician, especially not one from Alaska."

Chapter Ten

Kell Odin straightened his black suit jacket and fixed his silver hair on the way to the board room on the thirteenth floor of his Juneau high-rise. He used the chrome walls of his private elevator as a 360-degree mirror, and he approved of his Aryan features in contrast to the olive-skinned clients he would meet upstairs.

The chrome capsule bobbed to a gentle stop and its doors opened to a sterile corridor that led directly into the morning sun. Odin snapped his head to the side and avoided the bright morning rays, shielding his silver eyes with a long, slender hand. He headed directly to his board room, letting the soft, unused carpeting absorb the shock of his determined stride. Although he had spent more time than usual at his Alaskan corporate headquarters lately, the sterile smell of the room reminded him that he had not held a meeting large enough to occupy it in over a year.

Standing head-to-toe in tailored perfection, Odin subtly surveyed his guests before striding the length of the olive granite table that accentuated the rich mahogany wainscoting on all four walls of the room. The darkness of the room relaxed Odin's eyes and filled him with a sense of privacy, unaltered by the intrusive sun.

"Good morning gentlemen," Odin bowed slightly, yet still towered over his business partners who stood at attention. He eased into the forest green upholstery of his executive chair at the head of the table and rested his elbows on its surface, enjoying the coolness of the granite that emanated through his sleeves, giving his skin an icy jolt.

At the head of the table, Dr. Shing Zhào, CEO of the Republic of China Oil Reserve flipped through Odin's report with a skeptical eye. Eleven of his men occupied the chairs along the table chirping to each other in quick, unfamiliar syllables that began to grate on Odin's nerves. Alex Summit entered the room sixteen minutes late, and Odin snapped into action.

"Nice of you to join us, Alex," Odin said to his vice president of foreign affairs. "Did you bring the report from our financial offices with you this time? Our guests seem anxious to start."

"Anxious?" Dr. Zhào said. "China has almost completed work on the remaining four liquid natural gas tankers that you have requested. Meanwhile, we are awaiting your completion of our port's LNG facility and an estimation of when our first shipment of natural gas will arrive—that would make you anxious to get started too, Mr. Odin."

Odin looked his investor square in the eyes. "Your anxiety will be relieved shortly."

The lights dimmed on cue and monitors nestled within the granite tabletop illuminated as if out of nowhere, forcing the Chinese guests to lean into the cold stone to view the information.

"As you can see, the Alaska Natural Gas Contract has awarded American oil companies much more freedom in accessing surplus amounts of liquid natural gas. This fuel is slated for use by the United States through an expansion in the Alaskan pipeline down its northern slope and across Canada."

"And how does this endeavor help us, Mr. Odin?"

"Well, Dr. Zhào, with four of its top oil conglomerates rushing to the gauntlet, plenty of liquid natural gas will fuel the

United States pipeline. Aware of this, the Alaskan government has voted unanimously to increase funding for my personal projects as well. So they will receive more than enough fuel to satisfy their needs and I will be free to satisfy yours.

"And how much fuel can you possibly skim from this new operation?" Zhào asked. "Or have you also miraculously conned your country into delivering our fuel gift wrapped?"

"You will have your first private shipment from me within the month and we will finish construction on your LNG facility in the next two weeks. If you require any further gift wrapping, Dr. Zhào, I can work that into the price. Once you get me my fleet, I can supply you with one tanker of liquefied methane every two months. That is enough to ensure that you remain ahead in the oil industry—billions ahead."

"Promising, Mr. Odin—I am impressed. In fact, your deal sounds so promising that I would like to double my business upon completion of your fleet. My men will supply seven tankers to you by the first of the year, providing you ship us a full tank of LNG 12 months a year, not six."

Alex Summit immediately planted his face in Odin's ear, shoving him a bound copy of the Alaska Natural Gas Contract. Odin flinched from the invasive heat of Alex's breath and shoved the contract back into his employee's hands.

"Show the men the projected expansion of the pipeline along with the volume of LNG they are able to process," he whispered to Alex.

A blue glow shot up from the tabletop and the Chinese investors stared into their screens.

"While your offer is respectfully ambitious, Dr. Zhào, you can see that the Alaskan pipeline project will not be fully complete until at least two years from now. Without the pipeline, it would be very difficult to step up production enough to fulfill your request. I am, however, able to send your shipments bimonthly until the project is complete. Then we can renegotiate for a monthly delivery."

Amidst the dimly lit room and the glow of a dozen computer monitors, Odin could hear Zhào's men mumbling in a cacophony of inarticulate pitches.

"A renegotiation is out of the question," Zhào said after the pause. He motioned for Alex to turn the lights on. "Your broadcast was most impressive, but it failed to show me why I should continue supplying a fleet of tankers to a corporation that cannot fulfill my immediate needs. Two years is a long time to waste on marginal profits. You are a businessman…explain to me how I can possibly impress my investors now with a promise of great supply in two years."

"My current offer will supply more than marginal profits, Dr. Zhào, but I am willing to discuss alternatives."

"I want twice as much as you propose to ship to me. And in return, I will award you 50 percent over my asking price…to offset any inconveniences that you may have to endure during the first two years of our contract."

"Let me get this straight before we put this in writing. You are offering 150 percent on the first 24 shipments, provided I send them to you within the first two years of business."

"After which, I will be happy to renegotiate." Dr. Zhào said.

"Of course you will…you're handing over your right and left arms in this deal."

"…along with seven of China's top-rated LNG tankers." Dr. Zhào paused. "Do we have a deal, Mr. Odin?"

Odin stood from his seat and strode to the end of the table with a strong hand outstretched. He clutched Zhào's hand and gave it a firm shake. He took two steps backward and addressed the table with an elegant bow. "I believe we can accommodate those needs."

"What the hell happened in there, Kell?" Alex Summit followed Odin into his posh corner office in the penthouse of the high-rise.

"Watch your tone, Summit. And keep your distance." He scanned his desk and tilted his computer monitor away from Alex.

"One tanker a month? Are you crazy? We can't possibly skim that much fuel off the pipeline contract without anybody knowing about it."

"You just contact Jessica Hulbert in Financial so we can get this deal set up for the bank. I want seamless transactions once we get started."

"Sure, we'll get the accounts running through the proper, private channels. But after that, I want out of this whole deal. You can keep my Christmas bonus for this one."

"Excuse me, Alex?" Odin turned to face his employee square in the eye. "It's not that easy. And besides, there's nothing to worry about." His thin lips pursed into a smile.

"I think all that ice out there in the Bering Sea is getting to you, Odin. One shipment a month? We'll get caught."

"You sound like a broken record now, Alex."

"Kell, you said it yourself. Your own data showed it. Without the new pipeline, there isn't enough liquid methane to fill your US contract and Zhào's tankers. And as much as I love the smell of money, unless you've found a new way to turn greenbacks into methane..."

"You take care of the paperwork, Alex. There's plenty of that to keep you busy." He stared at his employee. "Let me worry about supplying the methane. I didn't exactly go into this business yesterday." Odin spun from his heavy granite desk to face the glacial view of the docks at the south end of the Gastineau Channel. "On your way out, tell my assistant to get Peter Ivanov on the phone."

Chapter Eleven

Sam Kiho stepped through the lobby doors of the Grand Aleutian Hotel and immediately breathed a sigh of relief upon noticing the large fireplace that stood prominently in the center of the great room. He removed his extreme-weather Gore-Tex gloves and jacket, and pulled the balaclava head sock from his head and neck to reveal a wild tuft of black hair that he immediately tamed with a cool swipe of his hand.

Sam let an older Chinese couple beat him to the plush seats next to the inviting fireplace, and turned his attention to the array of tourism brochures that aligned the route from the door to the check-in counter. He recalled the book on Alaskan crab fishing that he had nearly memorized during his flight from Honolulu, and grabbed a flyer on fisheries for comparison. En route to the front desk, he also snatched flyers on the Alaskan Maritime Highway, and grabbed several brochures that boasted the beauty of the local wildlife.

"Good afternoon, I'm Dr. Kamuela Kihomi. I believe I have a reservation," Sam said to the woman behind the reception desk.

"Dr. Kihomi," she replied with elation. "The Grand Aleutian is delighted to welcome you to our presidential suite for your three-night stay." She opened a folder and turned the registration form so it would face Sam. "As you can see in our fine print here, V.I.P. guests receive an array of complimentary hotel services that include private transportation and a personal concierge. As a V.I.P., you are also welcome to stay with us for up to three additional weeks without risk of relocation to another room."

"Do your guests find it that hard to leave Unalaska?" Sam motioned to the frost that accumulated on the exterior of the adjacent windows.

"We're accustomed to executives and government officials extending their stay." She glanced at the registration form. "The additional three weeks would take you up to Thanksgiving weekend. But honestly, you could very easily keep your room until January—our next big fishing season—without any problems."

Sam flashed his handful of brochures along with a kind grin. "But how could I possibly do it all in just two months?"

The Presidential Suite was nestled on the fourth floor of the Grand Aleutian Hotel, which gave Sam just enough elevator time to stow the twenty pounds of winter gear that had gotten him from the car to the hotel lobby. Underneath layers of fleece and down, he relaxed in a pair of jeans and a faded Quicksilver T-shirt that reminded him of the Oahu surf back home.

Having opted to carry his own things, Sam stepped from the elevator clutching two heavy bags that made his biceps bulge under the distressed shirt. His left hand held an array of winter clothing he had pieced together the night before, and his right hand clasped a HALO laptop with additional hardware, encased in ten pounds of steel and rubber. The door to his suite was at the far end of the hall.

A thud resounded down the hallway as Sam dropped his bags in favor of sliding the keycard and opening his door to a waft of fresh-smelling fabric cleaner that filled the room. He had barely grasped his bags from the floor when he tossed them on one of the queen-sized beds in the room. He turned the thermostat up to 72 degrees on his way to a large window that looked across the shore to the lighthouse at Dutch Harbor. In the distance, a ferry raced across Unalaska with the unmistakable speed of the Alaska Maritime Highway fleet, which comprised mostly high speed ferries that carried passengers up and down the coast.

Turning to the table behind him, Sam noticed a large gift basket filled with a sample of local treats. He plucked the card from the top of the basket and read it.

Dr. Kihomi, welcome to Unalaska. On behalf of Kell Odin himself, the Asgard *is honored to make your acquaintance tomorrow for a tour of our state-of-the-art operations. In the interest of efficiency, Mr. Odin's personal helicopter will meet you at 8:00 a.m. tomorrow at the Amaknak Vertiport, located at the main fishery on Amaknak Island. The Grand Aleutian will provide you with transportation. We regret that Kell Odin himself will not be aboard the* Asgard *at the time of your arrival, but Dr. Alena Saenko, our chief research scientist, will assist you onboard.*

We hope your stay is a good one.

Sincerely,
Captain Peter Ivanov

Sam tucked the card in his back pocket and began to outfit himself in winter layers once more. Before pulling his glove liners back on, he rang the front desk.

"This is Dr. Kiho…Kihomi in the presidential suite. I'd like transportation to Dutch Harbor immediately," he said. "And I would like information on an establishment called 'The Wheelhouse'."

*   *   *

"Did you just come here to stare at me, Ian?" Sarah tried to busy herself behind the bar while Ian rolled his empty shot glass on its side.

"I told you, I came to apologize for what I said at the fishery the other day…and to see if there's anything I can do to help."

"Anything you can do for me?" She faced Ian and cupped her hand over the shot glass, stopping it from rolling. "After you humiliated me at the docks? Forget it, Ian."

"You humiliated yourself, storming in there like a madwoman."

"Opening an apology with an insult, I see." She let go of the glass and stepped back. "Thanks for the help, but there's nothing you can do. It's been over a week since Jack supposedly got back, and I haven't seen a dime, let alone the man himself. The bottles are running dry in here and I won't be able to keep this place open without some cash."

"Did you try the credit union again?"

"I'm pretty much banned from that place after I ranted like a lunatic when the account was empty last week. And don't dare say you'll loan me the money."

"You could charge more for drinks."

"With the booze I've got left, I'd have to charge fifty bucks for this bottle of vodka just to break even." She held up a bottle holding one swig of the clear liquid.

"Jack will come through, Sarah, just hang in there."

Sarah looked Ian in the eyes. "Do you honestly still believe that?"

"No, I don't, alright? Of course I don't—I just wanted you to change the damn subject for once." Ian pushed his glass aside and clutched both of Sarah's hands, holding her in his gaze. "I worry about them too, but I force it out of my head. In two months, the season picks back up again and the sea will be colder and meaner. Ninety ships will take off for Opilio season and they can't get psyched-out now with the thought of a missing crew. Jesus, Sarah, just the thought of washing away out there was enough to keep you off the *Westender* forever. I haven't Opies in years because of it. We can't go raging through town spreading the idea that something happened to an entire crew on that boat. It's not fair and it's not safe for the guys heading out there."

"I understand what you're saying, Ian. But what if something did happen out there? And what if it happens again?" She pulled her hands free. "I've been looking at Jack's route online, and it ran damn close to Opilio territory, where the guys will be fishing in a couple months. There's a tanker from Odin Energy called the *Asgard* up there researching that area, and I just have this gut feeling that there's something wrong."

"Wait, Odin Energy?" Ian laughed. "Sarah, that's a good thing. It's all over the news. If you'd get a TV in here, you'd have seen it. Odin Energy just had this huge press conference about their research to supply Alaska with a crazy amount of natural gas. They projected it would be enough to expand the pipeline and maybe even ship fuel overseas in the future."

"I've heard of it, Ian. But why should I be doing cartwheels about it?"

"Odin's research could open up the fuel industry big time in Alaska. They projected a 200 percent increase in jobs around here and down the pipeline, which means more of us tired crab guys could get out of the Bering Sea and work safer jobs. Isn't that what you've always wanted? Leave the fishing to the young migrant workers and keep Unalaska alive."

"You're starting to sound like Kell Odin himself." Sarah smirked.

"My point is Odin is pushing for a better standard of living for us. If his tanker is in crab grounds, it's only doing something good. And if something happened to Jack's boat out there, I'm sure that tanker was equipped with enough hardware and staff to fix them up and send them on their way, safely. His headquarters is in Juneau—he could have even given them a flight if anyone was hurt."

"I don't know, Ian. Since when are oil tycoons that altruistic?"

"Hey, the thought got a smile on your face, anyway." Ian grabbed his coat. "Since you've got no alcohol in this shack, why don't you come with me…I'm putting the finishing touches on the addition and I can use a fresh opinion on it."

"You finished your house already?"

"Just about, so don't be too honest with that opinion. What do you say? I'll keep you for dinner and get you back here with plenty of time left to worry."

"I guess it couldn't hurt to get out for a little while." Sarah untied the apron from her waist and wiped her hands. "My coat's in the back room…help yourself to that fifty-dollar bottle of vodka while you're waiting."

The setting sun didn't give Sarah a break. At four in the afternoon, it barely squeezed through the window in Jack's office, offering little more than a gray glow to guide her to her jacket. She halted at the light switch, aware that shedding light on the desk would only tempt her to jump back into work. Her hesitation lasted seconds before Ian's voice pressed through the door.

"Hey Sarah, there's some Inuit guy here to see you." he shouted.

"Inuit guy?" Sarah asked more to herself than to Ian as she headed from the office toward the bar. At the end of the bar, a tall, sturdy man packed in layers of winter clothing patiently removed his hat and Gore-Tex shell.

The stranger waited until Sarah reached the bar before removing his gloves. "Sarah Reid?" He extended a suntanned hand. "I believe we've already met online. I'm Dr. Kiho, from the University of Hawaii…and HALO. You asked me about methyl hydrates the other day and…"

71

"You could have replied online." Sarah spoke slowly and stared at Sam as she returned his gentle handshake.

"I'm sorry. I've taken you off guard." Sam stepped back to address both Ian and Sarah. "Sarah's questions about the research taking place in the Bering Sea intrigued me. I have a research grant in the same area." He turned to face Sarah. "After our dialogue the other day, I had to come see this place for myself—and I've never been known for my patience."

"Nice try Dr. Online Predator or whoever you are, but we were just heading out, so you'll have to stalk Sarah another day." Ian stood to match Sam's height and Sarah blushed.

"Sam, this is Ian," she said. "And he was just leaving."

"Ian," Sam shook his hand. "I see I've given a false impression here. Sarah's a student of mine. She took my online class from the University of Hawaii last semester. We discussed the Bering Sea quite a bit and I'm just here to do a little exploring. I wanted to ask Sarah some questions about the area, if she doesn't mind."

"Sarah, I can stay here," Ian said as he sized up Sam.

"I'm fine, Ian. Why don't you go work on your house and I'll come by later, okay?" She shoved Ian's coat toward him, pushing him to face the door.

"Fine, but I'll be back soon," he promised as he left.

Sarah motioned for Sam to take a seat and she quickly made her way around the bar, leaving the counter between them while Sam removed layers of winter clothing.

"I apologize again if I startled you by showing up unannounced. I got so accustomed to our online discussions that I forgot we haven't actually met." He pushed his coat aside and leaned slightly away from the bar, adding to Sarah's personal space. "You're a lot more talkative online."

"I'm sorry. You...you did surprise me. I guess I pictured you, well, differently. You really are Hawaiian, aren't you?"

"Samoan, if you want to get technical. But I know what you mean. I'm supposed to look like a scrawny pale guy with glasses and an oversized lab coat. That's the stereotype, right?"

"You forgot old, too." Sarah smiled. "Can I get you a drink? Maybe something to warm you up a bit?" She looked at the pile of excess clothing Sam had placed on the barstool.

"Coffee, if you've got any."

"That's about all we've got these days. This is the bar I mentioned in my email. We're down to almost nothing. Unfortunately, you've picked the wrong season to vacation in Dutch Harbor."

"I'm not exactly here on vacation." Sam sipped from the hot coffee Sarah had poured into a cold mug. "Cutting to the chase, I'm visiting the *Asgard* tomorrow. I thought it only right to see you first. You're the one who peaked my curiosity, after all."

"Wait a minute, didn't you tell me contacting Elvis would be easier than getting hold of Kell Odin? How did you manage to hitch a ride on his boat?" Sarah leaned into the bar.

"There's the Sarah I've met before." Sam relaxed his shoulders and smiled. "And I said that you would have a hard time getting hold of Odin. Right now, I'm the leading ecologist focusing specifically on methyl hydrate research. Let's just say it would be a faux pas not to let me onboard."

"I'm duly impressed, Dr. Kiho. But why come to me? Right now I'm one of the top lunatics on Amaknak Island. And in case you haven't noticed, the folks around here think Kell Odin is the second coming."

"Please, call me Sam. And I came to you because I was hoping you could help me with my little tour tomorrow."

"I can come with you?"

"That's not what I meant." Sam pushed his coffee aside, half empty and no longer steaming. "You mentioned you were concerned about Odin's tanker out there in the Sea, specifically in the middle of your friend's crab fishing route. I want to know more about the fishing loop out there and the effect you think Odin might be having on those ships."

"I can show you tons about fishing, but like you said, I'm no scientist. I'm just going on instinct, and I haven't slept much lately, so who even knows how reliable that is."

"Call it an official scientific hunch if you must, but something you said about your friend's ship and Odin's tanker hasn't left my head either. I also can't figure out why on earth he would need a supertanker that far northwest of St. Paul Island to conduct research."

"Didn't you say methyl hydrates are created at cold temperatures? It doesn't get much colder than northwest of St. Paul."

"Methyl hydrates are formed far enough below the surface that any point in the Bering Sea would suffice. So why would Odin stick his tanker that far north? Am I correct in assuming ice patches get quite rough up there?"

"Ice can consume over half the sea during Opilio season alone, in January. In a tough year, ice can take over even more than that. Listen, I appreciate you coming up here, Sam. And I know you're a renowned scientist and all, but..." Sarah stopped herself in favor of taking Sam's mug to the sink.

"But what, Sarah? I want to hear your concerns. That's why I came here first."

"But you're Hawaiian—Samoan, I mean. If you've never been in it, the Bering Sea's going to seem like a different planet compared to the Pacific Ocean. And I don't know how I can help you with your trek to the *Asgard*. I'm just a bartender. There are scientists and universities around here that I'm sure will answer your questions."

"Don't doubt yourself, Sarah." Sam met her at the far end of the counter, where she stood at the sink. "You were my best online student. And weren't you the one who told me everyone around here is so oblivious that they looked the other way when a whole ship came back without its crew? Sure, I could contact universities, but I want to know what questions you have about that tanker. You've been out there on that exact ship. I want to know what you think could have happened."

"I'm really grateful that you listened to my concerns, but I'm sorry you came all the way out here." Sarah hung her head. "The Bering Sea's not exactly a close friend of mine. The ice patches rip through gear and eat through the boat hulls—the sixty-foot rogue waves can shoot out of nowhere and...I can't explain it."

"And knock a 200-foot ship on its side at the least? Shut down your equipment and take you offline without any contact to the outside world for days? Rock you uncontrollably and leave you hoping your ship will right itself before it capsizes and leaves you stranded, or worse, dead?" Sam looked into Sarah's eyes. "I know those waves, Sarah."

Sam took a deep, calming breath and sat down before continuing. "My home, Oahu, is in the middle of the Pacific Ocean, leaving nothing to calm the waves before they reach the shore. The Hawaiian Islands are made of rough, volcanic rock and during January, waves can reach more than fifty feet in height. They can stir from out of nowhere and cause disaster in seconds—sound familiar?"

Sarah nodded. "The next thing you'll tell me is that Hawaii really is located next to Alaska in that little white box near Mexico on most maps."

"No, but with the exception of weather, the oceanic movements around Hawaii parallel those of the Bering Sea. Twin currents exist at almost exactly the same times during the year. That's what has allowed me to study polyethylene deposit zones across the Pacific coast of North America without moving from Hawaii. The Hawaiian Islands and the Aleutian Islands are carbon copies of each other. I know those waves, Sarah. But I'll

75

need your help if we want to find out exactly what Odin is using them for—and exactly where your friends are."

Sarah hid behind her cupped hands and rubbed warmth back into her flushed face. As the blood rushed back into her dizzied head. "In that case, Sam, I have about a hundred maps and websites that you should probably look at before your trip to the *Asgard* tomorrow."

Chapter Twelve

Sam sat comfortably in the back seat of the Grand Aleutian's executive limousine as it rumbled over what locals named, "The Bridge to the Other Side," which connects Unalaska to Amaknak Island. Outside the window, the black volcanic terrain reminded Sam of Hawaii's big island. But the jagged, snow-covered jetties in the distance told him that he was miles away from home.

The limo pulled passed Dutch Harbor's main fishery, which was blanketed in large crab ships that were covered in morning frost. It slowed at an indistinct field covered in morning flurries. Sam zipped his coat up to his nose and pulled a skull cap over his head and ears. He gave the driver a generous tip and checked the charge on his cell phone before pulling his gloves on and exiting the vehicle.

"Sir, wouldn't you rather wait in the car?" the driver asked through his rolled-down window. "I'm not running a meter and it's nice and warm in here."

"It's a tempting offer, but it's 7:59 on the dot, and Kell Odin is known for his punctuality."

"Suit yourself, Dr. Kihomi. I'll wait until you have boarded, then I'm just a phone call away when you need a lift back to the hotel."

"Thanks, and please, call me Sam." Sam would have given more of an eloquent 'thank you' to the driver, but his voice already became overpowered by the Turbomeca Arriel 2S2 engines of the Sikorsky S-76D helicopter that approached. As the giant bird landed, its rotors whipped icy wind into Sam's face, forcing the snow around the field into what looked like a crude crop circle. Sam stood off guard as the doors opened and a tall man clad in black fatigues approached him, wearing only a black cap and gloves to protect his skin from the cold. A squiggly black wire ran around his head into his left ear.

"I'm picking up Dr. Kihomi now," the man said into the thin wire.

Sam extended his hand to the stranger. "You must be from the *Asgard*," he yelled over the rush of the rotors. He waited for an introduction, but received a gesture from the man to follow him into the helicopter.

Once inside the S-76D, Sam unzipped his jacket and relaxed into comfortable leather seats. His chaperone sat beside him and secured the doors.

"Nice ride you have here," Sam said to the man.

"We will arrive on the *Asgard* in just a couple hours. Dr. Saenko and Captain Ivanov will greet you onboard when we land." The man sat back and did not utter another word.

Sam tried to relax next to the daunting guard beside him. He looked down at the black, choppy waters of the Bering Sea and held his tongue as it wanted to marvel at the aerial beauty of the Aleutian Chain. From 5,000 feet in the air, St. Paul Island, home to less than 1,000 residents, looked like an abandoned crop of land just barely poking its head above the water. In late November, it seemed closed for business.

Miles of turbulent sea passed again before Sam's eyes rested on what seemed big enough to double as another island. Well aware that supertankers stretch to almost a quarter of a mile in length and span nearly a football field in width, the *Asgard* still seemed inappropriately huge in Sam's eyes.

The helicopter descended and the *Asgard* grew. As the skids hit the landing pad, Sam noticed a slender woman in a white lab coat emerge from the group of workers on the deck of the giant ship. Accompanying her was a stocky man holding his captain's hat to a tuft of greasy black hair. The rotors slowed and Sam's escort opened the doors to the helicopter, motioning for Sam to stay seated.

Sam watched the man in black share brief words with the ship's captain. A nod of the captain's head allowed the woman to approach the doors and greet her guest.

"Dr. Kamuela Kihomi, I am Dr. Alena Saenko. It is an honor to welcome you to the *Asgard*." She extended a delicate, bronze hand and led him onto the ship while the other swept wispy locks of black hair from her porcelain face.

Before Sam could reply, Captain Ivanov ushered him from the helipad. "Dr. Kihomi, I am Peter Ivanov, captain of this vessel." He wrenched Sam's hand with a powerful grip. "I do hope you find your visit today insightful, but remember this is a working vessel," he glanced at Dr. Saenko. "I know you are eager to see our laboratories, but we will start your visit in our main conference room, if you will follow me."

Sam tried to adjust his gait to keep up with Ivanov's brisk pace while falling back just enough to include Dr. Saenko in the trek to the conference room. Traipsing the length of the giant vessel, Sam forced his mouth to remain shut again, taking Ivanov's silence as a cue. He did, however, manage a nod and a smile from Dr. Saenko as they passed by a large crane on the ship's port side. It hoisted a 20-foot windowless submarine from the water, and Sam could see in Dr. Saenko's dark brown eyes that he would learn about the submersible later.

The trio trudged up countless stairs from the deck of the *Asgard* before finally entering the conference room, which looked like an antiquated version of the ship's bridge. Although dimmed by winter, the morning sun poured through a wall of windows, amplified by the many pits and scratches imbedded in the glass. In the middle of the room, Ivanov and Saenko pulled scratched wooden chairs closer to an old pine table that seemed warped by the years and the weather.

"I told you this was a working ship," Ivanov said with a growl, noticing the look of disappointment in Sam's eyes.

"No, I understand completely," Sam said. He eased into one of the chairs and pulled up to the table. "Besides, I'm here for the science, not the interior design."

"We are the world's largest pioneers of methyl hydrate research at the moment, Dr. Kihomi," Ivanov said. "And while we appreciate your company, you understand that the work being done on this vessel is for future commercial purposes, and as such, requires some degree of confidentiality. We don't want our competitors getting their hands on all our hard work. So I'm not sure there's much we can share with you."

"Well, one pioneer to another, Captain, I'm sure you understand that an operation of this size is bound to grab some attention."

Captain Ivanov pulled the usual public relations packet from a nearby counter and slid it toward Sam, who did not receive the packet before Dr. Saenko intercepted it.

"With all due respect, Captain, Dr. Kihomi is above this marketing jargon." She held the folder underneath the table in Ivanov's view and pointed to the prominent gold lettering on its cover that quoted Sam's dissertation word-for-word.

"I believe the best way to accommodate your needs is with a tour of our research laboratory. You will find that with all of the new equipment and staff we have acquired, this converted super-tanker offers just enough space for our research." Saenko said.

"You must have some super spectrometers down there. I have four in my lab, which is half the size of this room."

Before Ivanov could cut in, the door to the conference room creaked open and a silent crew member served Sam a cup of steaming coffee. Sam had almost forgotten his frozen hands but the coffee's swirling steam reminded him of the bitter, wet air that crept through the walls of the conference room. Nevertheless, he embraced the mug in a patient grasp and slowly sipped from the cup. As the steam reached his nose, his thoughts escaped back to his homeland.

"Kona coffee, Dr. Kihomi. The chef had it shipped in from the mainland with the last order of supplies when he heard you were coming. A little taste of home for you," Saenko said.

A little diversion from the Captain, Sam thought. He peeked over his cup at the counter where Odin's PR packets rested in a ray of bright sunlight. "I see from your brochure that you are familiar with my research."

Dr. Saenko blushed and Sam continued. "Listen, I am not here to ask for samples or to leak your information to competitors. Rather, I ask for your courtesy in sharing some of your research methods, as you have obviously benefited from mine."

Dr. Saenko tapped the PR folder in her lap, aware that Sam had her in a tough spot. She lowered her eyebrows and stared at Ivanov until he nodded back with a look of resignation in his eyes.

"You have a good point, Dr. Kihomi. I'm sure there are some aspects of our research that we could share with you." Dr. Saenko swung her seat around to the counter behind her and pulled a laptop from it. She swiveled back to the table and opened the screen so Sam could easily see. She turned back toward the counter, plucked a cordless mouse and activated the screen. Immediately a picture of the *Asgard* appeared online.

"Welcome to the *Asgard* research vessel," Ivanov said.

"I believe we've met." Sam urged Saenko on with a flick of his wrist.

81

"Our research vessel has been plying the waters of the Bering Sea for the past six months collecting data on the sea floor in hopes of developing a means to safely extract methane from methyl deposits that lie along the sea floor." Ivanov motioned for Dr. Saenko to advance to the next slide, which displayed a map of the Bering Sea.

"This map displays the territory where we have performed sonar and ultrasound readings on the sea floor to develop computer models depicting where the largest concentrations of free methane exist. It also helps us determine the thickness of the methyl hydrate crust," Dr. Saenko said. She clicked the mouse and a familiar picture appeared on the screen. "The submersible you saw being lifted onboard by our crane, is one of three on board. It collects samples of the crust, which we analyze for mineral content, strength and concentrations. We have two JSL's as well, so our crew can get a visual of the collecting process for added security."

"You perform all this testing onboard?"

"Yes, Doctor. With millions of dollars in the latest analytical equipment added to the submersibles and the hardware needed to maintain them, your question concerning the size of our operation should be answered now." Ivanov said.

"I don't question the size of your ship's deck and laboratory space, but if you don't mind my asking, why a supertanker? Isn't that cargo space going to waste?"

"As a researcher of methyl hydrates yourself you understand the importance of stability when dealing with methyl hydrates. When necessary, we fill the empty tank with sea water to stabilize ourselves. Perhaps because you flew out to meet us, you do not understand the turbulence of the Bering Sea."

"An extra 300,000 ton ballast tank?" Sam turned to Dr. Saenko. "I can see by your map that you've been traveling around the Sea quite a bit."

"We...well, we've been here for..."

"We put anchor on this spot when we heard of your desire to visit," Ivanov cut in. "An order from Kell Odin himself. Otherwise, we would have been out of range for the helicopter to land here. As you can see on our map, we have been moving closer and closer to the Russian coast. It is important that we complete our research before January brings the Arctic Ice. So you have, in effect, caused a temporary halt in operations, Dr. Kihomi."

"My apologies." Sam gulped his coffee. "With such a large ballast tank in this ship's belly, I just assumed that you anchored quite often. But you probably want to move out of here before the Opilio season begins as well, am I correct?"

"We're secure from the crab fishing industry." Ivanov snapped back. He stood abruptly and smacked the laptop shut. "Perhaps you should take Dr. Kihomi for his tour now, Alena. I have to get back to my staff on the bridge. Supertankers don't run themselves."

Actually, they pretty much do, Sam thought as he bit his tongue to stay quiet.

Led by Dr. Saenko alone, Sam found the weight of the air around him lessen even though he was stepping below deck. Dr. Saenko stopped him in a mud room just outside of a large metal door and instructed him to remove his cumbersome winter gear. Looking him up and down, she passed him the largest lab coat she could find and entered a numerical code into the door's electronic panel.

The doors whooshed open and the smell of stale ice and sea air immediately left Sam. He and Dr. Saenko stepped into a quiet and extremely brightly lit laboratory.

"We don't want our scientists to suffer from seasonal affective disorder." Dr. Saenko gestured to the bright fluorescent lights.

"This is a laboratory? It looks more like an airplane hangar."

"We converted most of the hold into an open space laboratory without all the walls and corridors to get in the way of the researchers. We've found that the open floor plan encourages the researchers to share ideas amongst different teams, which brings about innovative solutions to problems."

Sam gazed around the 40 or 50 lab benches, and listened to the purr and whistles of more than 100 lab instruments. Most of the instruments were automated, with robotic arms picking vials, piercing their caps with needles to take samples, and placing them back in their racks. His eyes followed the walls of the lab, overwhelmed by its size. But taking a closer look, he began to detect a pattern to the chaotic space.

The lab was broken into several smaller areas devoted to specific tests. On his left he recognized a large area dedicated to water testing equipment, an elemental analysis section full of atomic absorption spectrometers, UV spectrometers and infrared spectrometers. Beyond those toys, scientists worked at several sample prep areas. On his right, a majority of the equipment consisted of top-of-the-line gas chromatographs and liquid chromatographs.

The instruments before Sam's eyes were nothing out of the ordinary, but something about the front left of the lab intrigued him. He felt like he was in the middle of a *Star Trek* film. The wall was covered with LED lights, meters and LCD screens. Five chemists studied the displays, recording values on notepad computers.

"You seem right at home here." Dr. Saenko nearly shoved Sam toward another section of the lab, away from the foreign equipment.

"I see you do a lot of GC and mass spectrometry here." His gaze returned to the lab benches.

"Yes. Every soil sample that we retrieve from the seabed is

brought into this lab, dried out to remove the water, and then analyzed on the GC's. The way we've configured them, each GC can separate out over 150 different compounds in the soil, from simple compounds such as methane, to complex pesticide residues that may have collected there over the years."

When we see an unidentified compound, we continue on to the mass spectrometers, which determine the molecular weight of the unknown molecules. On the far side of the lab we have two nuclear magnetic resonance instruments and a few infrared spectrometers to also analyze them and tell us what components make up the molecules. We usually can identify an unknown in a matter of a day or two."

"I understand spectrometry." Sam watched Dr. Saenko's golden skin blush. "What are the most common compounds you've found in your research?"

"The usual blend of organic compounds. This area is like a collection basin in the Bering Sea. Over thousands of years, organic matter from plankton, plants, dead fish and crabs is carried by currents to this part of the seabed, where bacteria consume it and convert it to methane. As you know, the methane here is under enough pressure and at the right temperature to form a methyl hydrate. Over the centuries a very good amount of it has built up here.

Dr. Kihomi, if you don't mind my asking you a question…what is your business here now? I heard you have taken a step away from methyl hydrate research in favor of another area of study."

"Actually, I'm glad you asked that question. I like to dispel the myth that I've given up on methyl hydrates. I haven't abandoned my research at all. I've been studying the deposits of plastics on the ocean floor. As you know, polyethylene bottles break down over time in the ocean and are carried into deposition zones just like this one in the Bering Sea. But without conditions favorable for methyl hydrate formation, they build up as a fine layer of sand-like particles on the ocean floor. At HALO, we have begun to track the movement of waste to determine likely spots for the formation of methyl hydrates."

"Very interesting, but with the lack of civilization in these parts, I don't think you'll find much plastic waste here. Most of it is organic. Dead sea life."

"Like I said, I just want to learn from your research methods. Contrary to Captain Ivanov's beliefs, I am accustomed to turbulent seas and would love to know how your on-site testing works. I'm also curious about your success in testing sites like this one, off St. Paul Island. I've learned during my stay in Dutch Harbor that the fishing industry pretty much overruns this territory with its fleet. Aren't you afraid this will damage your testing site?"

"That is why we stay in motion. The king crab season has not affected us yet." Dr. Saenko's voice trailed and she cleared her throat. "Because we are somewhat funded by the US Department of Energy, they've set clear boundaries to ensure our operation goes undisturbed. Of course, we still hope to move out of this area before the next fishing season begins—out of courtesy, at least."

"I can imagine you also stay in motion to protect the integrity of the methyl hydrate on the seabed beneath you."

"Excuse me?"

"As a specialist in this area, I'm sure you're aware that too much drilling, even for samples, can upset the methyl hydrate's structure and cause catastrophic disaster, especially with fishermen cruising by, dropping hundreds of pounds in steel crab pots."

"Like I said, fishing boats have stayed out of this area." Alena snapped. "We are scientists here, Dr. Kihomi. Kell Odin has not poured billions of dollars into research just to end up creating what we're out here to avoid—the disaster of breaking the methyl hydrate under the sea."

"I'm sorry to insinuate…" He straightened his posture. "But I thought Kell Odin has not poured billions into this operation, the US Department of Energy has. And with all due respect, Odin is the moneyman here, not the scientist."

"Dr. Kihomi, I believe I have shared with you everything I am allowed to on this vessel. Captain Ivanov explained that much of our work here is confidential, even to scientists like yourself. I would take you to the bridge to see the captain, but he is preparing to take this ship to our next destination. I'm sorry to cut the tour short, but I think it's best to have Mr. Bergin escort you back to the helicopter now."

"That's fine, Dr. Saenko. I'm sorry to have imposed on your operation. I was under the impression that we could work symbiotically, but I see here that you are well-established without my assistance." Sam shook her hand. "Would I at least be able to thank the captain in person?"

"I'm certain the best thanks you can give us is to let Mr. Bergen escort you directly to the helicopter. This is Alaska, Dr. Kihomi. The sun will set soon and the clouds will roll in, and Mr. Odin would like his chopper back in Juneau safely."

"I'm sure it's his only one." Sam smiled, trying to look content with his tour.

Chapter Thirteen

The wind at Dutch Harbor changed from wet to freezing as the sun fainted behind the rocky horizon. Against the dead winter ground, the stratus clouds deepened until they lit up like charcoal amidst the blazing orange sunset. Automatically, the lights around the fishery buzzed in rebellion, refusing to let darkness shroud the hundreds of docked boats that lined the harbor.

One hundred feet away from the payroll office, Sarah pounded her fists into the canvas pockets of her Carhartt jacket and waited for fishery manager Paul Dorsey to stop making judgmental faces and make up his mind.

"No," he said.

"That's it? No application? No interview?"

"Sarah, you've caused me nothing but grief this season. There's no way you're working at the fishery in January."

"Grief? I've been here three times during the whole season and for less than ten minutes each time."

"My point exactly. You drive up here crazed, nearly knocking my men off the dock, then you storm my office files, which are confidential...and you've already wracked up three moving violations—one for a boat you don't even own."

"That's not grief, Paul. I had a good reason for every trip I've made here."

"You're right, that's not grief. Grief would be kind. You're a walking citation."

Paul turned to leave but Sarah hooked a heavy hand around his arm, spinning him nearly off his feet. "Please, Paul, I need the money. The bar is dry and…I know everything about the fishing industry."

"Then go fishing." Paul pulled his arm from her grip and motioned to Captain Brian Eriksson, who stepped from his car in the distance. "The *Adrienne Anne* needs a new deckhand for Opie season."

"You're an asshole, Paul." Sarah turned from Paul, whipping her long ponytail into the air, nearly striking his face with her heavy locks. She ducked her chin down and stomped into the wind toward her car.

"Easy there, kid," a pair of gloved hands clamped around Sarah's arms and she looked up startled.

"Sorry, Brian," she said after recognizing his truck, then his face under the floodlights above.

Sam stepped out of the passenger side of Brian's truck and Sarah froze, unaware that her eyes had locked on his silhouette.

"I picked up this stranger in the field just by the fishery," Brian said. "He was looking for you. Says he's helping you with a marine biology class?"

"Dr. Kiho…Sam, of course—he's helping me work out some new crab routes for next season." Sarah extended her hand and Sam gave it a squeeze, warming her raw skin momentarily in his plush gloves.

"I'm sorry to barge in on you guys here, but my car never showed up at the Vertiport. There must have been some confusion at the hotel."

"How did you guys know I'd be here?" Sarah said.

"We didn't. I was just taking Sam to the nearest phone. What are you doing here, Sarah?"

Sarah let out a gruff sigh and relaxed her posture. "I'm begging Paul for work, but it doesn't look good. He hates me."

"Still no cash from Captain Jack, huh?" Brian looked directly over her head at the fishery. "Why don't you take your guest to the phone in the office and I'll see what I can do with Dorsey over there."

"Brian, I appreciate it, but you don't have to…"

"Nonsense, Sarah. Besides, this Hawaiian looks like he's freezing to death."

"Come on, Sam. Office is this way."

With at least half a foot on Sarah, Sam still had to trot to keep up with her anxious stride toward the fishery office. She doubled her pace as they strode by Paul and Brian, whose flailing hands marked a heated discussion.

"What's the rush?" Sam panted as he followed Sarah into the office.

"What happened on the ship?" Sarah took a seat on Paul's desk and scooted to its edge, leaning into the conversation.

Sam stretched back and tapped the heavy wooden door behind him, letting it close gently. "A lot…but we should talk about it later, somewhere else."

"No, I can't wait another second. Besides, the guys here think I'm crazy anyway. What's one more scene going to cause?"

"Unemployment?" Sam smiled and nodded toward the office window, where Paul could see Sarah sitting on his desk.

"You're right. Hey, how about a tour of the *Westender*? I have to clean her up anyway. Paul won't think that's weird."

Sarah jumped off Paul's desk and slipped out of the office. She led Sam around the front of the fishery down a dimly lit boardwalk that crackled under their boots. The sun had set completely and the sound of the water against the harbor and the wind whipping through the docked boats made the freezing air seem even colder. Sarah tugged her jacket around herself and tried to squint into the wind amidst her dry, stinging eyes.

"Here she is." Sarah stopped abruptly and Sam slid to a stop before knocking into her.

She wrapped her bare hands in the cuffs of her jacket and climbed onboard the *Westender*. "Be careful around this part," she yelled into the wind at Sam. "The deck's a mess—there's a gap in the floorboards."

She kept her eyes on Sam until he stepped safely on board, then motioned for him to follow her aft. The wind picked up, shoving the two up the stairs to the pilothouse of the ship. Sarah shook her hands feverishly, fighting the stinging air that numbed her dexterity. Her clumsy hands unlocked the entrance and she waited for another gust to pass before pushing the heavy steel door open and jumping into the wheelhouse.

"Windy enough for ya?" She smiled at Sam, who brushed bits of ice from his face. "And to think, we're still at port. Imagine this thing a few hundred miles out in the middle of the sea."

"Your friends are pretty tough."

"Nah, they're mostly crazy, poor, or just stupid." Sarah flicked on the lights and took a seat in the captain's chair, motioning for Sam to take the seat beside her. "Now tell me, what happened on the *Asgard*?"

"Well, for starters, my tour lasted about fifteen seconds longer than the one you just gave me of the *Westender*."

"So it was a fifteen-second tour?" She blushed. "I thought they were all excited to have you onboard."

"They were, until I started asking them questions about their operations."

"Well what'd they expect?"

"I don't know, Sarah. I think they assumed I was like Odin—more politician than scientist. They accosted me with a cheesy PowerPoint presentation about how impressive their research supertanker is, but I couldn't shake the feeling that their extraordinary operation is just an extraordinary waste of space."

"Did they say what they used all that space for?"

"They do have a lot of hardware—three submersibles and maintenance areas for each. They also had some space set aside for lab equipment. But for a ship of that size and a guy with that much dough, the conference room looked like a kid's tree house. And they conducted their presentation off a laptop. Not even a widescreen lap top."

"Sounds glamorous."

"It looked more like a storage room, which was odd in itself. A guy like Odin, who meets with investors and government officials, should have a better suited area to conduct meetings."

"Maybe he doesn't have meetings onboard."

"My thoughts exactly. Meaning that anybody who's anybody has not seen the *Asgard*—including Odin's investors."

"Interesting…what else? What did the lab look like?"

"The lab seemed legitimate. It was set up for the usual tests. And since they have three submersibles collecting samples, they can collect a lot more and run a lot more tests. Most of the equipment is automated, and there were some white-coats wandering about. But still, I didn't see why they needed that much room for testing. It's not like increasing the amount of tests you do is going to change the results."

"What about the tank?" Sarah scooted to the edge of her seat. "I'm dying to know what they're putting in there. I mean, it's big enough to fit this whole boat…and probably the *Adrienne Anne* too."

"Are you ready for this?" Sam leaned back in his seat and clasped his hands behind his head. "It's a ballast tank."

"The whole thing?"

"Yep. They just fill it with sea water and use it as a giant level."

"Are you serious?" Sarah rose from her seat. "That's ridiculous, not to mention anti climactic."

"My thoughts exactly."

"Why would you even need that?"

"You may want to sit back down for this ground-breaking answer," Sam paused for effect. "They said they need it to keep the tanker stable in the rough waters of the Bering Sea so they could gather and test samples more effectively."

"But don't the submersibles collect the samples?"

"You picked up on that too, huh? But wait, there's more."

"Oh God." Sarah slumped in her seat.

"They also claimed that they're in constant motion around the Bering Sea. They said they travel so often, in fact, that my visiting put a halt to their entire operation."

"That's bullshit. According to the satellite picture I have on my computer, the *Asgard* hasn't moved from that spot since at least early September. The picture has been updated a couple times, but the *Asgard's* always in the same spot. Every time I zoom out to the fishery, I can see the different boats in and out of the harbor...it picked up the beginning and end of brown king season and the *Asgard* is there for all of it."

"Has it moved even a little?"

"In one picture, the boat completely disappeared, but that was a satellite glitch. When I refreshed the page, the boat was back. It hasn't moved. Besides, why would they need that super ballast tank if they were in motion most of the time?" Sarah paused to think. "And why would they lie about their position?"

"My guess is to cover up that they're testing irresponsibly. If they take too many samples from the same spot, they could ruin the integrity of the methyl hydrate. But the scientists onboard know that, so I'm stumped as to why they won't move."

93

Sam sat back, seemingly in thought, and Sarah craned her neck to look out the window of the *Westender*. Before long, she swiveled back to face him.

"Hey, Paul's coming. Grab a mop and look busy." She tossed her mop at Sam and led him down to the ship's deck.

"It's about time you got that rig cleaned up!" The wind carried Paul's voice to the deck and Sarah began scrubbing until he turned back toward the fishery.

"Okay, you can stop looking busy." Sarah tapped Sam, who picked at the crab carcasses onboard.

"Mind if I take this?" He held up an adult female crab.

"It's junk. And it's spoiled."

"I don't want to eat it, Sarah." He laughed. "But if you'd show me to the galley…"

"Sam, you're scaring me." She made a sour face and waved her hand in front of her nose.

"Just take me to the galley…I want to perform a little operation on this girl."

"The galley's below the wheelhouse…but you're not going to bring her back to life."

Sarah looked once more for workers on the dock before she stashed her mop and joined Sam below deck. By the time she reached the *Westender*'s galley, Sam had plucked the crab from its shell.

"Wow, you are hungry. You know, normally you don't eat the head…"

"I told you I'm not eating it." Sam kept his face buried in his work. "The reason I got the crab out of her shell so fast is because she was molting, which is extremely abnormal."

"Crabs don't molt?"

"Crabs do molt." He looked up at Sarah. "But they only do so when they ably have to—because they're growing or if they're injured. This crab is neither."

"It could have easily been thrown around the boat and injured."

"I found this crab in one of the pots. There's not a scratch on it. And it's not too big for its shell."

"Maybe it just got bored." Sarah sat beside Sam at the table.

"Molting is a risky operation. The crabs have to pull themselves nearly inside out to molt—they risk death every time they crawl out of their shell. There's an over 50 percent chance of fatal injury each time it sheds its shell. "

"It's still not as deadly as crab fishing." Sarah spoke to the crab. "Crab fishing has a 100 percent injury rate…beat that."

"It can't hear you, Sarah." Sam pulled at the crab's insides, unfolding what looked like a cross between a gill and lung.

"That's why we don't eat the head," Sarah said into her hand, covering her nose from the foul smelling animal.

"Smell that?"

"Um, yes."

"Smells like passing gas, doesn't it?"

"You could just say 'excuse me' and get on with your work there, doctor."

"That wasn't me, it's the crab." He pushed the body toward Sarah and pointed at the crab's lung. "This crab was asphyxiated, that's why it tried to crawl out of its shell. There's scarring tissue on the lung…and that smell trapped inside. Do you know what this means?"

"That you tried to blame your flatulence on a dead crab?"

"It's methane. The crab suffocated to death due to an overabundance of methane."

"Uh-huh. You told me methane isn't toxic."

"It is when it displaces oxygen. This crab choked to death on a concentrated dose of methane. And since a molting crab can't crawl into a trap, it happened onboard, above the water."

"And that's not normal, is it?"

Frozen Tide

"The sea leaks natural gas from time to time—but enough to breach the surface and at a concentration powerful enough to asphyxiate…no, it's not normal at all."

Chapter Fourteen

Captain Peter Ivanov paced the length of the *Asgard*'s bridge, waiting for Dr. Saenko to answer his page. Behind him, Brenda Anderson sat in her seat paying more attention to Ivanov than to the navigation and weather screens in front of her. More automated than the usual supertanker, the *Asgard* required no additional staff in the bridge, especially while the ship sat motionless in the water.

"Peter, you knew the visit wouldn't be pleasant..." Brenda said.

"Shut up, I'm trying to think."

"About what? You conducted yourself as Odin asked you to...he would have been here himself if he was worried about Dr. Kihomi's presence."

"Odin hasn't been here in days. And that doctor saw right through us, I know he suspected..."

Before Ivanov could finish, Dr. Saenko stepped gracefully through the door wearing her white lab coat. She glided toward him with her head down and her hands busy poking a pointy black stylus at the screen of her PDA.

"Dr. Saenko, I see you're standing at attention as usual." Ivanov tapped his foot, waiting for her regard.

"Unlike this ship, captain, my lab doesn't run itself." She

slipped the PDA in her pocket. "You want to know about the tour—and Dr. Kihomi, no doubt."

"Where exactly did you take him?"

"To the spectrometry lab. I showed him the same equipment he uses to conduct his own research. Ours, of course, have more bells and whistles, but it was nothing to raise suspicion."

"Good. Then you believe he left here satisfied and not skeptical?"

"I didn't say that, sir. He's completely suspicious of our operations." She removed her black-rimmed reading glasses and looked directly into Ivanov's eyes. "He asked all the right questions."

"I thought you said you showed him nothing." Ivanov's breaths grew deeper and he began to pace again. "What do you mean by 'the right questions'?"

"The size of the tank...the route we've sailed...the methyl hydrate crust integrity...Oh, and he mentioned the crab fishing season as well."

"And your answers to these questions?"

"I showed him to the door, just as you asked."

Ivanov stopped, leaning his head into a clammy hand. He turned to Brenda, who answered him with a stern face and a shrug of her shoulders.

"What did he ask about fishing season?" his voice creaked.

"Same question as in the conference room. He asked if we had encountered any ships. And he asked if our activity around the methyl hydrate crust had caused any environmental disturbances—all very good questions."

"Those questions have been asked by others before," Brenda said. "So why should we worry this time?"

"Ms. Anderson, Dr. Kihomi is the world's leading scientist in methyl hydrate research." Dr. Saenko approached Brenda, who sat dwarfed by her looming posture. "If anybody was to figure out exactly what we're doing out here, Dr. Kamuela Kihomi would be that person."

Brenda rose from her chair and stepped forward into Dr. Saenko's personal space, forcing her to retreat several steps as she headed for the ship's intercom system.

"That will be all, Alena," Ivanov said. "You can return to your busy lab now."

Dr. Saenko graciously excused herself and glided out of the door.

"What are you doing?" Ivanov called to Brenda.

"I'm paging Erik Bergen. You heard what Saenko said. That doctor can blow the whistle on us. We need to take care of our little indiscretion now."

"Indiscretion? This whole operation is Odin's responsibility, we just work here."

"That's not what I'm talking about." She paused to place her call. Then she turned to face Ivanov. "I mean the fishing vessel. The one we 'took care of' without Odin's knowledge."

"That crab ship? That's in the past, Brenda. Besides, how could Dr. Kihomi possibly be on to that?"

"I don't know, Peter. But according to you and Dr. Saenko, he asked about the fishing industry more than once. I just think that we should come clean to Odin and let him handle this."

Ivanov paused. "You're right. This is Odin's area of expertise. And I only kept it from him to help him during the Natural Gas Summit. I believe I handled it as he would have, so he won't…"

"Oh, who cares if he's mad at you? We have to deal with the problem before he hears it from Dr. Kihomi or worse, the fishing industry. They could bring about an investigation that could shut us down in a heartbeat."

An uncomfortable silence swept across the bridge, amplifying the clack of the door's latch as Bergen approached. The powerful man ducked under the door's frame and towered over Ivanov and Brenda.

"You called?" Bergen said.

"It's time we tell Odin about our visit a few weeks ago from that fishing ship. Dr. Saenko believes it may impact our operations here."

"You're afraid that visiting scientist will say something?" Bergen flashed a shrewd grin.

"Just fall back, Erik, in case you're needed." Ivanov motioned to Brenda. "Get Kell Odin on the speaker."

The ship's speakers blasted Odin's ring tone and Ivanov rocked into the heels of his black dress shoes. Bergen stood motionless behind him, poised as if guarding the door.

"Captain Ivanov, I assume your visit went well this morning," Odin's voice boomed throughout the bridge. "Now get me off speaker phone."

Ivanov jumped to the intercom and plucked the handset, pressing it to his ear. "I apologize sir. We're joined only by Brenda Anderson and Erik Bergen."

"If I wanted to address the room, I would have called a conference. Now, how did Dr. Kihomi's visit go?"

"Not—not smoothly sir." Ivanov could feel sweat forming around the rim of the phone.

"Explain, Peter."

"He asked several, well, 'good questions' is what Dr. Saenko called them. She believes he's suspicious of our operations here."

Odin's heavy sigh blasted through the phone. "You conducted your conference with him as I instructed, didn't you? And you only showed him the appropriate areas of the ship?"

"Yes, sir. We did exactly what you asked."

"Then why the anxiety, Peter? This visit was intended to alleviate any uncertainty the doctor had about our operations here, not to create more questions."

"We have reason to believe he's…he's biased." Ivanov gripped the receiver tightly, feeling sweat ooze around his fingers.

"Biased about his own field of research?" Odin paused. "What are you really trying to tell me, Peter?"

"I—I did neglect to fill you in on a small matter that is most likely completely unrelated to Dr. Kihomi's visit. But Dr. Saenko and I deemed it significant, only in the slightest, to tell you."

"You're going on like a culpable child now, Peter. What did you fail to tell me?"

Ivanov looked at Brenda who immediately turned from his gaze. "There was a fishing vessel near our operations just a few weeks ago, Mr. Odin. You were at the natural gas conference and I instructed your security team to take care of the situation in your absence. It didn't seem important enough to bother you at the time."

"Yet you see it fit to bother me now. What happened with this fishing vessel?"

"They didn't approach us, but they were close and they seemed to be having troubles—they sat in the same position for quite some time. I instructed Bergen to take his team onboard and assess the situation. When he reported that the crew was incapacitated, I instructed him to take the ship back to its port at Dutch Harbor. I told him to be subtle—not to create a scene, if you understand."

"You mean you told Bergen to dispose of the crew and return the fishing vessel back to port under the guise that he was legitimately returning for the season as a crewmate."

"That about sums it up, sir." Ivanov listened to Odin's strong, even breaths over the phone.

"Peter, the disappearance of a fishing crew is the opposite of subtle. And Dr. Kihomi's visit came just weeks after the incident you mentioned, am I correct?"

"Yes, sir, but he can't be…"

"Dr. Kihomi is staying at the Grand Aleutian Hotel, in Unalaska. He's a stone's throw from Amaknak Island and the Dutch Harbor fishery where you instructed my very high profile head of security to dock that ghost ship."

"Yes, sir, but the two events are unrelated."

"You incompetent imbecile!" Odin shouted. "You let me invite the lead methyl hydrate researcher directly into what could only be construed as a colossal, potentially detrimental crime scene."

"But Mr. Odin, he's a scientist, not a detective or a government..."

"Do you know who his father is, Peter? Iohunakana Kihomi is the founder and chief operator of the Hawaiian Archipelago Laboratory Organization. I'm sure you've heard of HALO."

"It's a hippie, tree hugging, save the universe operation—and he's still just a scientist."

"HALO is connected to almost every political department I've worked over during our entire operation. If I had connections to every government official on this planet, which I nearly do, Iohunakana Kihomi has connections to them, their colleagues, their superiors—hell, he probably knows their wives, children and house pets. HALO alone pushed a government project to secure more than 90 percent of Hawaii's ecology. It has reign over half of the Pacific Ocean if not more than that."

"Look, I don't know a whole lot about politics, but I'm guessing that if the United States government had a choice between your tripling the size of its oil industry and HALO's shutting it down—well, you seem to have the upper hand, Mr. Odin."

"Which is why I'm going to take care of this." Odin paused. "I see I'm going to have to spend a lot more time on the *Asgard*, Captain. And I will also have to find a really subtle way to nudge Dr. Kihomi back to his own research in Oahu."

"I agree. Thank you, sir..."

"Believe me, Peter, the last thing you're going to do is thank me. Consider your throne on the *Asgard* usurped. And get Erik Bergen on the phone please."

Ivanov slowly withdrew the phone from his ear and passed it to Bergen, who snatched it readily with an eager grin on his face. Brenda cast a grave stare into Ivanov's eyes.

"Oh, stop giving that doe-eyed look, Anderson. I'm still the captain of this ship for now."

"So I heard it correctly then." Her voice quivered. "Odin is taking your position here? Jesus, Peter, what are you going to do?"

"You've been working for that lunatic too long, Brenda. It's just a job. And I was getting sick of it anyway."

Brenda held Ivanov's gaze. A solemn frown crept across her face.

"What? So he'll put me on a dinghy for a while or dock my pay…I'll get over it."

Brenda motioned to Bergen, who nodded as he pressed the receiver close to his head. A maniacal grin crept across his face and his glassy eyes settled on Ivanov, scanning him from head to toe. When the conversation ended, Bergen pulled the receiver from his face, holding it like a trophy as he stepped between Brenda and Ivanov. His strong arm flexed tightly as he passed it across Brenda's face to replace the receiver.

"What the hell are you so smug about?" Ivanov said.

Bergen eyeballed him. "Kell Odin will be here tomorrow to take your position on this ship, captain." He turned to Brenda. "And he has just promoted me to first mate."

Brenda's posture broke and her eyes immediately welled up with tears. Ivanov felt his nostrils flare and his face burn as he stood motionless, panting.

"Come on, you two, buck up." Bergen grinned. "This isn't how you want to spend your final hours…onboard the *Asgard*, I mean."

Chapter Fifteen

Sarah swept through a soft layer of ash-blonde hair, pulling it from her face so she could look more carefully at the arctic environmental atlas she had printed from the Internet. She followed the tectonic plates to find her home on the Ring of Fire. They stood up and passed the bar toward an oceanic map Sam had given her.

"This place is dead, Sarah." Ian's voice grumbled over the sound of clanking ice in his empty glass. "You should be working on a way to revive it."

"In a way, I am." She returned to her map, which rested on the opposite side of the bar.

"Brian said you were at the fishery earlier, hitting Dorsey up for a job."

"Yeah, and I didn't get one, so I'm free to do some work of my own."

"Probably because Dorsey saw you with that scientist guy on Jack's boat."

"What?"

"The reason Paul didn't hire you—most likely because you've been running around town with that Hawaiian."

"Running around town? You act like I'm having an affair."

"Well, in a way you are." He looked into his glass. "Sarah, I thought we agreed to keep the *Westender*'s troubles to ourselves, at least for now. And here you are, taking some foreigner for a tour."

"The *Westender* is not some dirty little secret, Ian. And Sam's been an incredible help. Just look at all of the data he handed to me about the ecosystem right where we all fish. He's also the reason Jack was having such a good season out there before. He pointed out the migration patterns of the red kings." Sarah leaned into the table. "I need a calculator." She rushed back to the other side of the bar.

"He's not one of us." Ian shook his glass as Sarah passed him again. "And why are you burying your head in that junk instead of giving me a refill? I'm your only customer and you've got your mind stuck on—what is that stuff again?"

"Oceanographic maps and test results detailing the compounds in the water. Here I've got migration patterns and evolutionary data on hundreds of species of Alaskan crabs...I forgot my pencil."

Sarah turned back toward the other side of the bar and Ian grabbed her wrist. "I'm sure the evolutionary whatever is great, but all I and any other native to these parts want to know is how many pots and how many crabs are in them. You're going on like you're enrolled in another one of your online classes."

"That's not a bad thing." Sarah pulled free from Ian and raced toward a cup full of stubby pencils. "As much as you chalk your fishing seasons up to luck, it wouldn't hurt to have some knowledge backing it up. I could probably rake up some dough if I got a degree in marine ecology. I'd be the only Ph.D. on this island."

"And hell, you've passed the bar so many times, why don't you become the island's only lawyer too?"

"What?" She stopped.

"You're a bartender, Sarah. Sure, maybe once you were a killer deckhand, but now you can't get a job at the docks and you refuse to fish. And bowing out of the fishing industry in Dutch Harbor makes you one thing: a bartender. So give me a goddamn drink and stop burying yourself in maps and charts and online courses…and for the love of God, kick that foreigner out and save what's left of your reputation around here."

Sarah's shoulders dropped and her fingers went limp, letting the small pencil fall to the ground. She lowered her eyes, following the pencil and waiting for the sharp clack it would make against the floor. Instead, she heard a heavy knock.

"Who the hell is that?" Ian spun his stool around to face the door.

Sarah pulled her hands into the sleeves of her wool fisherman's sweater and trudged to the entrance, trying to make out a blurry figure through the art glass near its handle. She pushed against the wind to open the door and recognized Sam's puffy Gore-Tex coat and black balaclava.

"Sam!" She threw her arms around him then withdrew, blushing.

"Well, I'm glad someone's happy to see me." He pulled off his hat, revealing a wild tuft of static-teased black hair.

"Oh we're thrilled to see you," Ian called from the bar. "What are you doing here? You want your maps and shit back?"

"Don't pay attention to him, Sam. Would you like a drink?"

"What the…" Ian picked up his empty glass and slammed it into the bar. "I'm out of here Sarah. But remember what we talked about." He eyeballed Sam on his way to the door and exited, wearing only a lined flannel shirt to combat the cold.

"Did I interrupt something?"

"Don't mind Ian, he only acts that way when he's sober. What are you doing here, though?"

"You won't believe this one, but I got kicked out of my hotel."

"What did you do? I mean, you said you were a VIP there— why the change of heart?"

"They said they needed the room for a high profile client. They offered me a refund and a free week's stay next season though."

"Because Unalaska's tourism is so hot, no doubt. No offense, but they can't simply be out of room in the middle of November. Who's this high profile guy that's taking up every room in the off season?"

"I didn't ask and they wouldn't have told me." Sam took Ian's seat at the bar. "I see you're doing some research there."

"Nothing groundbreaking, I just wanted to understand a little more about the sea—so I could cut down on those stupid questions I keep asking you."

"Your questions are anything but stupid, Sarah. Remember, you were the one who told me about this place to begin with."

"And then the Grand Aleutian kicked you out. Do you have another place to stay?"

"Curiously, Unalaska only has one operational hotel during the dead season. But I'm sure I can find a place less local."

"You're welcome to stay with me." Sarah felt her face blush again. "I mean, Jack's office has a futon and it's relatively warm in there. Well, there are blankets."

"Tempting offer." Sam perked an eyebrow. "Irresistible if there's a computer in there."

"The computer's upstairs, in my room."

"Oh, I don't want to impose. I just—the hotel is holding my things until I find another place to stay. My computer is with my suitcase."

"You don't need to explain, Sam. Just go up the far staircase until the temperature drops about 20 degrees and it looks like you're going to climb right through the ceiling—that's my loft. The light switch is just outside the door under the casement window and the computer is, well, it's the biggest thing in the room. You can't miss it. It's already logged on, so do what you need to and I'll call the Grand Aleutian about your stuff." She smiled. "You know, you shouldn't trust your worldly possessions to a bunch of strangers."

"Thanks, Sarah, but only if it's not a bother…"

"Sam, you traveled hundreds of miles from paradise to this godforsaken place just to answer my questions. The least I can do is let you borrow my computer."

Sam stood and stretched, and Sarah took in every second of it. He crossed the bar and made his way up the loft on the wooden staircase that groaned under each step. Midway to the top, he stopped and gave a wary look at the rotting wood, then back into Sarah's eyes. She flashed a teasing smile and waved her hands at Sam, urging him to hurry upstairs.

With her eyes still fixated on the staircase, Sarah pulled the phone from its place under the bar and followed the tone of the keys to dial the Grand Aleutian Hotel. Her fingers had memorized the number after ten years of working in Jack's bar. She ordered Sam's belongings sent to her doorstep and hung up the phone.

Approaching midnight, Sarah pulled her apron from her waist, cast a look at the vacant bar and dimmed the lights. She strolled to the front door and slid the deadbolt to the locked position. Then she turned the bar's neon beacon off on her way toward the loft. A soft blue glow flickered at the top of the staircase and she smiled as she tucked her hands in her sleeves and climbed toward the light.

"The driver is away for the night," She said as she stepped into her loft. "They said they'll bring your stuff over first thing in the morning. They also offered to set you up with a return flight, free of charge due to the inconvenience of kicking you out on your…"

"Again?" Sam flashed an amused grin. "They've been offering me a ticket home all night. You think someone wants me out of Alaska?"

"What are you looking at?" Sarah leaned over Sam's shoulder into a foreign website.

"I'm just checking out a site through HALO. It's like a virtual tour of the Bering Sea bed. The thought of that ship taking samples from the same place has been nagging me all night…then there's the crab we found on your friend's boat."

"Do you think the *Asgard* caused the methane leak?"

"As a scientist, I shouldn't jump to that conclusion, but it would explain why a crab would die of asphyxiation onboard a ship. Jack's boat doesn't run on natural gas, does it?"

"Nope, it's got two diesel engines—you think the boat could have leaked methane?"

"No, it's not the right fuel. Besides, that crab didn't breathe-in exhaust and ships don't run on methane vapors. It would have to be liquefied to be used as fuel."

"So the methane came from the sea, most likely where Odin was taking his samples. It has to be the *Asgard* then."

"I keep coming to the same conclusion, Sarah. But we have so little evidence and Odin's guys made it painfully clear that they haven't been in the same spot." Sam rubbed his temples and Sarah sat down on the bed directly behind him. "They did have those submersibles though. A submersible could take hundreds more samples than we could do by hand. Maybe they're just taking too much too fast."

"Wouldn't they have noticed a methane leak though?"

"Not if they weren't breathing it in. On its own, methane is colorless and odorless. The only way you could see it is if it was bubbling to the surface of the water, and around a submersible, bubbles don't look so odd. Onboard a supertanker like the *Asgard*, you can't even see the water and nobody was working on deck, so nobody would have breathed it in."

"Why would it cause the crab to die then? Was it a small enough amount that it only killed that little crab?"

"No, that crab died because it was closer to the leak, on the deck of a fishing vessel that's designed to overlook the water. And if there's anything I've learned about life in the Bering Sea, it's that crabs have it all over us humans in terms of survival. Their natural habitat is closer to methane deposits than ours is, so they should be more equipped to handle exposure. For a crab to suffocate, it would have to take in air that had less than 18 percent of oxygen in it. People can't live in that situation either."

"So wait, that means if the crab suffocated on deck..." Sarah bowed her head in thought, hearing Sam turn to face her.

"Sarah, look at me." He placed one hand on her shoulder and gently lifted her chin with the other. "I said we have no evidence backing up any of this. It's speculation and I shouldn't have taken it this far anyway."

"No, Sam, you're right." Sarah looked into his dark brown eyes. "I know you don't like to speculate, but your theory makes sense. And if you're right, we have more than just Jack and Nate to worry about. Opilio season begins in a couple months and that testing site is only going to get more dangerous if we don't stop Odin now."

"I don't want to upset you anymore, but 'stop' and 'Odin' are rarely used in the same sentence. He's not only one of the country's largest suppliers of fuel; he's their new superman. He has also promised hundreds of jobs to Alaskan workers."

"And the other major industry here is fishing. 90 percent of the work in the Aleutian Chain comes from the fishing industry, so we can't ask them to stop their work either." Sarah fell back into her bed. "Sam, what do we do?"

"We find proof." Sam's fingers clicked feverishly at the keyboard. "You're right, we can't ask over eighty boats to stop fishing. Plus, they're helping the environment through population control. Odin's the bad guy here; he's the one we have to stop. But we need actual proof that..."

"That what?" Sarah sprung upright and craned her neck to sec the computer screen. "Your voice trailed off, what were you saying about proof?"

"Sarah, is this the satellite picture you downloaded of the *Asgard*?" Sam backed away from the screen and pulled Sarah closer.

"That's the picture. It refreshes every…" Sarah leaned closer into the screen, nearly touching it with her nose. "Oh my god, Sam, do you think that's…"

"It looks about the size of a fishing vessel, wouldn't you say? And it's approaching the *Asgard*—how do you find the date of this picture?"

"Give me the mouse." Sarah placed her hand over Sam's mouse-hand and clicked the right button, ordering the image to pan away from the ship. The *Asgard* left the screen and the cursor sailed the Bering Sea until it landed on Amaknak Island. Sarah zoomed in on the island, revealing the Dutch Harbor fishery minus 100 ships.

"No ships docked. It's late October," she said.

"Then that ship approaching the *Asgard* could be…"

"The *Westender*."

"The *Asgard*'s captain said no crab vessel had ever approached them. But according to the satellite picture, that smaller ship is just miles away from Odin's supertanker."

"So Sam, do we have proof now?"

"Not yet, I'm afraid. This is still a very blurry image and it doesn't tell us exactly which ship is approaching the *Asgard* and why. It could be a supply ship, for all we know."

"Supplies would come from the east, from St. Paul Island. This ship is coming from the south."

"Good eye, Sarah." He grabbed her hand from the mouse and gave it a squeeze. "Odin also doesn't get many visitors onboard and he arrives by helicopter. Maybe if we could get a

111

clearer image that we could update a little more quickly—it would definitely help."

"Logical request, Sam, but they make you pay extra for that." Sarah returned Sam's squeeze. "I gave this site ten bucks last week to learn that there was a signal error viewing this ship with more sophisticated imagery."

"The bastard blocked it." Sam slammed the mouse down, freeing both their hands.

"What?"

"I was wondering why Odin would let people satellite-view his ship in the first place, but it makes sense now. This photo on your screen isn't a satellite picture. These website satellites only detect the imagery. Then a lot of them get a chopper to fly by and photograph it—that's why it takes so long to update the image. When you pay money to see the better, more recent image, you're actually paying to see the satellite picture, no air-crafts involved. Odin must have blocked the satellite signal, but he had no control over the cheesy helicopter photography."

"So in a nutshell, this is as good as our picture gets."

"Precisely."

"Then we're screwed."

"Nah. I've conquered bigger waves." Sam swirled around in Sarah's chair, scanning the loft. "Do you have a phone up here?"

Sarah reached under a pile of clothing resting in the corner of her bed against the wall and plucked out a cordless phone.

"Do you mind a long distance call to Oahu?" Sam took the phone and grinned.

"Don't tell me you have your own satellite."

"Better, I have my dad."

Sam dialed what seemed like an inordinate amount of num-bers for an intra-country call, and immediately asked to speak to Dr. Iohunakana Kihomi. Although she knew Sam was speaking English, his jargon-infused responses to his father were foreign to Sarah. Nevertheless, she sat glued to the edge of her bed, watching Sam's expressive eyes widen and his strong jaw tighten in reaction to the conversation.

"Sarah," Sam asked with the phone still glued to his head. "Did you mention that one time the *Asgard* seemed to disappear on the satellite image?"

"Yeah, but the screen refreshed and it was back."

"Did weeks pass before the satellite picture updated?"

"Days, I think."

Sam returned to his phone call and Sarah continued to try and listen in. At one point, his voice reached a crescendo and he grabbed for a pencil. He scribbled names and percentages onto the back of an expired restaurant coupon that rested on Sarah's desk. She knew the conversation was coming to a close twenty minutes later, when Sam's responses changed from scientific gibberish to common thanks and salutations.

"Well, what did he say?" Sarah bounced slightly at the edge of her bed. "Can he get us a better connection?"

"Not a satellite connection, but he did find some interesting information from his political ones."

"Explain, please."

"The Alaskan governor just invited my father to a press conference called by Kell Odin himself. Odin basically designed it so he can toot his own horn about the recent supply of natural gas that he has been able to supply to the pipeline."

"Odin Energy supplying fuel—that's not front page news for us Alaskans, Sam."

"It is if you consider the amount of fuel he's managed to scrounge up when the Natural Gas Contract was ironed out only weeks ago. The contract was designed to encourage oil companies to gather surplus fuel and deliver it through an expanded pipeline to the United States in the long run—like a few years. Odin is bragging that he has the fuel now."

"So you think he was just sitting on a supply of natural gas, waiting for this moment so he could be first in line to deliver?"

"That's unlikely. I know Alaska has some reserve fuel, but to think Odin had a sizeable supply that he wasn't using…I don't see how he could do that and still make his business quotas."

"Okay, then how did he dredge up this surplus supply of fuel so fast?"

"That's only the first big question."

"I can't wait to hear the second."

"According to my dad's contacts, the shipment arrived for inspection this week on one of Odin's supertankers, but all of the ships in the fleet, including the *Asgard* were accounted for."

"So Odin has an extra supertanker."

"Odin has an extra supertanker that magically arrived in Juneau while all of his other tankers are working on the other side of the continent, in the Atlantic Ocean. No way. This extra ship had to travel to Juneau from only a few hundred miles away. Say, west of St. Paul Island?"

"That's where the *Asgard* is." Sarah paused. "But I still don't get it. The *Asgard* doesn't carry fuel."

"Remember when the *Asgard* disappeared and reappeared again?" Sam refreshed the computer screen, showing Sarah the satellite picture.

"On the monitor, yeah."

"I don't think that was a computer glitch. I think there are two ships, and your satellite image witnessed the changing of the guards—the *Asgard*s to be precise." He looked at Sarah, obviously waiting for her to fix her confused expression. "That's how Odin can have proof that the *Asgard* has been in motion, yet keep it in one place at the same time."

"But wait, why would Odin hide a tanker full of fuel just to conceal the fact that his research ship hasn't moved? It seems like an expensive way to cover up a lie."

"Not if he's trying to cover up the lie I'm thinking of."

Sarah raced through hypotheses, trying to catch up with Sam's train of thought.

"I have another speculation." Sam interrupted.

"Your speculations are scary, Sam, but they're all we got." She grabbed his hands and stared at him with wide eyes. "What's your theory?"

"Here goes—Odin isn't lying to secure illegal testing practices. In fact, he isn't even keeping the *Asgard* in one place to gather samples. And he hasn't concealed a tanker full of fuel merely as an expensive alibi." Sam paused, drawing in a deep breath. "I think Odin's drilling through the methyl hydrate crust. And he's filling his tankers with fuel, not sea water. The *Asgard* isn't a research tanker, it's an old fashioned supertanker— carrying liquid methane from the bottom of the sea."

"What?" Sarah let Sam's hands go and jumped to her feet. "Sam, you can't drill into a methyl hydrate crust, you said it yourself. It could expand to swallow ships and cause tsunamis. It would be..."

"Catastrophic, if the crust became too unstable. But that explains the ship full of scientists. They're not trying new testing methods; they're monitoring the integrity of the methyl hydrate crust. Come on, Sarah, why else would Odin want to keep his ship in the same place? Why would he even have a supertanker, let alone two of them if he wasn't filling them with fuel?" Sam stood inches from Sarah, dwarfing her with his sturdy posture.

"Your dad said Odin just delivered a tanker full of fuel to Juneau when his fleet is drilling in the Atlantic?"

"He couldn't have possibly shipped that fuel from the Atlantic to Juneau..."

"You said that." Sarah felt a knot form in her stomach. "Your dad—did he have the same hunch about this that you do?"

115

"It's not fact until it's proven, and we shouldn't operate on hunches, but…"

"But he did. And if you guys are right, then it's not just possible, but probable that methane came up from the sea at that site and killed the crab on Jack's boat. And we can tell, even by the fuzzy satellite picture, that the *Westender* did travel into the *Asgard's* path. And if enough oxygen was displaced that it suffocated the crab…" Sarah felt her vision begin to blur and her knees turn soft. Sam grabbed both her arms and guided her back down to the bed, where he sat beside her. "Jack, Nate…the crew is dead then, Sam. And if we can't stop Odin…Alaska's next, aren't we?"

Chapter Sixteen

Dr. Iohunakana Kihomi tapped his fingers lightly on his keyboard, without actually pressing the keys. Behind him, the sun rose and illuminated the harbor surrounded by his laboratory. The lab arched like a tunnel over the water, allowing the shore to rest undisturbed by architecture. From his office window, overlooking the bay inside HALO's research building, Dr. Kihomi could see his workers preparing the research vessel for another trip across the reefs of the Pacific Ocean. He let out a heavy sigh, aware that he would not join them in the sun and surf today.

"Still checking your email, Ione?" Dr. Kihomi's wife and fellow research scientist asked.

"I've been checking every five minutes for the past couple of hours, Lalena. Not a great way to spend my time, I know."

"Hey, trying to help our son is the best use of your time. What exactly are you doing now?"

"I'm waiting to hear from Odin's suppliers in Gothenburg, Sweden. I figure the easiest way to find out what Odin's doing out there is to assess the equipment he's ordering. I also have several connections at their shipyard. If they're sending any supplies, I could get one of my guys to go along and take a look at the bowels of that ship."

"I don't understand. I thought Kami already took a tour of that ship. It was the reason you sent him to Alaska."

"And he found something that scared Odin." He faced his wife. "I put Kami up at the Grand Aleutian as a VIP, and shortly after his visit to the *Asgard* he was mysteriously sent packing. He said they offered him first class tickets home the next day. The G.A. is a wonderfully accommodating hotel, but they don't hand out plane tickets, not even to their VIP's. Someone wants him out of Alaska."

"My, my, Ione are we operating on hunches these days?" Lalena smiled.

"They're starting to pay off." Dr. Kihomi opened a new email message and read, unaware that he was grunting in reaction.

"What does it say?"

"It's peculiar. Gothenburg said Odin cut their contract short. They didn't build anything on the *Asgard* and he didn't order any new parts from them. What's worse is this is the final shipbuilder on my list. There's only one other place he could have gone for a supertanker of the *Asgard's* size and capabilities."

"He didn't."

"He did. He went to China—he had to. They are one of the largest shipbuilders in the world. Without going to any of our usual suppliers for any other work at all, it's the only place he could have gotten that much equipment for twin tankers without anyone here knowing."

"Twin tankers? There are two *Asgards*?"

"It's speculation as well." Dr. Kihomi paused. "But Kami and his student in Alaska confirmed that the *Asgard* remained in the Bering Sea while I watched it dock in Juneau at a much publicized press conference."

"Are you kidding me? Even if Odin was hiding a ship out there, you think he would be smart enough not to bring it out in the open while his other ship was obviously still in the middle of the sea."

"Kell Odin is wealthy, powerful and certainly bold, but nobody ever accused him of being intelligent." Dr. Kihomi paused. "I do know where his confidence comes from though. Think about it. If he knows he can supply the United States with an unimaginable amount of alternative fuel—enough to save us from an oil crisis and eliminate our dependence on other countries—then he knows most businessmen, conservationists and definitely politicians will gladly look the other way and refrain from asking how and where he's finding this fuel."

"And where do the Chinese suppliers come into this plan?"

"There's no doubt that Odin is getting his fuel illegally. Possibly by drilling into the methyl hydrate crust of the Bering Sea." He paused to let the color drain back into Lalena's face. "It would suit his needs to have our biggest competitor build his ships. China would gladly keep the secret for a cut of the fuel— after all, they rival us in the squandering of oil. And Odin's deal would make him the prime supplier to both the United States and China, the two largest oil consumers in the world. That kind of power is…it's unimaginable."

"This is serious speculation, Ione. If that man is drilling into the crust like you say, it could upset the structure and cause tsunamis that could wipe out the entire west coast of North America and no scientist on his boat could predict when it would happen. It would be instantaneous and inescapable."

"I know, Lena. That's why I'm assuming the worst. If we can work with our son to put a stop to this operation, we might be able to work damage control in that sea. Now I know it sounds trite, but try not to worry until we're sure we have something to worry about. And you know our son. Kami will take care of everything. Lalena," Dr. Kihomi cut his wife off before she could reply. "Our own research vessel is getting farther from the harbor every second. And I can see by the adorable wet suit you're wearing that you would like to be on it." He smiled.

"Fine, I'll go. But I won't stop worrying about my boys." She kissed Dr. Kihomi on the cheek and darted out of the lab.

Dr. Kihomi turned back toward his computer and tapped his fingers gently over the keys again, waiting for inspiration to strike. He pictured Odin's supertanker as Sam had described it, assessing the equipment in each area of the ship. But he had checked out all of the hardware he pictured and suspected that they were supplied by Chinese shipbuilders who he could not contact, for fear of drawing attention to his intent. He pictured the boat again, this time following Sam's footsteps as he exited Odin's helicopter, passed the submersible being loaded on deck, and headed to the conference room.

"Hah!" Dr. Kihomi jumped from his chair and began striking keys.

Onmark Food Service, was the first name he entered into his computer. Data flashed onto a public relations website touting the company's leading role in supplying fresh food and beverages throughout working Alaska. Noting the company's outpost on St. Paul Island, Dr. Kihomi grabbed the cell phone from his pocket and dialed the toll-free number on his computer screen.

Sam awoke on Jack's couch to the MIDI theme song of *Hawaii Five-0* broadcast from his cell phone. He knew his dad was on the other end of the call.

"I got it!" Sarah yelled from the bar, pulling the phone from Sam's jacket pocket. "Should I answer?"

Sam hobbled into the bar half-awake, pulling a flannel over his T-shirt. He held out his hand for the phone and Sarah handed it to him with a grin on her face.

"I clean up better, I promise." Sam toyed with his hair and flipped the phone open. "Hey Dad, what's up?"

Sam listened, then put his father on speakerphone and placed the phone on the bar.

"Can you two hear me?" Dr. Kihomi said.

"Hi Dr. Kihomi," Sarah called at the phone. "Good morning."

"Sam, Sarah, I found some information that I think both of you should know."

Sam looked to Sarah for her approval and she nodded back. "Go ahead, Dad."

"I spent the night looking for a way to get to Odin's ship. I contacted all of the shipbuilders who could possibly have any deliveries to make to the *Asgard*. And I found out something that...well, that makes our little project here more like an urgent mission."

"Sounds enticing, Dad, what'd you find?"

"It started with a hunch, but a contact of mine overseas confirmed it minutes ago. Odin is working with a Chinese shipyard...he dumped all other suppliers and had both *Asgard* ships built by the Chinese. I believe the theory that we had about Odin drilling for methane is more involved than we thought. I think Odin struck a deal with Chinese investors."

"Supplying alternative fuel to the U.S. and to China—that would certainly put him in the God seat pretty darn fast. Impressive work, Dad."

"It sounds like we have a criminal and a motive here, guys, but what do we do to stop him? Sam's pretty much made it clear that the authorities can't lift a finger."

"Sam's right, Sarah, they won't. Not without some kind of proof of what Odin is doing. And even that might not be enough. We're talking about an answer to a globally financial and ecological question. An untapped fuel source is too good to question."

"It has been until now." Sam leaned into the phone. "Dad, we still need to find proof. But if what you're saying is true, we'll also need to find a way to destroy Odin."

"I found a way for you to get back on the *Asgard* for a little reconnaissance, but that's it. Taking down Kell Odin won't be easy, and it certainly won't be pretty…in fact, I've been up all night thinking of a way to do it and I've come up with nothing. We can't make two supertankers disappear, and even if we could physically destroy his operation, we'd most likely destroy ourselves in the process. And you can be sure someone would take Odin's spot at the helm."

"Back up a second, Dr. Kihomi. What did you say about getting on to the ship?" Sarah looked at Sam. "If the situation is this desperate, we have to try anything, right?"

"I like your spirit, Sarah. Sam, I did find a way you can get on that ship if need be. Onmark Food Service runs a biweekly shipment of supply to the *Asgard*. I posed as a corporation with similar needs and they told me that it takes eight staff members to bring the supplies to the ship. Three of those workers actually board the ship to unload and collect any storage bins that need to be refilled. They take a quick inventory as well, which eats up at least an hour of time."

"Excellent, Dad. Can Onmark place the *Asgard* in the sea at the same time the other *Asgard* was delivering its oil at the press conference? At least that would confirm the presence of two ships."

"That would be convenient, Sam, but they didn't have a shipment scheduled that week. Odin's pretty impetuous, but he's not that stupid. Instead, I was thinking that you could use Onmark to gain access to the *Asgard*…this time without a chaperone. The supply ship leaves this Friday from St. Paul Island and will go directly to Odin's supertanker. If you could pose as an Onmark employee and get on that supply ship…"

"Great idea, Dr. Kihomi, but I know Onmark supplies," Sarah said. "They used to deliver to The Wheelhouse before we stopped serving food here. Their St. Paul staff does have a high turnover, but there's a slim chance that they won't recognize a new face onboard, especially a Hawaiian one. Besides, Odin's guys already met with Sam. They don't even want him in Alaska, so imagine what they'd do if they caught him on their ship."

"I understand, Sarah. But it's the best way to get to that ship without drawing attention to HALO's involvement. I'm sure Odin has already begun to prepare for our return after Sam's visit."

"All the more reason to let someone else pose as an Onmark employee." Sarah looked at Sam. "I've been around those types. I can even fake their strange, pseudo-Canadian accents. And nobody on the *Asgard* has ever heard of me."

Sam shook his head at Sarah and grabbed the phone, taking it off speaker. "Thanks for your help, Dad. We'll find another way. Maybe we can do something about this satellite image…you know…unscramble the block Odin's got on this thing."

"To even try and take him down, we'll have to prove that he's doing something unthinkable, like drilling for methane. And to even suggest that he would put the entire hemisphere in danger, we need to catch him in the act. I know it's a long shot, but whatever we expect to find, it has to be on that boat. The next supplies shipment leaves on Friday, Sam. Let me know if you find another way." Dr. Kihomi hung up.

Sam looked at Sarah, who stood wrapped in her wool sweater, pulling at the cuffs with both hands. He looked up at the clock, as if he could will it to give him more time to think. Then his eyes dropped back down to the phone.

"Sam, my best friend and my baby brother are most likely dead. I've alienated my friends, my work—basically this whole town—for the chance that I can at least figure out what

123

happened and stop it from happening to anyone else. If you don't let me do something, I really have lost everything." Her brown eyes widened into an almost hypnotic gaze. "It's just a boat ride, Sam. I've done it a thousand times."

"I won't let you go alone. I'll follow you from a distance if I have to and…"

"Put a LoJack on my ass if you have to, Sam. Come on, what will he do, shoot me? I'm just delivering food. So I'll get a little lost and wander around. I'm a silly little blonde girl." She smiled and began to twirl her hair. "I can't possibly understand what's going on in that big boat."

"I must be insane." Sam ran both hands through his hair. "But do you know where we can get a lift to St. Paul Island by Friday?"

"Does the Grand Aleutian still owe you? Because I know they can get a chopper over here within the hour."

Sam looked at Sarah's soft smile and slender frame and a knot grew in his stomach. "Let's not rush too quickly into certain peril. It's only Wednesday."

Chapter Seventeen

Kell Odin stepped into the *Asgard's* makeshift conference room with a look of disgust on his face; the look had not faded since he had taken over as the ship's new captain. He squeezed past the splintered wooden table that consumed the room and headed toward the back counters with his hands up, as if at gunpoint. Tiny unidentifiable particles swam through the sunlight and Odin ducked in a futile attempt to control what he inhaled.

A line of sawdust and dirt skirted his suit jacket, and Odin noted that the garment would earn a trip directly into the incinerator for such a hygienic betrayal. He made a mental note to kill the crewman in charge of maintenance in the abandoned room, and to deliver the same punishment to the caller on the ancient corded phone that had beckoned him to the room.

"Odin," he said into his silk handkerchief that covered the dust-covered receiver.

"Mr. Odin, this is Dr. Shing Zhào calling from our conference room in Dalian Shipyard. Several of my colleagues have joined me."

"Dr. Zhào, I did not arrange for a conference call while I am onboard the *Asgard*." He already detested the choir of Chinese partners who mumbled on the other end of the call. "What is the meaning of this impromptu meeting?"

"Mr. Odin, I regret that you have been inconvenienced, but there is a pressing matter at hand that may or may not terminate our contract."

"Terminate? Explain yourself immediately, Dr. Zhào."

"You have explained it quite well yourself, Mr. Odin—in Juneau last week. In fact you have made it somewhat international news that you have double-crossed us."

"What on earth are your talking about, Zhào?"

"You have delivered a supertanker full of methane to the United States for your own profit, am I correct?" He paused while Odin waited. "I am also correct that you owe the Republic of China Oil Reserve that exact amount of methane. Are you so insolent as to cheat us under the lucid eye of the American press?"

"You use big words for somebody who has no idea what he's talking about." Odin sat gingerly on the edge of a dirty wooden chair. "I recall with quite some clarity that our agreement allowed me until the end of the month to deliver your first shipment. So you see I have not squandered your supply. I have to keep up appearances Dr. Zhào, and that is why I have offered my first shipment to the United States."

"You have to keep up your end of our deal, Mr. Odin." Zhào paused while his choir mumbled in crescendo. "You have one week to supply us with a supertanker full of liquid methane, or we will stop production of your new fleet and terminate this agreement. And let me tell you, Mr. Odin, it will not make for positive press when I siphon payment for my time and resources out of every possible corner of your corporation."

"Dr. Zhào, it is not wise to threaten me when I hold the bulk of your commodity." Odin stood, looming over the phone as if it was Zhào himself. "You will receive your shipment in full on the thirtieth of November and you would be wise to bury your paltry threats."

"And now I should take your word after you dishonored me

in front of my men? Don't forget, Mr. Odin, you are the one operating outside of your law in this contract. And as far as commodity is concerned, I can cease production of your fleet and repossess your precious twin supertankers with a wave of my hand. I can also divulge our little contract before you can bow down and kiss the feet of your precious American press. Without your resources, I may endure a financial setback, but without my compliance you would be…"

"No need to end that statement. I see I have caused more than just a fleeting concern in your corporation." He noticed his voice begin to soften and loosened his collar to reclaim his elocution. "To make up for the inconvenience, I will promise not one, but two shipments of methane to you by November 30. Hopefully this will assure you that I do have the necessary resources to fulfill our contract. After all, I alone drew up the documents that sealed this deal."

"Two supertankers in one week, Mr. Odin? I don't know whether to think you a demigod or a suicidal madman."

"You will find your answer at the close of the month. Now don't ring this ship again, Dr. Zhào." Odin immediately hung up the phone, recoiling from its base as if it had stung his hand. He stepped backwards, into the dingy light sliced by the pitted Plexiglas windows, and took a deep breath. The sting of old sawdust and mildew assaulted his sinuses and he made a sharp turn toward the door.

"Mr. Odin, I need to talk to you right away," Dr. Saenko met him as he descended the stairs from the conference room toward the ship's deck.

"Can't it wait, Alena? I have business to attend to." Odin surveyed his accosted suit and walked robotically as not to let it touch his skin.

Dr. Saenko stepped directly into Odin's path and jammed her fists into her slender waist, causing her white lab coat to flare with the wind like a cape. The angle of her thin, black eyebrows and the flow of her long brown hair into the wind matched the lift of her coat, creating a supernatural urgency to her stance.

"What, Alena?" Odin crossed his arms, shivering at the material that assaulted his skin.

She stepped aside, allowing him to descend the staircase as she spoke. "I've read my staff's reports, and we can't keep working in this location. All the instruments indicate a high amount of methane leaking from the water. It could cause marked ecological damage."

"And in all your infinite wisdom, what do you suggest we do?"

"I think it's necessary to vent the collection pipe and get out of here. I hate to drop this on you, but this resource is used up and if we don't vent the pipe, the gasses could build under water and warm the methyl hydrate crust. That could be disastrous."

"Venting millions of dollars worth of fuel could be financial suicide right now, Alena. Nevertheless, I do agree that we should create several drilling sites in the long run. Believe me, I am securing the supplies."

"That's not what I suggested, sir. The implications of one unstable methyl hydrate crust is bad enough, but drilling in several areas would magnify the potential for disaster by…Well, nothing even I can fathom. We need to stop drilling completely; at least until the methyl hydrate crust can recompose itself. You see, the carbon dioxide we're using is warming the crust significantly, which could…"

Odin waved his hand, silencing Dr. Saenko. "You're suggesting we stop production entirely and wait for nature to fix herself? That is completely out of the question.

Alena, might I remind you that humans have been helping nature along since we first walked the earth? Lesser animals are equipped with the physiology to adapt to nature, but humans—

we are equipped with the one survival tool that makes us kings—Impatience. We do not wait for our bodies to adapt to nature, we adapt nature to ourselves. Through our own design, we have given ourselves wings and gills, speed and ferocity. And we will afford ourselves the ability to take from the bottom of the sea whatever we desire.

"Listen, Mr. Odin. Taking a break from production only seems like a setback, but in the long run…"

"The long run? Alena, this is business. And I have just promised to double our shipment to our client as of next week. If anything, we need to step up production twofold."

"In this unstable area? Are you…" She stopped herself and followed Odin's glance to the ship's bridge, where the lone silhouette of Erik Bergen shone through its windows.

"I am your captain now, Alena. And you tell your crew to compensate for any disturbances caused while we're drilling—that's your job. Meanwhile, I will instruct my crew to begin assembly of a second collection pipe that we will place in a separate, more secure area…that should please Mother Nature for now."

"Sir, that's not a compromise, it's suicide. It took months to secure this area and we haven't even tested a new collection site yet."

"Then you'll step up production on this one, like I originally ordered," Odin snapped. "I have a contract to fulfill and you can either buck up and do your job, or follow the illustrious career paths of Peter Ivanov and Brenda Anderson."

"Aye, sir." Dr. Saenko clutched her clipboard and scurried out of Odin's sight.

Chapter Eighteen

Sarah tapped on the scratched metal casing of the antique thermostat and listened for the gurgles and clicks that indicated it still worked. The old mercury thermometer hanging above only rose to 64 degrees and she knew Sam was faking comfort seated at the far corner of the room next to a busted iron stove.

"We may get carbon monoxide poisoning, but at least it'll get warmer in here," Sarah said, satisfied that the heat had kicked in.

"I don't think hot water heaters emit carbon monoxide, but the place could catch fire if that makes you feel edgy enough."

"I just love risks." Sarah laughed and headed toward Sam at the warmest wooden table by the only interior wall of the bar. She noticed his beer had disappeared and did a U-turn back toward the bar.

"I've never seen anyone pace so much, Sarah. Not even the eggheads in my lab."

"Sorry, taking Internet classes used to be my way of procrastinating. So what have you figured out about our plan? How am I getting onto the boat?" She walked back to Sam, carrying two bottles and sat down, offering him a fresh brew.

"I wish you'd stop saying that. I'm still trying to figure out a way we can learn what Odin's doing out there without you going on the ship."

"That's what you've been doing for the past six hours?"

Sarah knocked her bottle over, spilling the dark India pale ale across Sam's notes. "Don't waste time getting around the problem. We have to solve it."

"I was wondering why you brought yourself a beer when you don't drink." Sam stood up and wiped his soggy jeans. "Nothing's going to keep you off the *Asgard*, is it?"

"You heard your dad. If Odin's able to supply us with methane and strike up a deal with the Chinese, he's got to be drilling in that methyl hydrate thing. We have to either take him out, which is impossible, or collect enough proof to bust him. And we have to do this quickly, before Opie season. You may not care, but I have to live with the fishermen around here, and if January comes and they're grounded without my bar to ease the pain, a tsunami will be the least of my worries."

"You Northerners have an interesting set of priorities." Sam swigged from his bottle. "Did you at least call the food distributors to see if they really are sending a shipment to the tanker this Friday?"

"I did better. I found out from their general manager that Onmark usually employs day laborers to pack and unpack supplies. Most of them are probably Aleuts who live on St. Paul, but a lot of them are illegal immigrants from neighboring countries. Onmark doesn't ask questions, they just take any willing soul so they can load and unload shipments as fast as possible. I'm thinking it would be very easy for me to secure a job on that supply ship."

"So you're posing as hired muscle? Sarah, have you ever done this type of work? Not that I think you can't handle it, it's just that the deck boss may take one look at you and…"

"Do you know what I used to do for a living?" Sarah rolled the sleeve of her sweater to display her flexed bicep. "Crab fishermen move 700-pound crab pots without a second thought or a forklift, thank you."

"Impressive, for a girl." Sam laughed, accepting the punch in the shoulder that followed.

"So did you find us a lift to St. Paul?"

"I have to admit, you won this round. I didn't get anywhere with the Grand Aleutian. They're accommodating as hell when it comes to getting me out of Alaska, but asking for a flight to St. Paul was…"

"Like getting blood from a stone? I figured that much."

"Why? Are they competitors with St. Paul?"

"No, but they're definitely driven by some kind of extra incentive lately. Just think about it. You were a VIP at their hotel and they kicked you out on your ass, but are totally willing to send you home on a first class free flight. The G.A. would never do that to a guest unless someone else, someone powerful, asked them—or made them. Odin obviously got a little antsy having you onboard his ship, so he's trying very hard to give you a lift home without calling attention to himself."

"He doesn't win any awards for subtlety, does he?" Sam crinkled his soggy notes and tossed them aside. "You're the native here, how else can we get a flight to St. Paul?"

"Fortunately, dear tourist, there are more aircraft in this state than there are cars. I'll hit up some of the local private charters and you call the tourist places—tell them you want to take a day trip to see the seals. Seals are a huge thing in St. Paul."

Sarah leaned toward Sam to push out her chair and slide from the table. Once standing, she fixed her sweater and turned slowly toward Jack's office in search of the phone. She could feel Sam's eyes follow her to the office, and her face blushed with regret at her obvious move.

Jack's office was never lit, but this particular time, Sarah didn't mind rummaging through the clutter to find the cordless handset. She waded through Sam's clothing, inhaling deeply at the exotic mixture of musk and papaya that had followed him from Oahu. After her hands had brushed through an oasis of soft cotton, she finally felt the phone and pulled it into view. The charge was nearly gone, but it would last through a few quick calls. Shrouded in the door's shadow, Sarah paused to wonder what ingenious plan Sam was putting together from his cell phone twenty steps away.

"I got nothing." Sam slapped his cell phone shut and Sarah walked closer in amazement.

"What? I mean, where did you call?"

"I picked through some tourist charters from the brochures I stashed in my pockets days ago." Sam looked at his overly relaxed jeans. "I haven't really had the chance to do laundry."

Sarah smiled at how quickly Sam became human again, and how much she enjoyed it.

"I can wash those for you later. Now, what did the tourist places say?"

"They all have the same story. They quote prices and talk up their planes, but as soon as I give them my name and credit card information, they tell me it's the off season, so I'd have to make reservations ahead of time because they need to find a pilot."

"No pilots? Jesus Christ, Odin really isn't subtle. Finding a pilot in Alaska is like finding alcohol in a bar." Sarah looked at the bar's tap that had run dry six days ago. "Fortunately, nobody's threatened by a broke barmaid. Why don't I call some locals and see how far I can get?"

Sarah punched several different phone numbers that she had committed into memory. She spewed small talk to the familiar voices on the other end and slammed the handset on the table with increasing force each time she was rejected.

"Sarah…" Sam grabbed her arm, causing the phone to tumble from her grasp. "Maybe we should give the table a break and find a Plan B."

Suddenly embarrassed by her performance, Sarah ducked

under the table to release some foul language and retrieve the handset. Before returning to her seat, she fixed her hair and tried to breathe a less rosy color into her face. She sat back down and gently placed the phone on the table.

"What about a cruise? We're at one of Alaska's best known harbors, aren't we?" Sam said.

"You want to go by boat? You're forgetting that they all think I'm crazy at the harbor."

"Okay, so we don't go to Dutch Harbor. What about the Alaskan Maritime Highway? Doesn't it exist to ferry people around these islands?"

"These islands, yes. But St. Paul is a few hundred miles from here. The best way to get there is by plane or helicopter. And if any boats run there, they'll leave out of Anchorage and probably not in the winter."

"What about the locals? You've been getting them sauced up in this bar for a few years now, aren't you friends with some of them? What about that Ian guy?"

"Are you kidding? Ian hates you." She immediately placed a soft hand on Sam's. "It's nothing personal. We just...we used to date and ever since, he's gotten a little jealous of every guy in my life. Not that you're..."

"I get it. He's the jealous ex-boyfriend." Sam smiled and accepted Sarah's hand.

"He doesn't really take to foreigners either."

"Foreigners? I'm American." He nodded toward a yellowing world map posted on the wall behind them. "Alaska and Hawaii are neighbors, see? They sit right next to each other in that little white box next to Mexico."

"Um, neighbor, if we ever do get a boat remind me not to let you navigate."

"Wait, that's it." Sam pulled her hands, drawing her closer to him.

"You want to sail to Mexico?"

"No. But we can take ourselves to St. Paul Island. You have access to a boat right in Dutch Harbor."

"The *Westender*?" Sarah withdrew her hands and stood, placing them on her hips. "No way. Paul Dorsey would go nuts. And besides, it's not my boat."

"But you do have the keys, don't you? Sarah, it's Wednesday night. How long will it take to get to St. Paul by boat?"

"Good point." She slowly sat back in her seat, forgetting to exhale as her thoughts turned to the dock at Dutch Harbor and the 130-foot house-aft crab ship that rested at its end.

"Dorsey has a night guy at the port after ten. If we left tonight, nobody would miss the *Westender*. But without anybody knowing where we're going, we'd be completely on our own. No safety net, not even the Coast Guard watching our backs. And with the deck like it is now, we'd be a little unbalanced."

"Hey, I'm not asking you to take any unnecessary risks. We could think it over some more and find another way."

"No we can't, Sam. You were right. The clock is ticking and even if we do find a charter, it won't take us out until late tomorrow. We have to be on St. Paul by then if I'm going to get on the supply ship." She stood and began gathering what was left of their notes. "If we're taking the *Westender*, I'd better get online and check out the weather and possible ice coverage. It is late November after all, and coming from our neighboring state of Hawaii, you know that means storm season's approaching."

Although winter hadn't begun on the calendar, a 12-inch thick layer of heavy wet snow paved Amaknak Island. The sun had set completely by late afternoon, and at midnight, the temperature had dropped to well below freezing. Sarah rubbed her hands together in the driver's seat of her Ford Festiva and waited for the engine to warm. Sam had foolishly offered to scrape an inch-thick layer of ice from the car's windows, obviously unaware of its tar-like persistence.

"I can't believe you trust a Festiva in this weather." Sam squeezed himself and layers of warm clothing into the compact car, satisfied with the five inches of visibility he left for Sarah.

"That just shows what you know about driving in the snow. In a second, you'll want to bow down and kiss my baby's donut tires."

Sarah leaned into the only transparent portion of the windshield and eased on the gas. The Festiva's wheels crunched against the icy snow, but they rolled onto the road without a problem.

"Are we driving on top of the snow?"

"A little trick I learned at an outdoor concert in Tuktoyaktuk about five years ago—where I traded my useless pickup for this baby."

Sarah and Sam arrived under the orange glow of the Dutch Harbor fishery just after midnight. By late November, even vessels fishing for halibut, black cod and turbot had returned, leaving the harbor crowded with ships, but deserted by workers.

"So, I'm just assuming with your reputation, we don't want to announce our entrance."

"Excellent assumption, Sam. Paul's the main Sarah-hater on dock. But he's just the dock lead, and since there's no fish to be unloaded, there's no way he's here. This being an off-season, the port engineers might be busy doing some maintenance, but they won't ask any questions if we're sneaky enough."

"Wait a minute, Sarah. There's got to be more to hijacking a ship like the *Westender* than just hopping onboard and turning the ignition key. Even if we don't want our presence known, we need to get some kind of clearance so we don't run into anyone in the sea, or into any underwater dangers. It's also very hard to gas up and hide the sound of the ship's engine and all the lights onboard. So how do you propose we do all that without calling attention to ourselves?"

"Simple, we use oars." Sarah winked and snorted a laugh. "Seriously though, the radio operator is an old friend of the family...My dad's old drinking buddy to be specific. Since we're not actually catching anything out there, the cannery doesn't really need to keep tabs on us. But we should set a course and tell him we're at least scouting out there so somebody knows where we are."

"Is your friend going to ask for consent from the ship's owner? I mean, I'm assuming your dad's drinking buddy will at least be sober when he dispatches us."

"You just leave that to me." Sarah turned off the engine and reached in the back seat for her duffle bag. After rifling through the bag under her car's dim dome light, she pulled what looked like a contract into view. "So many assholes on this island have ignored Jack's disappearance...I figure if anyone has the right to take advantage of that, I do. Besides, after ten years of doing his banking, I can write his signature better than he can."

"And in the morning, when your buddy Paul comes to work and sees the *Westender* is gone?"

"You didn't notice that they're dense as hell around here? By the time he notices it's missing, we'll either be out of range or back at the harbor. Paul's just a bigmouthed wuss, there's nothing he can really do to me."

Sarah turned her headlights off and eased her car against a four-foot snowdrift. The white Festiva disappeared in the crude camouflage and she motioned for Sam to step out of the car and follow her in the darkness toward the fishery. She stopped at the entrance and pointed Sam in the direction of the *Westender*. Sarah slipped upstairs to the main office which she noticed was surprisingly unmanned. Within fifteen minutes, she had scribbled her projected course on a notepad and left it for the radio operator to read after the *Westender* was safely launched out of sight. Careful not to be seen, she slipped out the back door of the fishery.

"Sam!" Sarah gave a coarse whisper into the air as she stepped into the night.

"They all look alike, Sarah." His silhouette shrugged under a flood light.

Sarah pulled at Sam's coat, leading him down a path of slick black ice that ran along the boardwalk. The *Westender* distinguished itself as the moonlight hit the chrome railing of the ship, and Sarah instinctively placed Sam's hands on her hips and began to climb.

"Follow me, but go slowly. The rails are covered with ice."

"I'm learning that everything in Alaska is."

Sarah stomped her feet on the deck with confidence, aware of the torn floorboards two steps to her right. She straddled the gap and led Sam onboard, forcing him around the obstruction and immediately aft.

"This won't be easy, Sam. The crab pots aren't put away well and they can throw us off balance if a rogue wave hits."

"You have weather equipment on board, don't you?"

"Sure, but we're going regardless of the weather, right?" Sarah crept sideways up the staircase to the wheelhouse, leading Sam with her frozen hand tucked into his warm gloves.

After a short bout with the steel door, Sarah flung it open and shoved a hand at Sam, telling him to stay put at the entrance while she found her way to the lights. She only ran a knee into one chair before flicking on the flood lights that illuminated the ship's electronics.

"The battery should be in good shape." She booted up three computers that began to snap and chomp to life. "We have sonar, weather and geography on these screens, and Jack converted to a better satellite setup a couple years ago, so we have radio and phone if we need it. Do you know how to use this stuff, Sam?"

"It's a lot more high tech than I expected, but it's similar to the hardware we have on the research vessels at home."

"Good, then you stay here and make sure we get online, and I'm going down to the engine room to see if this tub's even working. Once we start her up, I can gauge how much fuel we'll need. It's probably best to top her off."

Sarah descended from the bridge and slid around the ship's deck as if her feet had never left it for land. She jogged down a small, dry staircase and into the galley, still smelling the familiar stench of Sam's dead crab. Beyond the galley, she rushed passed three staterooms and eight bunks, never moving her gaze from the floor. She grazed the entrance to Jack's stateroom and burst into the engine room, where she finally picked her head up to stare two Cummings 855 engines in the face.

"Sonny and Cher," she whispered to herself, squinting at the metal beasts. "Let's see what kind of shape Watson left you two in."

Sarah stood at the far end of the engine room as if preparing for a shoot-out. She breathed several deep breaths before stepping closer to Sonny, the ship's main engine. Cher was used mostly on reserve, when her partner threw his usual tantrums. As Sarah stepped closer, she could see right away that both engines appeared in better shape than Watson had ever left them, and a tingle ran up her spine.

She stopped in her tracks, just steps away from the main engine and felt a chill followed by a stiff push against her backbone, as if the room had suddenly become haunted. The engines emitted a glow under the floodlights above that shone them foreign and alive. And she knew when she started them, they would run without a sputter.

"Sarah, what's the holdup?"

"Sam." She jumped. "What...I mean, how'd you get down here?"

"We're online upstairs. Everything's functional. Is there something wrong with the engines?"

"No, I mean I haven't checked them yet. But they look tampered with."

"What?"

"They're too clean. I think someone tampered with them. Maybe we shouldn't..."

"Unless crab ships need some swarthiness to get going, I don't think running a clean engine is a threat. Time's a wasting, Sarah, we should shove off."

Sarah stared at the engines and knew she wouldn't move from her spot. Her eyes began to glaze over and she let her mind ignore Sam.

"Do you want me to start them?" Sam's voice cut into her head. "These babies look like a 1990s model. I can get them going, if that's what you're worried about."

Sarah remained still and tuned out Sam's advancing steps.

"Sarah, what's wrong?" Sam placed a hand on her back and she stumbled forward, nearly losing her footing. "You haven't been down here in a while, have you?" He moved away.

"I think it's wise to tell you that I haven't been out in this boat, or any boat, in ten years."

"You're afraid that you don't remember what you're doing? Sarah, it's fine. I can run this thing if I have to. A ship's a ship, right?"

"Not this one." Sarah turned to briefly face Sam before storming past him to the galley.

Slumped at the scratchy wooden table, she hung her head and let heavy locks of blonde hair form a curtain around her pale face. She could hear Sam's footsteps approaching, but could not for the life of her tell how far away they were.

"This isn't the time to be shy, Sarah. Tell me about this boat." He leaned against the cupboard across from her.

"It's cursed, or haunted. I mean, it's not haunted with ghosts—more like memories, bad ones."

"I didn't peg you as a superstitious sailor. So tell me about this cursed ship, because two minutes ago, you were ready to start her up."

"Have you ever played a contact sport or done something extreme where it's only fun when you're feeling invincible?" She lifted her head. "I was 20 when I started fishing with Jack. It was a wild ride and the waves were awesome—we froze our asses off, but the fishing was incredible. I never felt so alive and I was immortal."

"And then?" Sam sat down.

"We were out for Opie season one of the many times Jack deviated from his route. He told Brian on the *Adrienne Anne* that we were running close to an ice patch and we would turn back, but then the bug hit him and he followed a pattern of crab north, into the ice. We didn't even get to drop a pot when a rogue wave…A wave that looked like a damned high-rise just grew out of nowhere. First, it took out our light with a hundred-pound block of solid ice. When the ice hit the deck, it sounded like a bomb going off. Watson and I got wimpy and ran below deck, but the others stayed out there. The next wave hit and I'll never forget the feeling." She pointed to the range across the galley.

"I flew into the range and burned the shit out of my arm. Still have the scar. The galley was pitch-black and everything went silent. I thought I'd passed out, but I could feel my skin burning. It was so still and quiet, but I couldn't get up. Then Watson yelled that we were on our side, and it all started to make sense. The floor was where the walls should be. We were nearly capsized, floating at a 45 degree angle."

141

"Sarah, it's understandable that you don't want to fish again, but…"

"That's not it. Watson and I crawled up through the hatch to get a look at the rest of the ship. It looked like hell, close to what it looked like when it was brought back a couple weeks ago. Half of the pots were swept off the side of the boat and we both figured if one more pot slid to the port side, we'd be upside down. We didn't dare go on deck, so we crawled back into the galley in the dark and waited.

Later on, when we were finally rescued, we learned that we were down there waiting for three days…Which explains how completely delusional we were both feeling. Watson called us the walking dead. The ship was knocked offline in the accident and Jack couldn't get hold of the Coast Guard. It was the *Adrienne Anne* that found us after Brian noticed we weren't on the radio.

Ian was the deck boss on the *Westender* back then and he told me that just after I went below deck, three guys were swept out to sea. Ian just watched them drown without any way to help them. He blamed Jack for the whole thing and never forgave him. That's probably why he's got the fishery convinced that Jack's disappearance is a good thing."

"But Ian kept crabbing?"

"Crabbing is like an extreme sport…If you can get right back into it, you might be able to ignore the fear and become invincible again. I took too much time off and grew a brain, I guess."

"And now we're about to head back into the sea." Sam maintained his space from Sarah. "You should have told me all this before. We don't have to take this ship out. If it's too much, you don't even have to leave the island. I can go myself and…"

"We both know it's too late to change the plan now." Sarah sat up and wiped her face across her sleeve. "Anyway, it's my own fault. I went along with this plan like I was into it. The truth is,

I didn't expect the boat to run. But it does now and as much as you think you know these waters, you'll need a native to get you through it."

"But you've done a lot already. You're in no way obligated to…"

"Put a stop to an illegal drilling operation that could destroy the coast of North America? Jack and Nate are most likely dead and I'm sitting here crying over a storm that happened ten years ago. I think I'm a little obligated to do something, Sam. I have to stop being selfish."

Chapter Nineteen

"You can uncross your fingers, Sarah. I think we're here." Sam squinted through a patch of dense fog that covered the approaching landscape like soot.

Sarah watched his expressions from a safely-padded seat in the rear of the wheelhouse, where she had buried her face in the ship's computer monitors for more than 24 hours. She could hear the boorish pounding of the wind against the ship's windows and even though she felt the tiniest bit of relief, she wanted to hide from the familiar shore of the jagged island. Its landscape covered in black ice, Sarah always returned to the feeling that the Pribilof Islands were a fraud; they couldn't have possibly been formed by fire and molten rock. And St. Paul marked the point of no return for her, as colder seas always waited ahead.

"Your knuckles have been so white during the trip, I thought you'd be happy to see land."

"Turn the VHF to channel eight for port services," she said. "Then let's go over the layout of the *Asgard* again before I lose my nerve."

Sam contacted the port and turned to Sarah. He pulled a black marker from a clipboard hanging by the ship's intercom and rolled Sarah's sleeve back to her elbow.

"Even though it's a high tech research ship, it's set up quite old fashioned. It looks like the ship's hold is in the orlop deck, which I thought was odd. But now I'm guessing the lowest part of the ship isn't for cargo after all. It's probably where Odin hides his drilling machinery and whatnot." He drew a crude sketch of the ship's interior on her forearm. "Before you head into the belly of the beast, you want to go to the first deck directly below the galley. There are two doors and the right one leads to the lab I saw. I'm assuming the other leads to staterooms, storage, whatever. If anyone sees you, say you're lost."

"Sam, you can't draw worth shit, I will be lost."

"Just remember the lab is below the galley, and following a couple white coats couldn't hurt either."

"Got it." Sarah checked over the drawing on her arm. "What am I looking for again?"

"Anything suspicious in the lab. There's a *Star Trek* looking wall of LED lights that their lead scientist didn't want me to see, so I'd head for that. Chances are someone is keeping a log of the activity from that Lite-Bright, most likely on a nearby computer. If you can grab that log, I can decipher it to see exactly what they're doing over there. Meanwhile, if you see anything to do with the methyl hydrate crust or the ship's fuel tank, even a gauge, let me know about it."

"Got it, Kiho. Meanwhile, you stay on VHF 70. That's Onmark food supplies." Sarah pushed her cell phone under her sweater and pulled its hands-free microphone through her bra, attaching it to the strap. "I'll call you on the satellite phone, but I can't hang up or redial, so keep the connection."

"Make sure you're not on speakerphone too. Jesus, I hate leaving you wired with just a cell phone in the middle of nowhere."

"Well, I left my spy kit at home. Now you remember what you're doing on the island, right Sam?"

"I'm a deckhand from Dutch Harbor meeting with a guy from Technico to get the crane looked at on the *Westender*, right?"

145

"Good, and try not to look so freezing if you're going to pass as an Aleut." Sarah pulled Sam's crossed arms apart and smiled. "It shouldn't take long to get an estimate from the repair guys, so when you hear that Onmark is sending its ship to the *Asgard*, you'd better not be far behind."

"Hopefully you'll do your job and get back to Onmark's vessel unnoticed, but I'll be hanging out in the wings in case anything goes wrong."

"Sounds like a plan, Sam." Sarah let out an uneasy sigh as she took her first glance at the cliffs of the Pribilof Islands. "But don't stay too close out there. Odin probably remembers the *Westender* if Jack did sail into his path before. If they see the ship now, they'll know something's up."

Sam pulled the boat into the harbor and followed Sarah's cue to wait until the bulk of deck hands on shore made their way to his ship. Satisfied with the audience, she prodded Sam to exit the ship, and reminded him to make a grand entrance onto the docks while she slipped out a more hidden exit.

While Sam's confident voice fired in the distance, Sarah scurried to the other side of the harbor, where the Onmark cargo ship guzzled diesel from the fueling station. In the early morning, she could barely make out the silhouette of the fleet manager, who oversaw operations from behind a curtain of chalky mist. Before bringing herself into view, she pulled her cell phone from underneath her belt. She hunched into its LCD screen, feeling the tug of the attached microphone against her bra, and dialed the *Westender*'s satellite phone. The connection was patched through and she knew by the silence on the other end of the line that Sam was listening from an earpiece at his end of the harbor.

Sarah secured the phone under her jeans again and repositioned its microphone, careful not to show the contraption. She flattened her sweater and pulled its sleeves over her hands as she

146

headed toward the Onmark ship with a fake march of confidence.

"Mr. Fines, I presume?" She extended her hand. "I'm Sarah Reid. We talked on the phone the other day about your supply run to the Odin Energy tanker."

The man gave her an obvious once over and stared at her quizzically.

"I offered to load and unload supplies, remember?"

"You done this before Miss..."

"Reid. And yes, since I was a teenager." She stepped into his space. "You pay under the table like Ray Lee did before he retired, right?"

Upon hearing the familiar name, the man relaxed and checked his watch. "Go inside and see a guy named Warner. He'll get you the proper uniform. We're off in two hours. Coffee's inside, and it's four days old."

"I'd expect nothing less from the number one food service supplier," she mumbled and walked past the fleet manager into a trailer marked "Onmark General Office."

For the next two hours, Sarah held a mug of steamy tar and stared into the bowed wood paneling of the trailer along with three Native Americans who looked like they hadn't slept in years. Just as she thought her toes would freeze off, the guy named Warner strolled into the office. He threw white coats at her and the others, and told them to join him at the ship.

Sarah's hands ended six inches before the sleeves of her Onmark coat did, and she guessed that not many women signed up to work on the supply ship. But the other workers stopped hitting her with strange looks when she carried more than her body weight into the ship, proving that she belonged. After what seemed like days of loading pallets with her grunting colleagues, the ship's engines finally ground to life and it pulled away from the port.

The morning sun burned off a miniscule amount of thick

fog and the sea quickly replaced it with cold, nebulous spray. Sarah fixed her hair over her earpiece and searched around the island's coast for Sam and the *Westender*. Without his confirmation, she could only trust that he was following the supply ship, acting as her emergency lifeline.

"Sarah, don't say anything." Sam's voice finally whispered in her ear after an hour of silence. "I've got you on radar, but I have to stay pretty far not to be spotted. I'm here though."

Sitting on a cold bench with fifteen other workers in a poor excuse for a stateroom, Sarah finally relaxed and imagined Sam's warm breath flowing into her ear. She peered out a small window at a yellow layer of rotted plastic, and pretended that she could see the *Westender*. The ship smelled like stale ice and sweat, and she had at least another hour or two before Onmark would reach the *Asgard*.

A cobweb-encrusted green bulb let out an oscillating beam of light that swept across the room where Sarah and her colleagues sat. The men began to filter onto the ship's deck in response. Sarah pulled her white coat around her, displaying the Onmark logo and the embroidered name, Chad. The men slapped white hardhats over their stringy hair and Sarah pulled her hair around her like a skullcap to make the hat fit.

She stepped onto the deck in the face of a late November breeze that pushed through her clothing. A sharp bite on the insides of her nostrils told her the temperature barely reached ten degrees. She stared past the cloud of her own breath into a choppy sea of black waves and felt eerily at home among the smell of winter and salt air. The sky had only changed to a darker shade of gray and a frozen fog rose from the tips of the waves. Stray seagulls cackled like witches through the endless horizon off the starboard side, but on the opposite side, Sarah turned to meet a giant black wall of steel that swallowed the skyline. They had arrived at the *Asgard*.

The cold didn't cast nearly the chill that the giant super-tanker did. And although Sarah had grown up around large freighters and tankers, this particular ship seemed to dwarf any she had ever encountered. She pushed her hardhat close to her head as if it could squish out her unreasonable fear of the vessel, and plodded on with her coworkers in preparation to unload.

"Hey, Chad." The supervisor on board grabbed Sarah's sleeve. "Stay here with the other newbies and start unpacking."

"My name's not Chad. And I'm supposed to be with the loading crew on the tanker, not unpacking here."

"I'm sorry, is this not part of your job description? Would you like to file a grievance with the union? You're day labor, so start unpacking or I'm charging you for the ride out here."

Sarah turned around and spoke into her hidden micro-phone. "Can you believe this, Sam? How do I get past this asshole?"

"Just do something, Sarah." Sam's voice reverberated through the earpiece.

"Sir!" Sarah pulled at the supervisor's coat. "It's been four hours and three cups of coffee, at least point me to the head."

"You've got to be kidding me. Princess, there's no powder room on this ship. Now get to work."

"Come on, sir. There's got to be one on the *Asgard*. Just let me on for a second. I'll take a couple boxes on with me to make it worth your while."

"Dammit, Chad, just piss overboard like the rest of us!"

"Fine, boss man, whatever you say." Sarah flashed a smug grin, pulled her coat back and began to pull off her belt.

"Oh for the love of…Get the hell onboard that tanker, Princess." The deck boss shoved her forward.

"Classy move, Chad," Sam said with a robust laugh. "Remember, you need to get near the galley toward the bow."

Sarah didn't answer Sam until she was on the supertanker. Most of the workers turned aft as they boarded the ship, but she removed her hardhat and ducked as she hurried in the opposite direction. Giant pipes wove throughout the ship's deck like vines, and Sarah stared at her clumsy feet that swam in oversized green galoshes. She slid to a bumbling halt just underneath the ship's bridge and made sure the coast was clear.

"Sam, I'm under the bridge. Where's the galley?"

"If you're under the bridge, you're at the galley. Do you see a door?"

"Yeah, to my left. But what if there are people inside?"

"Chances are they're workers on break and they probably don't know everyone onboard. Blend in… Say you're from second shift or something if they ask."

Sarah pictured the orange immersion suit she would wear as a deckhand on Jack's boat, and the coveralls she had seen men wear on tankers and freighters that pulled into Dutch Harbor. She looked at herself and slumped against the door.

"Sam, I don't look like a deckhand. The Onmark uniform is just a white lab coat…oh, duh." Before Sam could answer, she tossed her hardhat aside and tucked her hair into a tight bun. She took her white coat off and turned it inside out, favoring unsightly seams over the bright green Onmark logo.

"Look at me, I'm a scientist," she said to herself, letting Sam hear.

Sarah took a deep breath and opened the door to the galley. To her relief, it led to a short hallway with the galley resting to her left, beyond a thin bulkhead. To her right, she saw a staircase heading down to a thicker door with two keypads next to its handle.

"I knew this was too easy, Kiho. I think I found the lab, but it's locked with a double keypad. Should I wait for someone to come out?"

"Let's make sure this is the lab first. Are there lab coats or goggles on a rack by the door?"

"Yeah...I'm getting an upgrade as we speak." Sarah took her coat off and replaced it with a better-fitting lab coat from the ship. "So how do I get in?"

"Try the key code. It's 6110, then 1501. I remembered something from my visit to the ship."

Sarah punched in the code and the door heaved a deep sigh, cracking open toward her. She stood to the side of the entrance and peeked into the room, satisfied that no scientists stood directly in her path and that the ones in the room looked just like her.

"I'm going in, Sam, so I can't talk much. Let me know exactly what to look at in here because I have to look like I belong."

She stepped through the door and Sam told her to pass the numerous lab benches and zigzag across the lab to its far end. Sarah obliged, convincing herself that in the tradition of Clark Kent, a simple wardrobe change and a pair of safety glasses were enough to hide her true identity.

"I'm here," she said into her jacket while staring directly into a panel of nondescript gauges and twinkle lights.

"Good. Can you tell what that panel is for? Are there any descriptions or switches? Is there a computer nearby or any read-outs?"

"Slow down, Kiho. There's something about compression and a few temperature gauges, I think. There's definitely a side marked 'input' and one marked 'out'...There's something that says 'venting channel'. I don't know what any of it is, but there is a computer here."

Sarah waited a long while before Sam's voice cut in again.

"Sarah, can you copy or send any of the files on the computer?"

She leaned into the screen and punched the space key on its keyboard to awaken the monitor. A desktop came to life bearing Odin's insignia and several online applications she didn't recognize. She looked both ways, felt for the flash drive in her jeans pocket and shoved it into the computer, cringing at the soft "ping" the machine sang as it accepted the drive.

"I'm saving everything I can to disk, Sam. But a lot of stuff is locked. I can't guarantee we'll be able to see what this stuff is on another computer."

"Just steal it. I'm sure my guys at HALO can make heads or tails of it later." Sam paused for a long time. His voice returned to Sarah's ear in a panic-stricken tone. "Sarah, the Onmark vessel, how long does it take to unload?"

Sarah felt a prickly rush through her body as if her blood had turned to needles. She looked around her again and ducked into her microphone. "Is the boat leaving?"

"Let's just say you've probably been missed. Just hurry and get back on deck."

The computer didn't give her permission to remove the flash drive, but Sarah snatched it anyway and stuffed it in her pocket. She turned around with her head ducked as if her hair, in its bun, would hide her.

"Security," a woman's voice bearing a Russian accent shouted into a nearby intercom. "Security, I need your assistance in the lab."

Sarah looked directly into the lead scientist's dark brown eyes and followed them down to the oversized green galoshes.

"Those aren't lab regulation," the scientist said. "Who are you?"

"Sarah, that's Dr. Saenko. Get the hell out of there." Sam's voice barked through her head.

"I'm sorry, Dr. Saenko, I was on deck doing tests earlier." Sarah could hear her own shaky and unconvincing voice.

The scientist nodded toward the entrance of the lab. "Security will come through that door shortly to help you find another pair of shoes then." Holding Sarah's gaze, the scientist passed her and headed toward another exit in the lab.

"Sarah, the Onmark guys are looking for you. Get out of the lab!" Sam shouted in her ear.

Unsure of the woman's signals, Sarah swallowed a knot the size of a watermelon in her throat and headed to the alternate exit. Judging by the ship's outside, she guessed the door led to its bow, directly underneath the bridge and possibly farther forward. She opened the door into what looked like a supply room at first sight. Her eyes scanned the dimly-lit room, adjusting to its darkness and searching for something familiar. In the back of her head, she wondered where the scientist had escaped.

"Sam, I'm in some sort of storage room out the back exit of the lab." She stopped to take a deep breath. "It's freezing in here. Like I'm outside."

"Hang on, Sarah." Sam paused. "The tanker does have an opening at the bow for refuse. Are you in a trash room or some kind of waste tank?"

"I'd smell that if I was." She stepped forward and the room started to present itself like a small bite taken out of the front of the ship. She tried to keep her pace, fearing that with each step, her foot could miss the ground and land directly into the icy water. She took another deep breath and noticed a familiar odor. "I smell rubber, like tires or a raft. Could this be some kind of dock?"

"Lifeboats!" Sam's voice stabbed through her ear. "You're in an escape hatch. Probably for the officers of the ship, should something go wrong. Supertankers don't usually have something like this but Odin must…"

"Odin must be directly over my head right now, if this is his little escape pod." Sarah felt panic begin to strangle her and her eyes started to sting with fresh tears. "Sam, get me out of here!"

Through the emergency exit, Sarah could hear a barrage of footsteps stampede through the lab. She knew the ship's Security and possibly Kell Odin himself was searching for her. Her eyes adjusted to the dark room and looked for its deepest crevice so she could hide while waiting for Sam's directions.

"Sam, I can't take it, I'm busted. What do I do?"

"Hang in there, Sarah. I'll find you a way out, even if I have to cause a diversion."

In her panicked state, Sarah began to rock to the floor, picturing what could happen if Security found her or Sam. But like a dream, her thoughts dragged her back onboard Jack's ship where she felt the waves would overtake her and she would be carried away. While she let the panic shut down most of her body, a tiny voice in her head told her to become invincible again.

Sarah grabbed the voice and rose from the dark crevice. She forced her shaky hands to feel for the rubber raft that slapped against a nearby bulkhead with every choppy wave the boat encountered. She pulled the raft until the resistance against her arms told her it hit water, and she felt for the raft's outboard engine. She gripped a freezing toggle on the engine with one hand and guided her body into the frozen lifeboat with the other hand.

"Sam, are you close by?" Her voice shook violently with fear and cold.

"I'm a few miles away, out of sight to the east."

"Well, you'd better haul ass toward the front end of the *Asgard*, because I'm coming at you and it's not gonna be pretty."

"No, Sarah! That's crazy—that's suicide."

"And I'm a crab fisherman." Sarah hopped into the rigid inflatable boat and gasped in the cold until her lungs burned. She fired up the motor and launched from the *Asgard*, warning herself not to look back.

Even though her heart pounded and her palms oozed sweat, Sarah felt her body start to convulse in the freezing sea air. She swallowed at the rushing wind, trying to steal oxygen from each violent gasp she took. Without any winter gear to protect her, she knew she was suffering from stage-one hypothermia, which made her less alert and more likely to lose control.

"Sam, where the hell are you?" Sarah yelled into her phone against the wind.

"The computer says just a couple miles…And you've got company, Sarah."

She swung her head around, nearly collapsing in the motion and caught sight of a RIB exactly like the one she had stolen. She counted at least four men on the craft and her gut told her they had weapons.

"Sam, I'm not gonna make it. You have to meet me…Pull up closer."

"Odin will see the *Westender* if I get any closer."

"We've already screwed-up, just get over here." Sarah leaned into the wheel of the boat and tried to face the horizon despite her aching feet and ankles that were drenched with sea water. After minutes she began to hear the buzz of an engine that was not hers. The other raft was gaining on her and she could not force her numbing hands to punch her boat faster. A permanent white mist slapped at her face and she hoped the men behind were just as blinded by the spray, but their warning shot told her they could see just fine.

Sarah crouched down as several other shots sliced into the water around her. Her muscles seized in inches of freezing water while she held the wheel blindly with her hands above her ducking head.

"Sarah, I'm here. I can see you off the starboard side. Look up and I'll toss you the ring buoy."

"No!" Sarah popped her eyes above the gunwale, catching sight of the *Westender* just a few yards in front of her. "I'll be a sitting duck in that buoy. They have machine guns, Sam."

155

"Then get behind the ship and I'll pull you up on the port side."

"No, they'll follow me. Sam, what do I do?"

"Get closer to me, Sarah. I have another idea."

Sarah tried to slalom the boat but her hands resisted and shots plucked into the flexible sides of the raft. Water poured in and she breathed heavily through the pain as it froze her. The enemy was close enough that she could see their faces tucked behind the sights of their machine guns. They took their aim and they weren't going to miss.

"Hang on to the boat, Sarah, no matter what happens!" Sam yelled into her earpiece and Sarah flung her deadened arms around the wheel. With a heavy tug, her boat spun around into the air and the first shot hit it like a piñata. Completely disoriented, it took her several seconds to realize what Sam had done. While she hid in the raft, he had hooked it with the *Westender's* crane and it now swung several feet in the air positioned as a shield with its hull between her and the gunmen. Sarah clung to the wheel until numbness began to pry her grip. She let go just as two strong arms wrapped around her body, pulling her safely onboard the *Westender*.

"Get to the wheelhouse and turn her around," Sam ordered, shoving her behind him.

Sarah stumbled up the staircase drunk with hypothermia. She burst into the wheelhouse nearly fainting as the heavy warm air wafted through her. Eyes filled with blotchy blackness, she stammered to the wheel and blindly turned the ship. Outside she heard the wind whip and the ship's engines whine, and she tried to drown out the sounds of a battle on deck between Sam and Odin's men. Sarah wasn't sure where she was heading, but she punched the engines and sped forward until the sea was quiet again.

After several minutes, heavy footsteps clacked up the staircase and Sarah awoke to the wheelhouse door crashing open.

"It's over, Sarah. Wake up." Sam raced over to her and she could feel his powerful hands rubbing down on her shoulders and arms. "No naps until you get some circulation back."

Sarah wanted desperately to sleep, but she followed Sam's cue and ran the heels of her hands up and down her calves, pushing at the pins and needles that crawled throughout her body.

"Did I steer us off course?" she asked with a shaky voice.

"I'll right us in a second. Sorry I asked you to drive."

"It's okay, you looked busy." She smiled at him.

"You know, you're pretty cute when you're blue." He pressed a warm hand against her freezing face, giving it a tint of color.

"So what happened out there? How did you beat four armed men?"

"I held them off with the ship's old shotgun for a little while. Then they turned away. I was surprised too."

"Why did they turn away? They could have taken us easy."

"They knew that too, but they were obviously following orders. Maybe sinking a crab ship was a little too high profile for them?"

"After what we just went through, I have a hard time believing that...But I'll take it. At least we're out of there."

"I hate to ask, but did you get any information off the ship?"

Sarah shrugged Sam's hands aside and reached into the neck of her sweater, she pulled a lipstick-sized flash drive from her bosom completely dry and unscathed.

"I got this for you." She grinned and handed the drive to Sam.

Once she had warmed up, Sarah offered to take the ship back into port and gave Sam some down time below deck. The sea was calm for winter and the ride was surprisingly peaceful. Sarah spent the night at the wheel and gladly took another shift throughout the morning into the afternoon. Evening rolled in again and they pulled into Dutch Harbor.

"Nice job, Captain. How does it feel to be home?" Sam stood at the door to the wheelhouse, watching Sarah steer the ship into the harbor.

"I've been at home for the past ten hours. Thank you for that."

"So is there anything we have to take care of at the dock or can we head straight to your place?"

"I've never seen this presumptuous side of you." Sarah began to flirt, but her tone changed as she approached the dock. "What's with the flashing red and blue? And the Coast Guard's here."

"Sarah, you said we were all set when we took the ship."

"They can't be here for us. I did everything by the book. I told the radio operator we were off to St. Paul for some maintenance."

"Maybe the *Asgard* or the guy from Onmark turned us in. I knew they let us off easy. Why else would the Coast Guard be here with the police?"

"Okay, fine. But what can they turn us in for? Stealing their secrets to illegally dominate the world? Not letting them gun us down?"

Sam flipped his cell phone open and began to dial his lab at HALO.

"Wait, hide out for a minute, Sam. I'll get their attention, then you sneak off the ship—the car keys are under the seat. I'll meet you at the bar later. Whatever's going on here will only get worse if they find out you're here too. Besides, one of us needs to look at this thing." Sarah handed Sam the flash drive she had taken from the *Asgard's* lab. Taking the wheel, she pulled the boat up to the dock and killed the engines. She slowly climbed out of the wheelhouse amidst a blinding reflection of red and blue neon that splashed across the ship.

"Sarah Reid," a disembodied voice called loudly from a bullhorn. "Step down from the ship slowly. You're under arrest."

Chapter Twenty

Covered in a heavy fire blanket, Sarah felt her itchy sweater sting her skin. She hunched at the space heater set by the police officer's feet and reluctantly pulled the blanket closer around her tired body. The folding metal chair she sat in only added to her torture and she wanted desperately to go home.

"What was the reason you took the boat again, Ms. Reid?" The officer asked the same question again and Sarah resisted throttling him.

"I told you, I took it to St. Paul to get the crane fixed. Is that illegal?"

"Stealing a boat is a crime, Ms. Reid. And stealing a million dollar commercial fishing vessel is a big one."

"I just took my best friend's boat, which I have worked on by the way, to get some maintenance. You're acting like I'm a commerce raider or something. I didn't hijack the damn thing and I'm not a pirate. I even filed the proper paperwork and left notice with the radio operator on duty."

"Yes, the radio operator who never saw you that evening."

"Well he let me take the boat. Besides he knows me, did he mention that?"

"I can assure you nobody at the dock will vouch for you. In fact, the dock lead mentioned that you were exhibiting disruptive behavior at the fishery throughout the season. And he turned you down for a job."

"Paul Dorsey? He'll use any excuse to badmouth me. So I ranted a little and asked for a job...Did I break any laws at the fishery?"

"You stole a ship, Ms. Reid."

Sarah let out a heavy sigh. "Listen, I took the *Westender* to St. Paul during the off-season to make necessary repairs for the upcoming Opilio season. Is that so strange and disruptive? Even the dock lead can't report me for that."

"But Mr. Dorsey didn't report you, ma'am."

"Then who did?"

"The owner of the ship did."

"Jack?" Sarah dropped her jaw.

"Yes, Jack Samuelsson. Evidently he did not authorize your taking his ship. Now let's talk about your trespassing charges as well. I have a complaint from the captain of a supertanker a couple hundred miles from the Pribilof Islands. He says that you crossed a sanctioned area. A food supply ship confirmed the report."

"Wait a minute. You're saying Jack Samuelsson came here in person and reported that I stole his boat? Was he here? Did he sign anything?"

"He called it in to the fishery and Mr. Dorsey filled out the paperwork. Now what were you doing east of St. Paul after the repairs had been finished? There were no reported weather hazards, so if this was just a maintenance trip, why didn't you return? You realize there are heavy fines and jail time involved in poaching."

"Now I'm a poacher? Where did that come from? Did you see any crab in the holding tank? Besides I was the only one on board. That ship needs at least four deck hands and a captain to catch crab. Are you sure Jack Samuelsson called? Did he say where he was or if he's coming in?"

"Mr. Samuelsson is really none of your concern right now." The officer slid a clipboard to Sarah. "Read over your information and sign if it's correct. Then you can make your phone call."

"Phone call?" Sarah looked at the clipboard then back at the officer. "You're locking me up?"

"Well we don't send felons home, Ms. Reid."

Sarah left her personal effects with a familiar officer who took her behind a locked door to an area that looked like a large kennel and smelled like the locker room at an underprivileged high school. In the center of the area was a narrow hallway with empty holding cells to either side.

"You're lucky. You're the only one here tonight," the officer said. "It shouldn't be that bad."

"Andy?" Sarah recognized her neighbor's voice. "I didn't know you became a real cop. I mean…"

"That's okay. I didn't know you were a real felon. Here's a quarter and there's the phone." He pointed toward the end of the hallway where a pay phone rested under the room's only window.

"Andy, you know I didn't steal Jack's boat."

"Make your call. I'll wait."

The officer turned and marched to the end of the hallway as if he had never met Sarah, and she felt a chill run up her back forcing her body to shudder. She trudged to the pay phone, dropped the quarter inside and closed her eyes, trying to remember Sam's cell phone number.

"Hello, Sarah?" Sam's eager voice picked up on the first ring.

"Sam, you wouldn't believe what's going on."

"Are you all right? Where are you? Can I come get you?"

"God, I wish. They think I stole the *Westender* and they accused me of trespassing and poaching." She felt her voice quiver into the phone. "They're keeping me locked up in here. This is my one phone call."

"Sarah, don't worry, I'll be right over to bail you out."

"No." She hated her answer. "It gets more complicated. You'd better lay low at least for the night."

"What do you mean more complicated? Did Odin turn you in?"

"Something really weird is going on. Odin's guys only reported that I came too close to their little research area. That's a fine, not a felony. The officer who questioned me about the ship said Jack Samuelsson turned me in."

"But Sarah, that's impossible—Jack is…Well, he wouldn't have turned you in like that anyway, right? You're like family."

"For a second, I wished Jack really did call. That would at least mean someone has spoken to him. But you're right, it sounds damn unlikely." Sarah turned to see Adam several feet away, tapping his watch. "Listen, my time is up. Get some rest, Kiho, and try to figure out what I downloaded from the *Asgard*. Bail me out tomorrow, so you don't look attached to any of this."

"Okay, and Sarah, at least you're in a safe place. Maybe Jack did have a hand in this after all." Sam paused. "We will get this straightened out, you know."

"I know." She leaned into the phone, picturing Sam at the other end. "Goodnight," she whispered.

*   *   *

Sam hung up the phone, but kept it close by on Sarah's desk next to her computer. He had turned away from the screen to talk to her and could now return to a bright blue monitor with an icon displaying her flash drive. Sam double-clicked on the drive and a jumble of unreadable files opened. They were all labeled Odin Energy.

Without a second thought, Sam grabbed the phone and

dialed his father's lab at HALO. Although it was after midnight, he knew one of his parents would be up working.

"Hello, Kami." His father's voice picked up on the third ring. "What's wrong? It must be two in the morning over there."

"I need you to read some files for me on your computer. Can I email them to you?"

"Go ahead."

Sam attached a sampling of Odin's files to an email message and sent them to his father's computer. He waited three excruciating minutes until his father spoke again.

"Kami, where did you get these?"

"Sarah got them off a computer in Odin's research vessel. What are they?"

His father paused, answering only with loud huffs and grim "uh-huh's."

"Dad?" Sam asked after several minutes.

"Kamuela, this is unbelievable. We're in bigger danger than we imagined."

"What's going on, Dad?"

"The files you sent are measurements of carbon dioxide levels at the bottom of the Bering Sea, where Odin is keeping his ship."

"Yeah, well Sarah and I suspected that Odin was using carbon dioxide to turn the gaseous methane into liquid for storage."

"According to this data, there's more to it than that. From what I can tell, the files are readings from an extraction pipe that leads from the ship into the methyl hydrate crust. He's pumping carbon dioxide into the crust from an outer pipe, and then extracting the methane in its gaseous state through an inner pipe. And according to these readouts, there's quite a bit of residual CO_2 surrounding the crust."

Sam stared into the unreadable icons on his desktop imagining the data his father was reading miles away on his lab computer.

"Kami, you realize what could happen if Odin is heating the crust with carbon dioxide, don't you? Breaking the structure that way is like dropping an ice cube into hot water. It can cause simultaneous fissures throughout the crust instantly."

"I know. It would be hundreds of times worse than just boring one hole into it with a drill. But there's another danger, Dad. Hang on." Sam searched the Internet for a list of countries and their carbon dioxide emissions. He narrowed the list to include only areas where moving tectonic plates had left unstable cracks in the ocean floor. "Dad, are you still there?"

"Yeah, what were you thinking, Sam?"

"I'm thinking about the Ring of Fire—the whole Pacific Rim. All the islands in the Ring of Fire are products of moving tectonic plates. If the makeup of the sea floor was compromised, say with a buildup of heat from unnatural carbon dioxide emissions…"

"My god, Kami…you're suggesting the carbon dioxide could eventually release its pressure and reactivate the Ring of Fire."

"It would be like a choir of volcanic activity across the Pacific, from Alaska to Hawaii at least. The oceans wouldn't be the only death trap; all those underwater geysers would release carbon dioxide, enough to gas millions of people. So those who don't get wiped out in a probable tsunami would most certainly die of asphyxiation." Sam took a deep breath and tried to steady his thoughts. "Dad, what do the readouts say? How bad are the CO_2 levels now?"

"It's hard to tell without a frame of reference and just a few files, but it doesn't seem to be critical yet. So far, it looks like just stray methane is being released."

"I never thought we'd find something so horrible that we'd be putting a 'just' in front of stray methane."

"Well, you should be relieved that you did find this information. Send me all the files you have right away. This should be enough to report Odin and keep him away from the oil industry and humanity, for that matter…now where's Sarah? She at least deserves my thanks for the work she's done."

"Oh no, Sarah!" Sam sprang to his feet, nearly dropping the phone. "Odin's guys saw her stealing the information."

"What? Do they know you're involved?"

"I'm sure they suspect it, but they saw Sarah."

"Kamuela, if Odin knows what she stole, he's not going to let her get very far with it. Where is she?"

"In jail, she got arrested for stealing a crab ship."

"Good, she's probably safest there for now. Start sending me those files. I'll need a few hours to scan through them and put together a legible report to send to the authorities. Once I've got the evidence on its way to Washington, I'll give you call. Then you can bail her out."

"It's gonna be a long night, Dad. Thank you, by the way."

"Don't mention it. I can put in some overtime to save a few billion people."

Chapter Twenty-One

"Bergen, tell me again what Alena said she saw at the lab." Kell Odin inched to the edge of the leather seat in his S76-D helicopter.

"Dr. Saenko just said a strange woman was snooping around the console, but she scared the girl off before any damage was done. She said it looked like one of the Onmark employees, but unless she was a scientist, she didn't know what she was looking at."

"She may not be a scientist, but she sure as hell is working with one." Odin sat back and leaned into the window, overlooking the dark waves of the Bering Sea. "I doubt that woman worked for the food suppliers—she must have known exactly where to look in the lab, too. She must be working with HALO, which means we have to handle this delicately, Erik. We don't know how much she knows and I will not have any bad press linked to my name. I'm sending a tanker to the Chinese buyers in one week and I can't afford any mistakes."

"What do you suggest, Sir? Should we eliminate Kihomi or pay him off?"

"Dr. Kihomi is an environmentalist, and his family certainly doesn't want for cash, so bribery is out. And he's way too high profile to be eliminated. But he is obviously linked to that fishing boat, so he at least knows that we were responsible for its missing crew. And I'm guessing that girl he came in with is also tied to that damn crab ship. But don't worry, I know his type. He's a true boy scout…And they all have the same weakness."

Fifteen minutes before the chopper landed at Amaknak Island, Odin relayed his plan to Bergen, keeping it fresh in his mind. By the time the helicopter's skids hit the ashen ground of the nearby Vertiport, a black Town Car sent by the Grand Aleutian Hotel was waiting for them. Odin paid the driver of the car to take the night off, and he ushered his pilot to the wheel.

"You sure the driver won't say anything?" Bergen cracked his knuckles into a fist.

"Anything for a kill, huh Erik?" He looked at the worn leather interior with disgust. "Although I'm certainly not happy that I just bought this piece of junk."

The sun barely began to rise by the time the car pulled up to the police station. Odin buttoned his coat around himself, pulled the hood securely over his head and wrapped it in place with a black cashmere scarf. He angled his face toward the ground as he stepped out of the vehicle, careful not to show himself. Bergen stepped out after him, slouching unnaturally in civilian clothes.

Upon entering the station, Odin slunk to the corner of the dimly-lit lobby and hid amidst dusty cobwebs and the rainy sound of termites chewing the timber frame above. He forced himself to stand still and watched Bergen approach the guard on duty.

"Excuse me, I'm here to post bail."

The guard looked at the clock overhead. "Our hours start at six."

"I see, and it's a quarter 'til." He flashed a smile. "Can I get started on any paperwork beforehand? I'm just very eager to get Ms. Reid out of jail. When she called me last night, I said I'd be right over, but then I just couldn't scrape the money together.

She's probably convinced herself I'm never going to come by now and I'd hate to see her upset."

"You're here for Sarah Reid? Oh bless you." The guard handed Bergen a clipboard. "We've been seeing her upset for the past six hours. Believe me; you've got a handful to deal with."

Bergen filled out the paperwork and pulled out an envelope stuffed with fresh bills. "The bank and the post office are still closed, so I'll have to give you cash, if that's okay."

"We'll take it." The officer grabbed the envelope. "Now you understand that once Ms. Reid is released into your custody, it is your responsibility to make sure she stays in town until her court date, which is on the back of this slip. If she doesn't return, you don't get your hard-earned money back."

Odin leaned deeper into the corner as the rising sunlight crept through the station and illuminated the faces inside. The clock flashed 6:00 a.m., and he finally caught a glimpse of Sarah walking toward him from the far end of the room. In his mind, he had pictured his nemesis as a statuesque creature, with a beautifully strong frame and a cunning smile lashed across her face. It insulted him to see he had been bested by a slouching bundle of wool and denim with tired eyes and scraggly blonde hair.

"This way, Sarah." Adam led her to the front desk where Bergen stood smiling.

"Nice to see you survived the night, dear." Bergen gritted his teeth into a stiff smile. "Let's get you home now."

"Who are you?" Sarah brushed her hair aside revealing two dark brown eyes that squinted in the sunlight to study his face. "Did Sam send you?"

"Honey, just sign on the dotted line and you're out of here," the guard said as she handed Sarah a ballpoint pen.

"No, wait. Sam didn't send you." Odin watched Sarah stare deeper into Bergen's eyes and he tried to remain hidden in the corner of the room.

"I know who you are. You tried to kill me!" Sarah spiked the pen to the ground and turned directly into Andy, pushing him back several steps. "I'm not going anywhere. Put me back in jail."

"My god, she's delusional," Bergen said. "And it's no wonder. She looks exhausted, and there's probably lead based paint in this dump. And didn't you people feed her anything?"

The guard rolled her eyes at Andy, who wrapped both arms around Sarah to hold her steady. Odin let a satisfied smile creep across his face, justified that she had turned into a worthy opponent after all.

"Sarah, stop it! Your court date is a week from now and this man is bailing you out, which is more than anyone else in this town is going to do for you." Andy let her go and she teetered off-balance, slumping to the floor with a thud. Staring intently at the display, Odin mistakenly locked eyes with her and recognized the immediate shock on her face. He instantly sprung from the corner and raced to her.

"Let me help you, miss." He wrapped one arm around her, cloaking her with his coat. Underneath the garment, his other hand placed a .32 Seacamp pistol into her ribcage. After carefully concealing the small pistol between his gloved hand and her sweater, he straightened his coat and nudged Sarah to stand upright next to him. He pushed the pistol until he felt the barrel ease through the loose wool stitching of her sweater to the skin underneath. Sarah shuddered and Odin gave a fulfilled grin to Bergen.

"Why don't you sign now, Sarah?" Bergen passed her another pen.

Odin sandwiched her between himself and Bergen, and she signed the paper with a trembling hand.

"I know you're tired, Sarah, so let's walk slowly to the car. It's nice and warmed up for you," Odin said.

169

Bergen led the others to the Town Car and slid into its back seat, leaving room for Sarah and then Odin. Once all three were inside, the driver punched down the car's automatic locks and rolled up the privacy partition.

"You were a smart girl not to try and run," Odin said. He retracted the pistol and tucked it in a small side holster that looked like a cell phone case. "Even in the middle of a police station, I could have killed you on the spot and spun it like you were the one at fault. So buck up, you just avoided a bullet and a murder charge."

"You think you just spared my life?" She tilted her head and stared at him with glossy red eyes. "You only delayed the inevitable. The work you're doing is going to kill thousands, millions even."

"Isn't it a little early in the morning for an environmentalist lecture? Besides, you wanted a tour of my ship. And that's exactly what you're going to get."

"Go ahead and kidnap me. Kill me for all I care, but you'll still get caught. I'm just a barmaid."

"My dear, I believe Dr. Kihomi, you're more than just a barmaid. And if you're important to him, then you're important to me. You're going to tell me what exactly you were doing on my ship, then together, we'll make sure Dr. Kihomi doesn't…"

"Turn you in? Well if that's your plan, shoot me now. Because I'm not talking and Sam won't risk the lives of millions of people just to save me."

Odin stared at Sarah until her weak frame was too infuriating to bear. Her insolent words gnawed inside his head, and he breathed deeply to keep his hand away from his pistol.

The Town Car pulled into the Vertiport at 7a.m. and Sarah didn't resist when Bergen pulled her from the vehicle and into the helicopter. Odin climbed in behind the two and sat opposite Sarah and Bergen, relieved that he no longer had to keep close contact with her because she could not possibly escape the aircraft. She twisted away from Bergen who still kept her at gunpoint, and Odin relaxed into his seat. Outside, the sun pushed against a patch of gray clouds and nothing but a black Town Car stood in the field where the helicopter lifted from the ground.

Chapter Twenty-Two

The fan squealed, letting out as much air as it could, but the heat in the Ford Festiva had yet to pour through its vents. Sam jammed the plastic ice pick against the car's windshield, merely taunting the thick frozen sheet that had usurped it over night. He glanced down at his watch and noticed the hour hand sweep toward 10 a.m.. All evidence in place, his father had just given him consent to pick up Sarah at the police station.

After a marathon of scratching at the frozen shell around Sarah's car, Sam accepted that he would have to find the police station through a barrier of scratched frost. He jumped into the driver's seat and yanked it back several inches. Enduring several miles of squinting into blinding sunlight refracted by pits and scrapes, Sam arrived at the police station. He had barely shoved the car into park before storming toward the small building. He didn't bother with his hat, gloves and jacket.

Sam burst through the door directly into the stale smell of propane from a crude heater that burned like an engine in the corner of the room. It didn't look safe, but it was warm. The lobby of the station was just small enough to fit Sam and one other gentleman who had come to dispute a parking ticket. And the receptionist seemed engrossed in picking out a fungus that had crept into her yellowed fingernails.

"Excuse me." Sam spoke softly as not to startle the receptionist. "I'm here to post bail for Sarah Reid."

"Sarah Reid left this morning." The woman didn't lift her head.

"What? You mean the charges were dropped?"

"No, sir. Two men bailed her out."

"Any idea who they are or where they went? Was it Ian?"

The woman looked up. "Are you Dr. Kihomi, by any chance?"

"Yes, did Sarah leave me a message?"

"No, but the men who picked her up did. They told me to give this to an Aleutian-looking man named Dr. Kihomi." She slid a business card to Sam.

Sam immediately recognized the Odin Energy logo on the card and his heart skipped a beat. He turned the card over to read a phone number and the message: 'It is rude to keep a lady waiting.'

"You let her go with two strange men?" Sam clenched his hands, trying to keep his calm.

"She went willingly, sir. Now if you don't have any more business here…"

Sam stepped away from the desk feeling the fire of the propane heater prickle like a slap across his skin. He tossed a glance at the receptionist who returned to her fingernail examination, and bumped his way out the door with his eyes fixed on the business card. His skin crawled with nervous energy and he stormed back into the Festiva, shaking the entire car with a slam of its driver's side door. The liquid crystal display on his cell phone took two minutes to wake up in the cold, but Sam was already punching the numbers from the card. After three angry misdials, he took a deep breath and carefully touched the correct keys.

"Dr. Kihomi, I presume." Odin answered before the phone even rang.

"Been waiting for my call, Odin?" Sam held his breath as he spoke and choked down the anger in his voice. "Where's Sarah?"

"You wanted her to see my ship, didn't you? Well my new chief mate, Mr. Bergen is giving her the grand tour right now."

"I know about your grand tour, Odin. It ends in the bottom of the Bering Sea. Now what the hell do you want?"

"Don't be stupid, Kihomi. And do not for one second take me for a fool. Now how much do you think you know about my operation here?…And choose your words carefully, because I've received full backing from the state of Alaska and the federal government."

"Aren't you forgetting the Chinese?"

"What?" Odin paused.

"Your Chinese buyers. Yes, Mr. Odin, I know about your deal to supply oil to the Chinese. For an intelligent man, you don't cover your tracks very well. I also know that you're using carbon dioxide to extract methane from the methyl hydrate crust at the bottom of the sea. But there's a problem with your little plan that extends far beyond my turning your ass in. By deciphering your data, my scientists have discovered that you've allowed far too much carbon dioxide to accumulate at the sea floor."

Odin's breath crackled through the phone.

"You see, Odin, you're worried about my foiling a little deal you've worked out with your buyers, but you're sitting on top of a land mine. If you continue to destroy the methyl hydrate and pump the water full of carbon dioxide, you could destroy the entire west coast of North America, not to mention your little operation and your life. So perhaps you don't hold all the cards."

"Let me give you the facts now, Dr. Kihomi. I graciously had my top scientist give you a guided tour of my ship at your request. After seeing the advancement of my technology, you hijacked a commercial fishing vessel for the purpose of trespassing on my ship and stealing privileged information. You then tampered with this information to try and discourage my corporation from merely studying the same natural phenomenon that you have built your reputation upon.

Dr. Kihomi, America does not want to know that there is no hope for the fuel industry. Americans love their private transportation and their gluttony of energy. So they would much rather believe me when I tell them that in order to save your own status as the world's top scientist in this field, you were willing to deprive the United States of salvation from an impending oil crisis by tampering with my research."

"That's ridiculous, we have evidence."

"No, Kihomi, you have computer data. And I have your friend locked in my cargo hold. I'll give you instructions soon. Meanwhile, you keep your data to yourself, and stay away from my ship and all other Odin Energy operations." He hung up.

By the end of the conversation the Festiva had barely warmed up and its fan belt squealed against the cold morning air. Sam controlled his shaking hands and threw the car into drive. Inexperienced in the snow, he skidded back toward The Wheelhouse like a drunk.

Sam yanked the doors open and ran upstairs to Sarah's computer, leaping over several steps and giving the staircase a violent shake. Once seated at her sleeping computer screen, he took a deep breath. Then he called his father.

"Dad," Sam spoke before his father could say hello. "You didn't send any evidence anywhere yet, did you?"

"I'm on hold as we speak, Kami. What's wrong? You sound like you just ran a track meet."

"Odin's got Sarah."

"What?"

"He bailed her out of jail before I got there and now he has her on his ship. He's threatening to kill her and destroy our credibility if we blow the whistle on him."

"That's insane, Sam. He's going to kill her and try to destroy us anyway because he knows we could ruin him. This is just an elaborate stall for time." His father paused. "I'm sorry, son, but we spoke about the implications of Odin's work. We can't possibly sit back and let him cause a catastrophic disaster that could kill millions of innocent people."

"Dad, I know, but..."

"We also can't let him hurt your friend. And I have definitely worked too hard establishing a good name for HALO to let an imbecile like Odin ruin it by smearing your name."

"So what do we do?"

"Sam, this is very quickly crossing into your area of expertise. I'll play the desk jockey and you'll have to be the superhero. We still have a couple days while I prepare the data for the authorities. So in the meantime, you rescue Sarah."

"I understand you need to send the data, Dad. But you have to give me more time to figure out a plan. I can't exactly come up on the *Asgard* guns blazing with the Coast Guard at my back. He'll freak-out and kill Sarah on the spot."

"Come on, Sam, think. Eventually Odin will want the evidence you stole. Arrange a trade. Make him think you believe he would give you Sarah for a lousy computer file—anything to get on that ship."

"He knows I'm not stupid...I'd never agree to a trade like that. It's suicide."

"But he is stupid, Sam. And he knows he's facing destruction from two countries if he doesn't do away with us. He may be eager to get whatever he can from you, and he's probably chomping at the bit to destroy you on his turf. If I know Kell Odin, he's making this up on the fly, just like we are."

"What if he arranges to meet with me here, at Dutch Harbor?"

"It's not likely. A man like Odin can not stand inferiority. He must be the Alpha at all times. Besides, if he kills a prominent scientist, he's more likely to get away with it on his own little island…That godforsaken *Asgard.*

"Dad, I'm a Hawaiian environmentalist, he's an oil tycoon who owns half of Alaska. This whole place is his turf. I could really use some backup from our friends at HALO."

"That's out of the question, Sam. Odin is already threatening to ruin our reputation. If he succeeds, I won't let him take down HALO too. It's up to you, Sam. You need to get to Odin's boat by your own means. And go by ship, you'll never get clearance to land a helicopter on that tanker."

"Ship? That's exactly what I can't do. As we speak, I'm sure Odin's making my life difficult on this island. I'll never be able to rent a boat."

"Then use Sarah's connections. She's a native. She has to have some friends in Dutch Harbor who wouldn't like to see her…" He paused. "Just find her friends, and fast."

Chapter Twenty-Three

Sarah pulled her knees closer to her chest, hearing her boots scrape against the wet ground where she sat in the dark. Her body smelled like stale ice and metal, and her hair dangled in frozen clumps around her ice-cold face. Returned to the same cargo hold she had earlier escaped, she found herself confined by rigid metal bulkheads to her back and a callous pitch-dark sea ahead. The *Asgard* remained incredibly still, but the whoosh and slap of the waves tossed her aching head into a dizzy spin.

Sarah dug her hands around her kneecaps and tried to silence their uncontrollable shuddering. She steadied herself against a large metal door that let a garbled conversation slip from the other side. By the numbness in her lips as her breath rushed over them, she could tell she had been confined in the area for close to an hour. A thick rubber tarp kept her body just warm enough to feed her consciousness, and sanity held out to award her ears pieces of a heated argument from the ship's lab.

"We should do away with her and cease production, Mr. Odin." A very strong female voice boomed through the metal door.

Odin's calm, quiet voice seemed to mumble to the contrary. Its indiscernible pitches seemed colder than the water that licked at Sarah's boots.

"The data that woman stole proves the same thing I have been trying to tell you. The site is unstable. We have to stop production."

"We can't move to another site now, the fleet isn't ready." Odin's voice rose.

"We should stop production completely. Don't you get it, Odin? The methyl hydrate has been breached and who knows how large a fissure we've created and where it could go. Keeping hostages is not going to convince the seabed to cooperate with us!"

"I'm not concerned about the seabed, I'm concerned about Dr. Kihomi and the evidence that girl got to him. I'm concerned about reaching my quota; I have deliveries to make. It's a big sea, Dr. Saenko, and it's not going anywhere, so you just keep doing your job. Meanwhile, I'm getting that hostage off ice. She'll have to survive a few more days if we're going to keep Kihomi's attention."

Sarah grabbed for her jeans and pulled herself into a tighter ball, feeling fear battle hypothermia in her clouded head. A boom resonated through the door and she could hear metal scraping metal and a soft whoosh as Odin stepped through.

"You have a hell of a nerve still shacking up here."

Sam spun around from his slumped position on the barstool to stare Ian square in the eyes. The sunlight that spewed through the windows of The Wheelhouse reminded him he had worked through the night.

"We know you orchestrated this whole thing, Hawaii. You stole a ship and...What the hell did you do to Sarah?" Ian said, advancing toward Sam.

"Hold it, I'm not the bad guy here." Sam leapt to his feet and instinctively swung his fists into a blocking position that

showed off his muscular physique. "I've been here all night trying to figure out a way to get Sarah back."

"Back from what?" Brian stepped from behind Ian and Sam
let his hands down. "You just bailed her out of jail, right?"

"Is that the story you got?"

"You got something different?" Ian stepped closer to Sam,
poised to swing.

"For Christ's sake, Ian, calm the hell down. Sit down, guys.
I've actually been trying to contact you all night."

"Contact us, why?" Brian sat, but Ian remained standing.

"Kell Odin bailed out Sarah. And once you hear my explanation, I'll seem like Mother Theresa compared to that asshole."

"Right, Kell Odin the giant oil tycoon bailed Sarah out. Did
he bring the President of the United States and Elvis with him?"

"Shut up, Ian and let him explain." Brian motioned for him
to sit. "Okay, Sam, you have exactly three minutes to convince
me not to join Ian and pound you."

"It started with the *Westender*, and Jack's fishing season. You
haven't heard from him yet, have you?"

"No, but there's a reasonable explanation for that…"

"And have you figured out that reasonable explanation yet,
or are you still feeding on the idea that he retired to a tropical
island?"

"You're changing the subject, Kiho. What the hell does Jack
have to do with your wacko idea that Kell Odin has done something with Sarah?" Ian said.

"Odin killed Jack, Ian. And he disposed of the rest of the
crew as well. Sarah was the only one who noticed something had
gone terribly wrong, and since you simple-minded primates
wouldn't lift a damn finger to help her, she contacted me. I had
the resources to look into the area where Jack's ship was, well,
breached, in a way. And it had everything to do with Kell Odin."

"I'm dialing 911 in ten seconds, buddy, unless you can convince me this story of yours makes sense. As a ship's captain myself, I can't let you screw with tall tales about fellow fishermen. Jack's like a brother to me…"

"Jack was like a brother to you, which is why you of all people should shut up and listen to me now, Brian. Kell Odin has a research vessel squatting in the middle of the sea, where Jack's ship was last heard from. It's a supertanker called the *Asgard* and it is claimed to be a research vessel. Well, it's not. Odin's been using that ship to extract methane from a methyl hydrate crust that lies at the bottom of the sea."

"A methyl, what?" Ian rubbed his face and crinkled his brow. "Can I kick the scientist's ass now, Brian?"

"You could, but then you'll never be able to help me save Sarah. Odin has her because she uncovered evidence that he was tampering with a very volatile crust at the bottom of the sea. If this thing leaked, it could gas the entire west coast of the United States to death. I'm damn near positive that your friend Jack experienced a dose of the noxious gas right before it took him and the crew of the *Westender* during their trip to Odin's turf."

"This is ludicrous!" Brian jumped from his seat. "You want us to believe that a wealthy oil tycoon has killed Jack in an effort to harvest natural gas and now he's kidnapped Sarah for uncovering his harebrained scheme? You're a madman, Sam."

"Just listen to me. My research organization, HALO, has uncovered dealings between Odin Energy and Chinese buyers. He has also just delivered a supertanker full of liquid natural gas to the United States before the pipeline expansion project has even begun. He's left his satellite office in cushy Juneau to commandeer a supertanker in the middle of the Bering Sea. And Sarah was bailed out by two men, who left me their business card." He pulled the card from his back pocket and slid it to Brian who read the Odin logo from the front.

"This is way too much information to digest, Sam. But suppose you're even a tiny bit right…You couldn't possibly prove it."

"Actually, I could. And I need your help to get to Sarah. I'll need a boat about the size of a crab ship, outfitted with at least one powered winch and a crane, if you catch my drift."

"Now you want the damn *Adrienne Anne*? You're not a scientist, you're a fucking pirate! I suppose if we don't just hand it over to you, you'll steal it, like you hijacked the *Westender*." Ian said.

"I'll earn my ride," Sam said. "What if I can take you to Jack and his crew? I know it's devastating to think that your friends could have perished in the sea, but if they did, you'd want to at least recover their remains, right?"

"So you claim that Odin disposed of the crew and returned the *Westender* by himself?"

"I'd bet my life on it, Brian…and Sarah's."

"Well, even if you're right, how could you possibly find them now? The sea is huge and my ship's sonar can't locate underwater obstructions like that on its own. You'd have to get me within a couple miles of the remains."

Sam pulled a map from a disheveled pile of papers he had strewn across the bar. It looked like a topographical picture of the moon, but it was labeled "Bering Sea."

"This is a map of deposit zones—places where the ocean's current usually spools around and dumps off most waste. Given the time of the *Westender's* return and the estimated time Odin could have disposed of the crew, I'm almost positive we could find Jack's body in this zone here." He pointed to a sketched divot in the map just past St. Paul Island.

Sam watched Brian's eyes dissolve into the map. He studied

the contours of the sketched lines as if he could read the topography as well as Sam.

"You're not going to give this lunatic a ride, are you Brian?"

"It is far fetched." Brian looked up at Sam, who stared back with honest, pleading eyes. "You touch anything while you're on my boat and I'll have half the island tearing you to shreds in a heartbeat, Kihomi."

"So have I at least earned a ride?"

Brian paused and placed both hands at the small of his back. He propped his chest and let out a grunt as he stretched. Sam followed his eyes to the support beam in the center of the bar. Photos of Jack and his crew, and of Sarah and Nate, stuck to the beam with yellowed Scotch tape. Their corners curled and some were torn off, but the faces in the pictures stared back.

"Sam, if what you're saying is even the least bit true, I don't have time to play skeptic. Ian, get the *Adrienne Anne* signed out, gassed up and ready to go. We'll leave in a couple hours."

Chapter Twenty-Four

By early December, a thick coat of snow lined the shore of Dutch Harbor, flaking toward a tapering sheet of ice that cracked under the choppy waves. The noon sun warmed the air enough to top each wave with a mystical cloud of ice crystals and condensation that pitched into the air. Cackling seagulls swarmed the harbor, seemingly in the know about the upcoming fishing season and the free fish guts it would scatter about the shore, which was in its early stages of bustling.

Ian had already donned his full immersion suit by the time Sam reached Brian's ship. To Sam, he shone like a bright orange highway cone atop the 200-foot steel vessel that was the *Adrienne Anne*.

"You've been aboard the *Westender* recently, but don't assume you know what it'll be like out there," Brian said, following Sam to the ship. "I want you in full immersion gear, just like Ian. The water's below freezing in parts and the storms are growing every day. The only thing I can guarantee is a rough ride, and with just the three of us, I can't guarantee a safe one. So this had better be worth our efforts, Kiho."

Sam looked into a muted sun that attempted to push through the winter sky. The air that whisked off the sea stung his face, and he followed Brian onto the ship with his eyes on Ian, hoping the thick orange jump suit would keep him warm.

Once on deck of the *Adrienne Anne*, Sam began heading aft to the wheelhouse, only to find he had gone in the wrong direction. Brian's ship wasn't only larger than the *Westender*, but it was a house-forward ship. Sam casually squared a sharp turn and headed to the bow, hoping Ian hadn't noticed.

"This way, Hawaii—unless you want to steer the ship by its crane!"

Sam held back his retort when he saw Brian emerge from below deck with armfuls of rolled-up maps.

"We're not completely numb around here, Sam. I don't know exactly what you need for our trip, but I grabbed some geological maps of the seabed, some tidal maps and navigation charts. We do have your online gadgets too, and that's where you'll find a lot of your info as we go. You know, weather and such. We have a GPS and a direct line to the Coast Guard, too." Brian stared Sam in the eyes. "Should anything happen…"

"Hey, like I said a million times before, I'm here to help." Sam pulled some maps from Brian's arms and nodded to the wheelhouse. "Once we get all this stuff laid out, I'll be able to explain a little better what we're doing."

"Good, because I've never purposely charted a course to roam aimlessly before. I gotta say, it doesn't leave a good feeling in my gut, Kiho. You'd better know what the hell you're doing because with the wind and waves we've been having in the past couple days, we got one shot to do it right. And if anything, I mean anything goes wrong…"

"We'll take this ship right back to port and it's my ass, I know. Brian, I wouldn't put you, Ian, or your ship in jeopardy unless it was the only way to…"

"Explain it all to me upstairs."

Although the helm of the *Adrienne Anne* was large enough to comfortably house an expansive console worth of online sonar and navigational equipment as well as communication devices and controls to steer the ship, it seemed a tight squeeze to Sam as he ducked Ian's angry glare. Upon entering the wheel-house, Brian took a seat at his usual captain's chair, which could have easily doubled as junk, and cut through Sam and Ian's deafening silence.

"Spread those maps out, Kiho, and tell us in more detail why the hell this deposit zone of yours is nowhere near Odin's ship, where the crew of the *Westender* mysteriously disappeared."

"Jesus, Brian, he's leading us into the middle of nowhere so he can scuttle our ship and kill us." Ian said. "He says he's a scientist studying some gassy shit and now suddenly he's a missing persons' expert?"

Sam looked at the two men. Ian's eyes narrowed into angry slits, bearing a tiny emerald glow where his full irises used to rest. Brian's brown eyes crinkled in disbelief and his lips pursed tightly together, and Sam could have sworn he was holding back a laugh.

"I'm not a pirate, Ian. And the gassy shit you mentioned does relate to the flow of refuse in the ocean." Sam pointed to the ship's sonar monitor, which displayed what looked like striations along the seabed.

"See how the seabed dips in certain places to form divots? Well, when sea life begins to drift in currents, it's usually carried to a central location on the seabed…usually landing in one of these divots. Now, if left long enough, this sea life biodegrades and emits the natural gas, methane, and if that divot is deep enough, the trapped methane becomes frozen and compressed, forming a methyl hydrate."

"The thing Odin's trying to destroy, or so you say." Brian said.

"Yes. Now in order to study where methyl hydrate deposits will most likely occur, I have spent an extensive time mapping the zones where biological trash will end up and decompose."

"Now you're calling Jack and his crew biological trash?"

"I wouldn't put it like that, Ian. But I did spend the night tracking where objects about the size of a fishing crew would drift if sunk in the Bering Sea just northwest of St. Paul Island in mid October. With the storm season approaching, any waste would have moved pretty far by now, and I'm guessing that even if he weighted the bodies, Odin wouldn't be stupid enough to leave them hanging around the *Asgard*."

"So Jack and his crew are the biological trash then." Ian said.

"For Christ's sake, yes!" Brian said. "So Sam, you got a good handle on where these boys would be if…"

"If math and science have anything to say about it, I have a damn good idea where those guys could be. The zone that we're headed is a new hot spot for waste, since the storm patterns have been slowly shifting in the past couple years."

"…yeah, global warming and all that shit."

"Global warming's not shit…" Sam looked at Ian, who studied his physique and clenched his fists. "Listen, you have no choice but to trust me. Jack and his crew have been missing for over a month now, right? And Sarah will be the next forgotten sailor if we don't head out, like, yesterday."

Ian's nostrils flared at the mention of Sarah's name and Sam sidestepped the warm cloud of carbon dioxide that fumed from his deep breaths. Meanwhile, Brian's silhouette ate up the sun in the windows behind them; he was peering out of the bridge, waving to a bright orange blur who trotted toward the *Adrienne Anne*.

"Simon Watson, our engineer," Brian said, turning back toward Sam. "A ship needs a crew, you know."

Seven hours into the trip, Sam fixed his eyes on the ship's GPS, paying no attention to the enormous swells that ate up the deck outside. Having made several trips into the Pacific on HALO's research vessel, he was accustomed to the comforting feeling of freedom that accompanied a horizon filled with nothing but ocean at every angle. But the Pacific's blue waters didn't compare to the tar-colored waves of the Bering Sea, and Sam kept his back to the windows in the wheelhouse.

"Brian tells me you're researching methyl hydrates." Simon Watson emerged from the belly of the ship with his hands coated in a thin layer of engine grease.

"You talk like you've actually heard of them," Sam said.

"I know what they are. I saw a special on the Bermuda Triangle and how those bastard little bubbles of methane can stall airplane engines thousands of feet overhead. I saw a graphic of those things swallowing up a ship." He peered out the window to survey the length of the ship. "Why are we heading toward one?"

"First of all, those specials are speculation. Some scientists want to blame all the crazy Bermuda mishaps on methane seeping from the ocean. Now, I'm not saying it couldn't happen, but it's unlikely it did to that extent in Bermuda."

"Then how do you explain all that wreckage?"

"You're an engineer, Watson. You've got a scientific mind. So you know there's only one explanation." He stared at Watson's intrigued face. "Aliens."

"For Christ's sake, Kiho, you're joking around about this? So, that methyl hydrate we're heading toward isn't really powerful enough to sink us?"

"Whoa, now. I said the methyl hydrate deposit in the Bermuda Triangle wasn't powerful enough to stall an air fleet and sink a Navy. The methyl hydrate in the Bering Sea, however, could cause a catastrophic tsunami that could sink the Pacific Coast. It could also gas-up the Ring of Fire, turning the entire area from Alaska down through Hawaii into a geyser-fest that could asphyxiate millions of people instantly."

"Jesus, you scientists got a sick sense of humor." Watson gave an uneasy grin.

"Kiho and Watson," Brian called from the wheel. "There's a report coming in from the Coast Guard that a freak storm is tearing up the waters very close to St. Paul Island. They're advising commercial fishing boats to dock at the Pribilofs and wait it out. If we continue on, we'll get fined and probably killed."

Sam looked at Brian, who nodded his thoughts back to him. "I've hit storms hard before and lived to tell about it." Brian said.

"Count me in too," Watson said. "My brother could be down there in Kiho's underwater trash basin and I'm not wasting any time at the Pribilofs wondering about it. I don't need the Coast Guard babysitting my ass. They can hang back at St. Paul without us."

The three men looked to Ian.

"Hell yeah, I'm in!" he said.

The waves stretching to the Pribilof Islands seemed calm. Without the Coast Guard's report, Sam could have easily misconceived that storm season in the Bering Sea was nothing compared to the 60-foot swells he would see at in Hawaii right now. Brian stared out the windows of his cockpit with a twisted look of skepticism across his face. The crinkle in his brow aged him twenty years and the dim Alaskan sun washed out his bronzed skin. Sam tried to focus on his maps and the ship's navigational and sonar devices knowing full well that every time he stopped to clear his mind, the image of Sarah sent a swift kick to his gut.

"Kiho," Brian called, this time punching at Sam's arm. "Sam, we're reaching the deposit area. Should I have Ian scan the sonar now or what?" It was the third time he had asked.

Sam walked to the windows of the bridge and stared into the sea, as if he could scan the bottom with his naked eyes. "Turn on the sonar."

"As long as this so-called storm keeps at bay, we should get a good reading of what's directly beneath us. But the seafloor is a few hundred meters down and even if we find something, none of us are equipped to go get it," Ian said.

"Just turn it on, Ian." Brian said.

The charcoal-grey computer screen blinked several times before revealing a rough sketch of the seafloor. A bright green line that looked like a second hand swept across the screen and revealed a garbled message that Ian's eyes translated immediately.

"There's nothing down there but maybe some lava rock and fish remains. It's not even a good place to drop a pot." Ian looked at Sam. "You're damn lucky this storm's holding out, Kiho. Because if you dragged my ass out here to find a bunch of tanner shells and dead sea slugs…"

"Remember, Ian, we came here to find trash, not king crab. Tanner shells and dead sea slugs may actually be a good sign." Sam said.

Brian leaned into the computer screen. "Be patient, Ian. We'll travel this route a little longer, then get out of here before the storm hits." He cast a glare at Sam. "When I think I've hit nothing, I always take it one mile longer…But that's it."

Sam felt a knot in his throat that must have matched that of a crab ship captain's, who had led his crew in the face of danger to nothing but barren waters. The GPS above the ship's sonar monitor counted the distance of Sam's allotted mile, and his skin began to chill.

"Now, that looks like a ghost pot." Simon's dry voice crackled to break the silence.

"Whatever it is, it's something." Brian looked to Sam and Simon. "I'll get closer. If it is a ghost pot, you two think you can help Ian pull it up? It doesn't have a buoy so it'll be a challenge."

"Not so fast, Capt'n. There are three more ghost pots coming up at the top of the screen."

"Shit, Ian, you're right. This really is a wastcland."

"Nature's garbage dump." Sam said.

"So which pot do we go for, if any?"

"All of them, until we find the crab pots numbered one and two"

"Crab pot number one? Are you kidding me, Kiho?"

"Wait, Brian. I know what he means. I hopped onboard the *Westender* too. Crab pot three tangled and crashed into the deck, meaning the last pot they dropped before something happened was pot one." Ian said.

"Jack must've had quite a catch if he went through all his pots and landed back on one." Brian passed the three men and stared out the windows of the wheelhouse. "Okay, crew, get on deck. Ghost pot season starts now."

Sam helped Ian wind a thick line around the ship's deck winch, taking intermittent stops to look at Simon atop the ship's crane, one hundred feet in the air. The sun offered little help, hiding behind a sheet of gray clouds, and the gulls squawked, aware that fishing for ghost pots with no markers or buoys was futile.

"Now usually, we see the pot's buoy floating on the surface, then we throw this line to tow it in." Ian lifted a coiled boat rope fitted with a steel grappling hook at the end. You being a greenhorn, Kiho, I'm betting you'd have trouble snagging a good pot on a sunny day. Now we're fishing for ghost pots with no surface markers, so I don't know what the hell we're grappling for."

"Judging by Brian's sonar, this is where ghost pots come to die. We're sitting atop a fortress of garbage in these waters and we're looking for anything that can link us to The *Westender*. Think you can catch some garbage from the largest trash heap in the Bering Sea? Or are you limited to neon buoys lighting the way for you?"

Ian turned from Sam and looked at Simon on the crane.

"When I catch your piece of trash, you just make sure you're ready to guide it to deck. Crab pots are heavy, Kiho—hope you've got some muscle under that smartass attitude."

Chapter Twenty-five

At 200 feet below the surface, the only light cast on the floor of the Bering Sea came from one of Odin's two unmanned submersibles. Strong LED strobes cast a gray glow over a dead sea floor and Dr. Saenko looked on through a monitor, safely onboard the *Asgard*.

The submersible relayed a visual of the seabed that an untrained eye could have mistaken for the moon. Dr. Saenko winced, aware that just months earlier, the seabed was crawling so thick with tanner crab that it looked coated in gritty brown sand.

She turned her gaze away from the desolate seabed to a long metal pipe that worked its way through the earth. Inside the metal casing, a smaller cylinder pumped metered amounts of carbon dioxide directly through the methyl hydrate crust at the bottom of the ocean. She checked the adjacent monitors, measuring the temperature and amount of carbon dioxide that ran through the pipe into eight horizontal wells that stretched from the central pipe.

Dr. Saenko turned her attention back toward the submersible, which had nearly reached its position over a second pipe, designed to collect methane as the carbon dioxide warmed the methyl hydrate crust. This pipe plunged 100 feet into the ocean floor and fanned into 16 horizontal wells.

"Position the submersible for sampling," she ordered to a technician beside her.

He nodded, and worked a stiff lever on the console. A large robotic arm swooped from the unmanned submersible on the monitor. A small probe reached directly into the earth, sampling just a few ounces of the seafloor.

"That's enough for our taste test," Dr. Saenko said. "Slowly pull that arm back and let's move the sub back onboard."

"That's it? No offense, Dr. Saenko, but our other samples have been much more detailed—and time intensive."

Dr. Saenko turned to her technician and lowered her glasses. "Are you suggesting I'm cutting corners?"

"I'm just, um...no. I just don't know what kind of data we can accumulate from one tiny sample."

"Well, if my one, tiny sample tests the way I expect it to, you'll thank me for not prodding around down there." Dr. Saenko stared at the submersible, which slowly climbed up the length of the pipe. She eyeballed the technicians to her rear, scanning their tense shoulders and gritting teeth. They steered the sub with stressful precision as it neared the ship's hull, easing it by the 13-foot propellers that acted as thrusters to help steady the ship over the pipe.

"You're expecting a problem, aren't you Dr. Saenko?" Kell Odin's voice stabbed her between the shoulder blades and she felt her flesh warm instantly.

"Mr. Odin, I didn't see you come in. I was just taking routine tests, sir. But yes, a problem could arise at any moment."

"I have enough problems on deck with that girl and her scientist without your tinkering getting in my way."

"Sir, the monitoring of a collection hub that is outfitted with 24 different channels flowing with two very dangerous gasses is not tinkering. You hired me for a job and I intend to carry out my duties to the best of my abilities...and beyond."

"Just don't get carried away, Saenko. I have shipments to deliver. And remember, the amount of fuel we're harvesting is enough to power Alaska and the entire United States oil-free for years to come."

"And the amount of power it takes just to stabilize your ship among rogue waves and 80 mile per hour winds is enough to power 40,000 homes," she said under her breath.

Odin glared at Dr. Saenko and her shoulders stiffened, sending knots up to her neck that she knew would last for days.

"Do I have to remind you that our pipeline is perfectly safe, Dr. Saenko? We've outfitted it with emergency valves to prevent a blowout of gasses."

"Mr. Odin, this isn't oil we're drilling. The pipe won't simply blow out and begin spurting oil and we can't fix the problem by drilling an adjacent well. You have 16 channels feeding methane into one collection hub. At the same time, you have eight channels pumping carbon dioxide through the same area. If that hub were to weaken, it could more than blow out. It would swallow our ship and cause a tsunami."

"Are you arguing with me, Saenko? Believe me, I know you are a brilliant scientist. After all, I only hire the best. But you'd think your scientific mind could comprehend by now that the methyl hydrate crust that we're drilling is perfectly stable. You helped select the site yourself."

"That was before."

"Before what, Dr. Saenko—and speak quickly, I'm growing tired of your complaints."

"We've bumped-up production to double our starting rate. And we've been operating at peak performance for quite some time. My theory, no, strong belief, is that our drilling is causing a cavity of methane gas to form in the seabed."

"Well that sounds like good news, Saenko. More fuel for us."

She took a deep breath and forced it through her flared

nostrils. "It's not good news at all. That cavity coupled with the weakened methyl hydrate crust is a disaster waiting to happen. If that crust were to rupture now, it could release a catastrophic amount of methane into the atmosphere. Not only would it suffocate all of us, but it would sink this ship and…"

"Overtake the entire universe in a tidal wave of epic proportions, right?" Odin slammed his fist on the consol in front of Dr. Saenko. "Just keep the pipes running, Saenko."

"And if my sample proves me right?"

Odin leaned into Dr. Saenko, pouring a hot breath across her face. She shivered and dropped her shoulders enough to reveal the monitor behind her.

"Your work is done here." He punched the keys on the console and the submersible took a jarring turn to the right. Its extended robotic arms shuddered and it began to drift out to sea.

Dr. Saenko spun toward the monitor. "You just destroyed your own sub. That was thousands of dollars worth of equipment that we need to…"

"It was unnecessary equipment."

"Sir, what about the collection pipes and the stability of the hub? If it breaks down, we won't be able to collect any more methane."

"Fine, Saenko, shut the pipes down for now. It's almost time to switch ships anyway. This tanker is near full and we'll get her on the way to China soon."

"Then we're finished here?"

"Hardly. The second *Asgard* tanker is arriving within days. You have until then to secure the area. We'll begin pumping when the second ship is secured."

"But Sir, the methyl hydrate won't fix itself in just days. And the stress of setting up another supertanker could blow the crust completely." She stared at Odin's unaffected glare. "What about the…the hostage on this ship? You can't change up ships with Kiho on your tail."

"Quite the opposite, Saenko. A change would be perfect. Our scientist friend will just be a little surprised when the *Asgard* he sees isn't the one bearing his sweetheart. She'll be on her way to China."

"If she's lucky," Dr. Saenko whispered to herself.

Chapter Twenty-six

Sam squinted on deck to catch Simon Watson's signal from his position atop the *Adrienne Anne's* crane. One of his bright orange arms hooked around the crane's rope while the other waved like a diver in trouble.

"Crane's fixed, Ian. Let's start pulling up more pots," Sam said.

Ian watched a heap of trash skate across the boat's deck, and turned to Sam.

"We're right in the zone, Ian. Trust me."

"The zone? We've been at this for hours and a storm's rolling in. We're running dangerously close to the zone where I kick your ass for wasting my time."

"Pots ahead!" Brian yelled through the ship's intercom.

"Where have I heard that before," Ian said.

"Hey, the last pot we pulled up came from the *Time Capsule*, and you said that ship was in the *Westender's* fleet."

"It doesn't work like that, Kiho. Pots don't line up in chronological order down there. We have just as good a chance at pulling the up the damn Heart of the Ocean necklace from the *Titanic* as we do of finding pot two from *The Westender*."

"Well then you'll strike it rich. Your captain ordered us to pull up some pots."

Ian stomped toward the boat's deck winch with heavy feet that broke through the ice on deck. He approached Sam with a shove and Sam accepted the slide he took four feet from the starboard railing.

"Back up, Kiho. I got a rope to throw…blindly at another ghost pot."

Sam gave Ian plenty of distance, watching him heave the grappling hook into the sea and pull it back easily, hand-over-hand. Ian turned toward Sam, dangling the empty hook in his hand.

"Nice skills," Sam said.

"Pushing my buttons isn't gonna magically make a crab pot appear any faster, Kiho."

Sam stood back and examined Ian's stature. Ian positioned his feet at a forty-five degree angle, stomping his right heel into the ship's deck to steady himself. His arm swung back, forcing his shoulder blade out, and Sam tightened his face, almost feeling the pain of a pulled scapula.

The rope flew from Ian's hand and Sam bit his lip, tearing through the chapped skin. The hook sank in the sea and Ian gave it a tug that pulled him toward the starboard railing.

"We got something, Kiho. Remember how to set up the winch?"

"I'm on it." Sam rushed to the winch. He set a thick metal guard in place and tightened his grip around the frozen lever, letting it bite through his gloves to his calloused hands.

Ian leaned over the railing and stared into the water. But Sam turned his head toward Brian, trying to numb the anticipation of another catch.

Off the side of the boat, the water stirred until a seven-foot area calmed around a large obstruction.

"Looks like we got a big one," Ian said.

Sam forced himself to keep looking at Brian, who inched toward the window, making the exhaustion on his face visible.

"Holy shit," Ian said. Sam heard the winch stomp shut.

Sam lowered his gaze to catch Ian dumbfounded, holding a buoy marked *W-E*. The number two was stamped on its side.

"Well, bring it up!" Sam slid to the winch and grabbed the lever.

"I can't." Ian backed up.

Sam placed a heavy hand on Ian's shoulder and signaled to a descending Simon with his other hand. "We got pot two!" He skidded to the ship's intercom and called Brian.

Simon met Sam at the winch and the two men watched it eat the yellow rope attached to crab pot two until the pot was visible.

"Good God." Brian surprised Sam, standing behind him.

"What is it?" Sam looked into the steel pot, littered with refuge from the seabed, and crawling with junk crab.

"That's Jack's immersion suit. It's…it's tied to the pot."

Sam looked at his own orange jumpsuit. "Brian, everyone wears those."

"Jack's has a cigar burn on the left leg. He wears it like a badge of honor. He's had it since I worked on the *Westender* with Sarah."

The three men stared at the dangling pot, letting it hit the side of the boat and squeal along its hull, until Simon grasped both hands around the metal cage.

"We have to pull it up. It's always better to find the bodies of lost fishermen than to leave them out to sea."

Sam joined Simon and they hoisted the great cage toward the ship. Its steel frame supported the carcasses of several foul-smelling dead crab and was encrusted in grime. The rope holding buoy number two had obviously been used to affix four orange jumpsuits to the cage's frame—their contents had been devoured by the sea.

"I think I'm gonna be sick," Ian said. He turned to the port side of the ship.

Simon helped Sam pull the pot onto the deck with a bang that shuddered the cage's remains onto the crab-sorting table. Brian sprinted from the deck up the stairs to the wheelhouse.

"What's he doing?" Sam said.

"He and Jack were like brothers. He's calling the Coast Guard to report this."

"Wait, wasn't your brother part of the crew of the *Westender?*"

"I knew Mark was gone the moment he passed. Brothers just feel these things. But I didn't go raging through town about it like Sarah Reid. Now I think maybe I should have."

"Holy shit, Sarah!" Sam's hands jerked from the cage. "Did you say Brian's calling the Coast Guard?"

"It's protocol."

"He can't! Remember why we're here, Simon. We found the bodies to prove that they were murdered…to prove that Kell Odin had them murdered—because Kell Odin has Sarah."

"Slow down, kid, what are you saying about murdering?"

"Simon, look at this rope." Sam tugged at the frayed remains of the buoy line that held an immersion suit to the wall of the cage. "These guys were affixed to the cage and the cage was dropped. Someone wanted these bodies lost."

"You think this Odin guy tied the crew to a cage and drowned them?" Simon backed away from the cage.

"No, let's backtrack. Remember, the *Westender* came upon Odin's ship where it may have run into a fissure in the sea bed that let out methane gas."

Simon stared at Sam in silence.

"My theory from the get-go is that the crew of the *Westender* never knew what hit 'em. They were suffocated by an outburst of gas and killed before Odin ever reached the ship."

"So why hide the bodies then?"

"Odin caused the gas leak. If the *Westender* was found, people would know the dangers of Odin's operation. He's leeching methane from the seabed. I have the proof and he has Sarah." Sam grabbed Simon's shoulders and gave him a firm shake. "If Odin sees the Coast Guard cruising up to this territory, he'll think I turned him in and he'll kill Sarah for sure."

Simon squinted into the sun behind the wheelhouse. "It's too late, kid. Brian's been up there for a few minutes now. You know he called for help."

"Then we have to beat them to the *Asgard*, it's the only way."

"That's impossible, Kiho. The Coast Guard's got choppers and RIBs that can kick this ship's ass."

"We have to try, Simon. We already lost the *Westender*, we can't lose Sarah too."

"You're right." Simon stared at the stairs below deck toward the engine room. "One regatta, coming up."

"Dr. Saenko, the *Asgard II* is approaching. Mr. Odin is giving direct orders to turn off the collection pipe and prepare to disengage it from the ship." Erik Bergen's voice reached the control console in the ship's lab, where Alena Saenko monitored the methane collection pipe.

"No," she whispered into the intercom, aware that Bergen would not hear her.

She placed a hand on the keypad that controlled the valves in the main collection pipe and typed the code that would block the valve from venting. Her index finger hovered over the "enter" key.

"Dr. Saenko, the *Asgard II* is approaching. Are we waiting the storm out before switching ships?" Her lead scientist said.

"No, Mark. We're disengaging right now and switching ships. There should be a 30-minute lag while we unlock the feed on this ship and connect the collection pipe to the next ship. We've been ordered to block all gasses from venting out of the pipe while we switch ships."

"But the temperature of the methyl hydrate…can we turn the valve off and let the pressure build in the pipe system for 30 minutes? The tests indicate that the temperature and pressure…"

"I know, Mark. We should have vented the pipe gradually throughout the collection process in a safe fashion that would let the buildup of methane and carbon dioxide vent slowly, without causing much damage to the life on the seabed. But Odin did not want to waste precious fuel.

Realistically, with this storm approaching, we're facing 30- to 60-foot rogue waves. The thrusters on the *Asgard II* will have to work overtime just to balance it above the collection pipe. It'll be nearly impossible to complete this action at all, let alone in 30 minutes."

"But Dr. Saenko, does Odin understand that if the pressure in that pipe is allowed to build up, it could blow?"

"It could do more than blow, Mark. It could backwash a buildup of carbon dioxide and methane gasses into the entire pipe system that runs throughout the methyl hydrate crust. It would shatter the entire crust."

"That could destroy the entire seabed."

"Not to mention the western United States and possibly parts of Russia. It would asphyxiate everything in its path and could vent gasses that would destroy millions on the mainland. We've known this for quite some time."

"You said Odin had everything under control. Why the hell are we doing this?"

"You took the paycheck just like everybody else here—without asking questions. We all wanted to believe Kell Odin had everything under control—just as his investors and the politicians do." She let out a heavy sigh. "It's as much our fault as it is his. Tell me honestly that you didn't know this would happen."

Kell Odin stared at a grey horizon speckled with yellow sparks of sunlight. The *Asgard II* approached the starboard side and shouldered the rising tides that swept off the sea in the increasing wind.

"Dr. Saenko, is the collection pipe locked and ready for the ship to disembark," he ordered into the ship's intercom.

He waited several seconds before receiving a faint "Aye Sir" in response.

"Bergen, radio the team on the *Asgard II* and tell them that I will not be sending Dr. Saenko onboard. I will also remain on the *Asgard I* en-route to China."

"Sir, you're not going to captain the second ship?"

"I have investors to meet in China, Erik. Besides, the second ship requires more of a martial presence, if you catch my drift."

"Sir," Dr. Saenko's voice boomed from the bridge's intercom. "We have disengaged the collection pipe, but we are concerned about the buildup of pressure should it require more than 30 minutes to attach it to the new vessel. I fear that with the approaching storm, we may run into problems if we don't immediately vent the pipe."

Odin grunted. "You are a scientist, Elena. You realized that venting the pipe could damage surrounding wildlife and suffocate our crew on deck."

"Of course sir, but we have prepared for this situation and we can assure you the crew would be safe below deck while the pipe vents. The death of surrounding wildlife is miniscule compared to the threat of a burst pipe and the impending chain reaction that would follow."

"Are we still doing this Elena? My ships are built to withstand atmospheric conditions. We have thrusters that will maintain the ship's stability while it connects to your pipe within your time frame. Wouldn't you rather we vent that pipe into our ship's tanks where the fuel could be profitable to us instead of venting toxic gasses into the atmosphere?"

Odin let out a relieved sigh and a self-congratulatory smile crept across his face.

"Sir, you might not want to relax just yet." Bergin pointed toward the ship's sonar screen.

"What in God's name is that?" He tapped on the screen as if he could push the blip off the monitor. "Another damn crab fisherman's wandering into our territory? Does a federally sanctioned boundary mean nothing to those imbeciles?"

"Sir, you have an incoming signal," an officer in the bridge said.

"It must be the damn ship's captain. Bergen, monitor the *Asgard II*'s approach and keep Dr. Saenko under your thumb while I take care of this."

"Approaching vessel, you are trespassing on government sanctioned waters. Turn about immediately or I will have to alert the Coast Guard," Odin said.

"Well that would put a damper on your plans to illegally leech toxic gas from the sea and destroy the United States in the process, now wouldn't it?" The voice replied.

"Kiho?" Odin's face grew red and he plunged his index finger between his neck and his collar, feeling a vein pulse against his touch.

"Bergen, is the *Asgard II* within range of the collection pipe yet?" Odin said.

"Mr. Odin, it's right outside." Bergen directed his attention toward the looming supertanker that mimicked the appearance of their ship.

"Excellent. Get yourself and your men on board now. Take Saenko's team with you, but leave her behind. You have exactly three minutes, Erik."

"Sir, why such a quick retreat? Is there a threat?"

"Arm your men and prepare to welcome Dr. Kiho to the *Asgard*." Odin looked into his computer monitor.

"Do you want me to take our hostage along?" Bergen nodded his head toward the old ship's bridge where Sarah's silhouette slumped in the sunlight.

"No, she stays with us. Now move so I can get this ship out of Kiho's sight. We can't let on that there are two ships. We need him to think nothing has changed by the time he gets here."

Bergen looked at the monitor. "That's his ship? It's just a few miles away. How the hell are you going to hide a supertanker in such a short amount of time?"

"Diversion, Erik, which is why you need to stop questioning my orders and move." Odin cleared his throat and radioed his second ship. "*Asgard II*, Erik Bergen will be on board shortly as your acting captain. Follow his orders precisely. Now get the engineers online and prepare the thrusters to steady the ship over our intake pipe. It is a suggestion of our lead scientist here that we hurry and vent the pipe. Time is money, people."

Odin ordered his own crew to pull the *Asgard* away from the second ship and out of plain sight.

Chapter Twenty-Seven

Sam Kiho watched Brian Eriksson press his forehead between his middle finger and his thumb, folding the skin toward his temples. He had forfeited his view of the ship's GPS in favor of navigating toward the sun, exactly where Odin's ship rested miles in the distance.

"We're almost there, Brian. It would be in plain sight if the sun wasn't in our eyes. You know you don't have to stare at it," Sam said.

"You don't know these waters, Sam. The GPS will give you direction, but it doesn't know that the sun gets an eerie orange glow before the freezing rain starts; then the wind picks up. You can almost time rogue waves by the smirk of that sun. It's blinding right before a big one hits."

"So you old captain types can really predict rogue waves? That kind of information would be invaluable to our guys at HALO."

Brian laughed. "Don't get too excited, kid, and don't call me old. 90 percent of running these rigs is instinct and at least half of my instincts are wrong." He thrust a hearty pat into Sam's back that made him stagger.

Sam sidestepped Brian and leaned into the sonar and GPS readouts. He cupped his hand over the screen to shield the sun.

"I know we're coming up on them pretty fast, kid. I haven't

been ignoring the technology." Brian stepped forward, casting his shadow across the console. "Easier to read now?"

"Holy shit, Brian, we're on top of them." Sam stepped back as if his body had physically bumped into the *Asgard*.

"Well son of a…you're right. Funny, I could have sworn she was heading away from us a few minutes ago. Maybe I have been staring at the sun for a while. Okay then, prepare to, um, what are we doing once we reach this ship?"

Sam tugged at his immersion gear to free himself from its buckles. "I have to confront Odin and somehow manage to get Sarah the hell off that ship. I'm much better at figuring out this shit on the fly."

"You don't have a plan?" Brian grabbed Sam's arm, scraping his chapped fingers against his flannel shirt.

"This is the improvisational stall, Brian. I have to buy some time while I figure out what's going on in Odin's head—and what he's got up his sleeve. It'll work out, don't worry."

"Work out? This is Sarah's life we're talking about. And you don't even have the common sense to keep your survival gear on when you're cruising stormy seas to another boat. How did you think you'd get to the *Asgard* anyway? Hovercraft?"

"I'm using the RIB, Brian. Drop it."

"I'm still the captain of this ship, Hawaii, and none of my men jump on a dinky lifeboat in the middle of a storm wearing jeans and a damn T-shirt. And I'll be damned if I'm sending a newbie to a supertanker without so much as a to-do list. This isn't a day at Kailua Beach, Kiho. This is some serious shit and you've got us all neck-deep."

"You think I don't know that? I got a whole team of scientists on Oahu holding a finger over the button to alert Washington to Odin's plan. I got the Coast Guard racing to the *Asgard* to accuse Kell Odin of murdering the crew of the *Westender* and I hold all the cards that could extinguish the career of a very power-hungry, world-dominating oil tycoon. Now I have to balance all these threats, not to mention save the world and win back the life of one woman. And I have to do it from the bow of an inflatable dingy in the middle of the Bering Sea at high tide…"

"So you agree then."

"What?"

"You should put your immersion suit back on." Brian nodded toward the windows. "It's cold out there."

Sam let a grunt escape from his chest and he pulled the orange suit back over his clothing. He tried to keep one eye on the ship's console as he dressed.

"What in the hell is that?" Brian grabbed for Sam's sleeve.

"What?"

"Sonar's picking up something strange underneath Odin's ship. It looks like a wreck at the bottom of the sea. A big one. And I've never seen such a lack of life down there on the seabed, especially not in golden king territory before fishing season has even begun. Sam, I think something weird's going on there. You might want to wait for the Coast Guard."

"We can't wait for the Coast Guard and they can't help us. And that's not a wreck, it's probably the collection pipe. That's how Odin is extracting the methane from the seabed." He leaned into the screen and followed a bright green blip across the length of the monitor. "But over there…that's not just a pipe in the ground, it's a network. And mother of God, that system is huge. It spans the whole seabed. At the rate he must be collecting methane, we're sitting on the equivalent of an active volcano."

"Well, sunshine, before you throw yourself into it, I gotta tell you that supertanker doesn't look too steady over that pipe of yours. I just got visual through the binoculars. I thought the *Asgard* needed to sit still for this shit. It looks like that ship is making adjustments to leave, or dock."

209

"With that network, I wouldn't worry about the *Asgard* going anywhere. Besides, as good a captain as you are, Brian, I don't think staring through the sun into those ancient opera glasses is really considered visual confirmation."

Brian tossed the binoculars aside. "You almost called me old again, Kiho. I should keelhaul you for that one alone. But since I'm not a pirate, I'll give you some advice instead. There's something very wrong with that ship over there. I can feel it. It just doesn't make sense, appearing and disappearing on the sonar, and now it's wavering when it should be standing still."

"It's the storm Brian. Either way, we need to make our move. I know Odin's up to something, that's part of the fun." Sam flashed his best Superman smile.

"We're gonna lose more than we bargained for on this run, Kiho, I can feel it. I'll hold the *Adrienne Anne* as steady as I can in this spot, but you don't have long."

Sam accepted Ian's hand to steady himself over the railing of the *Adrienne Anne*'s starboard side. Simon Watson used the deck winch to help lower him into the rigid inflatable boat that had sat as a reserve life boat on the crab ship since a storm shook the crew back in 1985.

"I worked on her all morning, Kiho. She's never seen battle, but she should start up just fine." Simon repeated the phrase for the third time.

Sam tried to take comfort in Simon's words, but focused more on his grip, which loosened around the frozen rope that guided him to the small craft. The freezing rain just started to pick up and the eerie orange sun stabbed at the corner of Sam's eye, promising a throbbing temple in seconds. *Brian, you'd better be wrong about those rogue waves hitting*, he thought to himself.

The first step Sam took into the lifeboat sent a chill through his body. The boat rested just inches off the rough surface of the Bering Sea and collected the full brunt of water and wind. Sam released his grip on the rope and signaled Ian to pull the line back onboard. He turned from the crew to start its 110-horsepower engine and paused to see nothing but black waters in front of him.

"Start her up, Kiho," Simon called down from the deck.

Sam took a deep breath. He placed a gloved hand over the ignition and powered the outboard motor. It grumbled to a quick start and the six-meter craft hopped above the first mogul-like wave. Instantly, Sam hydroplaned across the sea. The boat felt solid on the choppy waves, and began to take on water immediately, as Brian had promised.

No stranger to RIBs, Sam sidestepped the puddles on deck aware that the small boat was designed to fill like a bathtub and still cruise effortlessly. He gauged his speed at 70 knots by the way the freezing rain pelted his unseasoned skin. Sam suddenly admired Brian's ability to stare directly into the sun as his eyes watered, searching for Odin's ship.

Just about time to cut the engine, Sam spoke into his watch, reminding himself that a ten-minute cruise would put him directly in Odin's path, hopefully out of sight. The waves persisted, pitching three-and-four foot peaks toward the lifeboat, but Sam ignored them in search of the *Asgard*.

Within seconds, the glare of the sun disappeared and a cold wind struck Sam's face. The supertanker appeared on the horizon and grew to the size of a small island compared to the lifeboat. Sam let himself stare at the ship for minutes before he fought to cruise around to the *Asgard*'s stern, on the opposite side of the ship's bridge. But the waves surrounding the *Asgard* began to stir and toss the inflatable into wild circles.

"Brian," Sam said into the ship's antiquated two-way radio.

"Can you hear me? Do you detect a storm ahead? The waves are getting wild around here."

There was long pause and heavy static.

"Kiho, it's the pipe. There's heavy activity around the pipe."

Sam pushed his way along the port side of the ship, tensing his hands over the RIB's controls and wishing the small boat was any color but an obvious bright orange. The water calmed and Sam almost exhaled, until a fierce blast of air pushed a five-foot wave into the lifeboat's bow.

Sam looped his arms around the ship's wheel and hugged it until his biceps popped. A wall of freezing water rushed over his body, stealing his breath in an uncontrollable gasp. The RIB steadied itself like a sea kayak and filled with water that forced Sam's body into an abrupt seizure.

"Kiho, you okay there?" Brian's voice crackled.

"It's an air ram...some kind of weapon from the bottom of the ship." Sam swayed his body to the diminishing rocking of the waves. "Wait, scrap that. That blast of air wasn't meant for me. It's the ship's thrusters. It's steadying itself over the collection pipe."

"That doesn't make sense at all, Kiho," Simon's voice said. "The *Asgard* only needs to use its side thrusters to gain positioning. If it has been positioned over the pipe all along like you said, it would need to use its bottom thrusters to stay put. Those would point directly downward, sending a surge into the sea, not a wave on the surface. Something is definitely wrong there, Kiho. You need to..."

Sam disregarded Simon's advice and turned his attention to the silhouette of at least seven men rushing into an obvious formation on deck. He stared through the sun's glare like a deer in headlights until Brian's voice barked over the intercom instead.

"They're armed, Sam, get out of there," he said. "We got a visual. They're armed."

Sam's hand instinctively landed on the ignition and his arms forced the RIB to turn around and race out of the *Asgard*'s orbit. Before his head could catch up to his body's reaction, the boat skimmed across the sea, ejecting the gallons of taken-on water into the air like a thick storm cloud. The cloud masked Sam's position and he leaned into it, accepting the freezing mist. Bullets whizzed through the cloud, pecking teasing splashes in the waves beside him.

"Push it Sam, you're still in range," Simon said.

"I'm trying," he yelled, losing breath. "But this boat is too slow and it's holding the whole damn sea."

The freezing rain picked up and the sea sent more challenging waves into Sam's direction, slowing the RIB and spinning it into uncontrollable spirals. He gripped the wheel until he could feel the cold metal through his Thinsulate gloves. But suddenly, the RIB responded and his yank on the wheel began to oversteer him into a 360 degree turn. The water settled into an immediate calm and Sam stood dumbfounded, staring at the *Asgard* from several meters in the distance.

Brian and Simon's voices mumbled over the radio, but Sam stood transfixed on a football-field-sized flat sea that came to a halt under the supertanker. The horizon pushed large waves and icy spray in every direction across the sea, but the water underneath the *Asgard* appeared almost paved.

The armed figures on the supertanker made an easy target of Sam, obviously using the still waters and his halted position to their advantage. Instead of gunning the motor, Sam held tightly to the RIB and took in a deep breath. It dizzied him, as he expected. He wasted a split second to take a glimpse of an albatross, breaking formation over the supertanker and falling toward the sea.

"Brian, Simon, Ian," he spoke clearly into the radio and

tried to remain calm. "Get below deck immediately and cover your faces. Run."

Sam pulled his coat over his head and wrapped it around his nose and mouth. The men on the *Asgard* took aim, and Sam turned the RIB's engine on in spite of them. The orange boat and his orange jumpsuit made a perfect target, but more importantly to Sam, the nylon and crushed-neoprene made a suitable gas mask.

Before he could cross his fingers, a sound mimicking an Atlantic Northern right whale groaned from the sea. On cue, Sam turned the RIB and pushed away from the *Asgard* at top speed, but kept his head turned backwards, toward the supertanker. In less than a second, the sea rose in a wave that crested like a volcano. The wall of water surrounding the supertanker diminished it to the size of Sam's lifeboat and spray hissed from every side of the great mountain. Sam fought to keep his eyes open long enough to witness the watery peak swallow the 250,000 ton supertanker in one gulp. It disappeared completely.

Sam snapped out of his trance heading toward the *Adrienne Anne* at well over 70 knots. A shockwave from the giant methane bubble carried him across the sea on an unstable rogue wave that promised to pound him underwater at any second. Sam fought to keep his stance and stay on the skidding boat. Its small size and buoyancy worked to his advantage, hydroplaning over the wave like a giant surfboard.

Sam tried to relax into the surf of a lifetime, but remembered the ride he took in Sarah's Ford Festiva instead—a little orange underdog that could drive on top of the snow. *Brian*, he thought, not ready to think about Sarah.

"Anyone there? *Adrienne Anne*, are you okay?"

"Sam what the hell just happened?" Brian answered. "We're below deck but our ship's been hit by some kind of rogue wave.

Our computers are probably offline. I need to get to the bridge and check on them."

Sam uncovered his mouth on the exhale. "Cover your faces with your survival gear and get to the deck winch and the ring buoy. I'm heading to your ship fast and I'll need help getting onboard."

The wave began to crest and Sam knew he had seconds left before the lifeboat would fall captive to the pipeline below. Not ready to meet the full brunt of the sea, he pushed his body toward the gunwale of the ship, which approached the starboard side of the *Adrienne Anne* faster than he expected.

A ring buoy ascended over his head about a hundred yards off course—an impossible grab. Sam turned to the deck winch, unable to see anything but white mist. A loud rush of surf deafened him and his feet began to slide across the deck of the RIB. *Hold your breath, here it comes* he thought. Sam shut his eyes and let his body collapse under the drop of the wave's broken crest.

"Gotcha," Ian said clenching Sam's hand in his own.

Sam blinked several times to see that he had not fallen into the ocean.

"Hook him up to the winch, Ian. Those suntanned hands of his aren't gonna hold on long," Brian said.

Sam urged his muscles to come to life and help the men lift him onboard, but halfheartedly let Ian do most of the work.

"Keep your mouth covered, Kiho," Simon mumbled through a wall of neoprene stretched over his face.

"Thanks for the reminder. Have you gotten to the bridge, Brian?"

"Listen to this guy, giving the captain his orders. Yes, Kiho, the computers are back online. But you're turning a new shade of blue, so get your ass below deck and warm up."

215

"The *Asgard*..." Sam pushed against Ian, who tried to force him off the deck.

"Kiho, you got back alive. We'll take another swing at the *Asgard* once we stabilize this ship. We almost capsized while you were out playing tag with that supertanker."

"You don't understand, Brian. That rogue wave wasn't a wave at all. Why do you think we're talking through our shirts? That wave was a shockwave and it came from a giant methane bubble, that swallowed the *Asgard* whole."

"Sarah." Ian said.

Brian and Simon's eyes turned glassy and stared at Sam for an answer. Sam opened his mouth to speak, but found nothing to say to the three gaping men.

"We should get to the bridge and contact the Coast Guard." Brian broke the silence. "If that methane thing is breaking, it'll be our asses too."

Sam ignored the scraping of his knees against a wall of ice that formed under his clothing and followed the three men to the wheelhouse. The strong smell of propane heat made his head spin, but he welcomed the ability to pull off his makeshift gas mask. The others followed Sam's cue and pulled the neoprene from their faces.

Brian slumped at his console and scanned the Doppler radar for approaching storms. The sonar reported a barren seabed and the pipeline disappeared in a wall of heavy activity.

"Is all that stuff methane?" Ian pointed at the sonar screen.

"No, the pipe couldn't have cracked that severely or we would be riding a tsunami to Cleveland right now. The wave that hit us was just a burp. But we don't have much time."

"We should leave this place and let the Coast Guard handle this, Kiho. Now that Sarah's...Odin's gone, you can contact your guys, right?"

A daze fell over Sam and he didn't try to answer Simon's

question. He turned to Brian who slouched over the console and Ian who stared out the window as if waiting for the next wave to take him. Sam's body shivered, feeling the effects of stage-one hypothermia, but he forced his body to compose itself. He pulled his head toward his right shoulder until he heard a stiff pop in his neck, then cranked his head to his left. He let out a deep exhale and prepared to speak.

"*Adrienne Anne,* come in." A childlike voice squeaked through the radio before Sam could deliver his speech.

"What the hell is that?" Ian darted to the console.

"It's a signal, but coming through the satellite phone," Simon said.

"That's my number." Sam looked at the identification screen.

"Well it sure as hell ain't you. This is *Adrienne Anne,* who the hell is this?"

"Ian? Thank God I finally got you. It's Sarah. I'm onboard the *Asgard*—I don't have much time."

Sam snatched the phone. "Sarah, are you in the sea? Do you know your depth? Where are you? We'll come get you."

"In the…what? I'm in the *Asgard,* en route to China."

The men exchanged confused glares. "China?" they said in unison.

"The *Asgard* sank, sweetie," Brian said.

"No. There are two supertankers. The original *Asgard* is headed to China. I'm with Dr. Saenko…Odin will be back soon. We're taking the trade route to China. Brian, you know the route."

"Sarah, are you hurt? Where's Odin? Who was on that other tanker?" Sam said.

The men waited until they were answered by three loud beeps and silence.

"Signal's gone," Sam said.

"But not before I got their location." Brian pointed to a spot on his GPS. "You can check my math, but that new *Asgard* wasn't there for more than a couple hours, and if Sarah's ship took the usual route to China, they haven't gotten very far. They're just a few miles from the pipeline...which means we're heading back into the belly of the beast."

Chapter Twenty-Eight

"Tell Kiho the state of the pipeline…it could crack at any minute," Dr. Saenko whispered into Sarah's ear. "If he gets onboard the *Asgard II* he has to find the controls in the lab and vent the pipe or the whole network can blow."

"The *Asgard II* sank, and we lost our connection—cell's dead." Sarah threw the phone and watched it slide across the old conference room floor.

"No, Sarah! That means the methane is already leaking. It's begun. We're done for."

"And now you're concerned?"

"Listen, Sarah, I…"

"I still have faith in Sam. He knows where we are now and he'll get us out of here. And he and his guys from HALO will fix your mistakes. They'll save the sea and arrest your bony ass."

"Vent all you want, Sarah. I deserve that much, but this is more than just a rescue mission for Sam. That pipeline is holding a tanker's worth of methane gas at unspeakable pressure. It's already starting to blow and if…when the rest of it goes up, if that pipe isn't venting, it could cause a natural disaster larger than any we've seen in our lifetimes."

"Well, you should be proud of your work then, Doctor."

"What has Sam got? You've been working with him for some

time now. You must know what tricks he has up his sleeve. Do you think he can help us from that crab ship?"

"Let's see. I tell you everything Sam can do, I give away all his contacts, I divulge his plans, and you kill him the second he steps onboard this ship. Forget it, you're the bad guys, I'm not giving you anything."

"Sarah, we're already out of range. Nobody has shown up and the Coast Guard isn't going to let any ships or aircraft near a wave large enough to swallow the *Asgard II*, if it did indeed sank. Odin doesn't trust me and he sure as hell doesn't need you anymore. We're as good as dead, so you might as well tell me what glimmer of hope is left in your dehydrated, exhausted little brain."

Sarah sank against the rough wooden cabinets that lined the old conference room. Sawdust sprinkled over her head and her wool sweater scratched against her skin. She could feel her backbone knock against the metal hinge and she breathed a sigh through cracked, bleeding lips. Her stomach tightened through hunger pains.

"Sarah, I want to help. Please, tell me why you think Sam can still do anything for us. Please, tell me what he's got so I can try to help him onboard."

"You're just as much captive as I am. How will you help him?"

"Odin still needs me to work the technology in the lab. He may want to do away with me once we reach China, but until then, I can appeal to him for access...even if it's just a bluff."

"Odin's not that stupid."

"Maybe I'm just that smart."

"Yeah, you're brilliant. A genius. You managed to endanger half the world with one brilliant flick of your brilliant, manicured little finger. The second you get your bony ass back into that lab, you'll weasel your way back on Odin's payroll. I'll take my chances with Sam and the Coast Guard."

"*Adrienne Anne*, this is Captain Roberts from the US Coast Guard. We received your distress call and we are ordering you to clear these waters immediately due to hazardous conditions. Do you need assistance?" The voice shot across the sea.

Sam leaned toward the port side windows of the wheelhouse to see a tiny speck of orange skid closer to the ship. "Well son of a…they're sending a RIB full of guys to rescue us."

"Well screw 'em. We don't need their rescuing, we have to keep heading toward Sarah."

"Easy there, Ian. We can't skirt the Coast Guard, and they're right, we can't handle these waves on the *Adrienne Anne*," Brian said.

"But we're so close. The *Asgard* will be within eyesight in just a few more minutes. I can see it on the screen." Ian tapped the monitor.

"Let 'em on," Sam said. "Brian's right. If the methane creeps up again, we could be the sea's next snack."

The small Coast Guard craft sidled up to the *Adrienne Anne* and Brian motioned to the others to meet them on deck. Within minutes the small crew of the *Adrienne Anne* braved freezing winds to welcome the rescuers.

"Come 'round to the starboard side," Brian shouted to the RIB captain. The craft hopped away from the *Adrienne Anne* and temporarily leapt out of sight, behind the ship's stern.

"Okay, Kiho, you wouldn't feed us to the Coast Guard and leave Sarah out there any sooner than Ian would. What's your plan?"

"You know me so well already, Brian." Sam patted his shoulder. "Just get all those Coasties off that RIB and on deck here…oh and I'll need my radio and cell phone back from the bridge."

"Aye, Kiho." Brian winked. "Ian. Get Kiho his stuff. We got a Coast Guard crew to welcome…and keep welcomed."

221

Ian slipped on the freshly frozen surface of the ship's deck and ran up the stairs to the wheelhouse. Sam checked the thick suspenders that held his immersion suit tightly over his clothing and accepted Brian's heavy coat. Within seconds, a light spray announced the Coast Guard's reappearance at the side of the ship.

Brian extended a rope ladder to the crew and motioned for them to climb aboard. One man equipped with ropes of his own ascended the ladder and took Brian's hand to climb over the slick, frozen railing of the ship. He kept an eye on his footing but glanced at Sam more than once.

"You guys need medical assistance?" He asked once he had collected his feet on deck.

Brian looked at Sam and jerked his head toward three other rescuers, ready to carry a large backboard onto the ship.

"Simon Watson, our engineer. He might be hurt. Sam, peek your head below deck and tell him help is on his way." Brian winked at Sam.

"I'll tell him." Sam slid to the stairs that led below deck, keeping the Coast Guard men at a safe following distance. "Watson, you down there," he whispered. "Don't worry, the Coast Guard is here to help you with your neck injury." He annunciated the words and cringed, listening for Simon's response.

"Got it, Kiho. I'll be in the galley...and my neck is just killing me." His arm extended into view and a stiff thumbs-up appeared in the light of the stairwell.

Sam returned to Brian who coaxed the last Coast Guard officer onboard the ship. Ian tied the small craft to the *Adrienne Anne* with one hand and passed Sam his cell phone and the ship's radio with the other.

"Nice RIB, huh Kiho? It's a little bigger and probably faster than Brian's old piece of crap. I mean, it could get you to the

Asgard in about ten minutes flat if you were to head, say a few more degrees Northwest. If you hopped on it before I could tie it up, that is." Ian loosened his grip of the rope. "Man, this thing is hard to hang on to."

Sam watched three men descend to the galley in search of Simon, then turned toward Brian who ushered the other two men toward the ship's bridge.

"Bring her back safe, Sam."

"Don't worry, Ian. I'll save the sea and get the girl. Now get this ship the hell out of here before it does get eaten by the sea."

Sam placed his weight in Ian's hand and leaned outward over the ship's railing and toward the Coast Guard's RIB. From several feet above the craft, he could tell it was in much better shape than Brian's lifeboat. Still, a stiff wind pushed against his back, shoving him toward the side of the *Adrienne Anne.*

"Don't catch a cold, Hawaii." Ian grinned and tossed the rope to Sam who had just touched down on the RIB.

Sam grinded the motor to a quick start and tried not to catch the turning heads of the Coast Guard as he stole their boat.

By four in the afternoon, the hint of sunlight Sam had relied on disappeared behind a veil of charcoal clouds until the horizon swallowed it completely. The RIB scooted across waves that rose in response to a north wind, and sleet pecked at his face through the soaked collar he used as a mask.

Sam passed the grave of the sunken *Asgard* clone and followed the lubber line on his compass toward the heading Ian had given him to find the real *Asgard's* location.

"Wake up, girls. Slumber party's over." Odin stood in the doorway of the old conference room, visible as only a silhouette in the moonlight.

Sarah coaxed her eyelids to open and heard Dr. Saenko scurry to her feet.

"Kell, this is ridiculous. I have to get back to my lab and make sure the holding tank is pressurized. You don't need to keep me here like a prisoner."

"You're right, Dr. I will escort you to the lab personally, as soon as I finish with this one."

Sarah pulled her knees toward her chest and pushed her palms into the rough wooden flooring. Splinters ate at her cracked skin, but she pulled herself up with fading strength.

"What are you doing with her?" Dr. Saenko's arm shot in front of Sarah like a gate at a train crossing. "She can't hurt anyone. Besides, Kiho may still be on his way. We might need her to get information from him."

"If Kiho knew what we were up to, and I doubt he really does, even he wouldn't want to save this ragged little girl. Do you think the premiere researcher for the top marine recovery agency would compromise this sea and all of its delicate ecology for one girl? He'd kill her himself if it meant saving this ocean."

Sarah gave Dr. Saenko's arm a light push, lowering it out of her path. "It's okay, Doctor. This scraggly girl could use a walk."

"This is the end, you know. He's not coming for you, Sarah," Dr. Saenko whispered and helped her to her feet.

Sarah pushed past Dr. Saenko and met Odin at the door. She extended her wrists and tilted her head, letting out a gruff sigh as she did.

"I want to take you on a tour, Sarah," Odin said.

"Of the bottom of the Bering Sea, no doubt." She answered under her breath.

Odin stepped to the side and let Sarah precede him down the steps of the conference room to the deck of the ship. She descended the stairs planning each step, and realized why he hadn't bothered to grab her or tie her hands. The stairs were incased in a layer of slush that fought against her Timberland work boots. The railing was too cold to touch and she folded her arms around her body, feeling the diminished size of her chest and shoulders.

Sarah looked down at the steps, aware that stealing a glimpse of the horizon would land her a cold smack in the face from the wind and freezing rain.

"We're just going to the deck, Sarah. So you can get a glimpse of what I do here on this boat. My customers in China are very dependant on my services. So are citizens of China, and those of the United States. My fuel will bring them power."

"Your fuel will bring you power, nothing else." Sarah spoke with her head down, letting only the wind hear her.

Sarah's arms ached and her backbone felt like it would shatter in the cold. She nearly fell when she finally reached the deck.

"Don't worry, I got you Sarah." Odin grasped her arm and pulled her upright. "I want you to see the horizon where China will appear soon."

Sarah let Odin pull her across the deck of the ship. Her head felt dizzy and she tried to ignore the black splotches and silver streaks that danced before her eyes. She felt her shins knock against cold metal piping several times, but dared not stop to rub them.

"Do you see anything out there, Sarah?"

Sarah hadn't noticed she was leaning against the ship's railing until her waist began to freeze against the wet metal.

"Of course you don't see anything." Odin positioned himself behind her and reached around her body, placing both of her hands against the banister. "There's nothing out there. Sure, China will pop up eventually, but it'll take at least a day. Until then, it's nothing but us and the cold, dark sea. Funny, but as desolate and vast as this sea is, it just doesn't seem big enough to share with a tree hugging, uneducated little bartender."

Sarah blinked herself awake and suddenly realized her situation. She pulled her hand up against Odin's and felt her flesh tear where it had frozen to the beam.

"Come on, Sarah, you know I don't have room for extra passengers. And this will be a good stop for you. It'll only hurt for seconds, then your body will warm up—and who knows, you and your friends from that crab boat may have a little reunion."

"Sam," Sarah whispered. She envisioned him edging to the supertanker to rescue her.

"Don't worry, Sarah. Dr. Kiho is invited to the reunion too." He pushed his body against hers and pulled her hands from the railing, holding them out into the air. "Now give me a little jump so you don't hit your head on the side and bloody the water."

Sarah wanted to spin around. Her mind screamed, but her body stood frozen, not even shivering anymore. She felt Odin's body warm her back and she fought the decision to take the cold sea over his body heat.

"Time to go, Sarah Reid."

Sarah felt her feet leave the ground and her hands grasped at nothing but air. When she hadn't hit the water yet, she guessed that she had learned to fly, or had already drowned. Then a heavy object pounded her in the gut and sent her to the unmistakably hard floor of the *Asgard*. She opened her eyes to see a coiled rope the size of her torso pinning her to the ground. A bronze hand flew over the railing, followed by a black boot that landed in the head of Odin's silhouette.

"I'm here for the reunion." Sam's voice followed a fist into Odin's stomach.

Sarah pushed the rope aside and crab-walked under the spotlight on the ship. She rubbed her arms and blinked her eyes.

"Sam?" she said.

"Not now, sweetie, I'm fighting," Sam's voice replied from the distance.

Sarah watched Odin reach for his radio, and Sam's hand swat it into the sea. Odin kicked at his feet, trying to sweep him to the ground, but Sam had obviously found his sea legs and jumped over Odin's foot. He landed another punch into Odin's stomach and threw him to the ship's deck.

Large green circles filled Sarah's eyes and she could no longer make out the two figures in the light. She listened for Sam's grunts between the sliding of feet and the night winds until she finally gave herself up to sleep.

"Sarah, wake up, we have to get below deck." Sam lifted her shoulders and carried her to her feet.

"How did you get here? Where's Odin?"

"Odin's knocked out but he'll be up soon. We have to get to that lab and vent the methane collection pipe before it explodes."

"We have to get out of here," Sarah said. "This place is crawling with bad guys. We're headed to China."

"Soon, Sarah. Let's get you inside first."

Sarah felt a heavy, warm coat weigh her nearly to the ground. Sam's arm followed over her shoulders and her body crept to life.

"Dr. Kihomi," Dr. Saenko called from the stairs to the conference room. Her heels clicked on the frozen steps and the sound resonated across the metal piping that wove across the supertanker.

"Dr. Saenko." Sam stopped and pulled Sarah into his chest for warmth. "What the hell's going on? You realize the *Asgard* clone you sent after me got swallowed in a giant methane bubble."

"I know." She came to a stop in front of him and panted

clouds of hot breath into the air. "I heard Sarah on the phone with you earlier. You have to go back there. We have to vent the pipe or the entire pipeline will erupt. It runs for miles along the seabed. It's enormous."

"Mother of God, Saenko, why the hell did you let Odin do this?"

"Please, Sam, you have to vent that pipe."

Sarah pulled her head from Sam's chest to join the conversation, and in the moonlight caught Odin's silhouette rising to its feet. She tugged at his shirt and felt his head tilt down and his breath warm her head.

She looked up. "Odin's coming."

"Shit, Sam, I'll hold him off, you have to get to that pipe."

"Me? No way, Saenko. You can't take Odin on your own."

"We don't have much time, Sam. If I can get to the lab, I can try to remote operate the pipe and vent it. The pipe is back where you saw the other ship sink. If I can't vent it, you're our only hope. There's a manual shut off valve halfway down the pipe, about 50 feet under the water. We use a mechanical arm to turn it."

"And how the hell is Sam supposed to turn it that far down in freezing water? Does he look like he's wearing a dry suit and a submersible?" Sarah said.

"Odin's coming," Dr. Saenko said. "There's a way off this ship. Follow the main pipeline aft to the chopper. You can fly, can't you Sam?"

"I've never flown an S-76D, this must be brand new."

"Well it's your only hope."

Dr. Saenko shoved Sam's body forward, and Sarah nearly stumbled to the ground. Odin's silhouette disappeared under the moonlight and she felt a nervous chill run up her back. It gave her the strength to hurry Sam to the chopper.

The stern of the ship rested a hundred yards in the distance and the night seemed to grow darker as they approached the black helicopter. The wind pushed through Sarah's clothing and she hurried with it to the giant aircraft. Sam pulled the door open and lifted her inside. The passenger's seat was cold and Sarah clenched her teeth together, enduring the pain.

Sam jumped in the pilot's seat and clamped a huge pair of headphones over his ears. He handed Sarah a similar pair and they froze her temples. In the darkness, he punched several buttons on the front console and light finally appeared in the cockpit.

"You really know what you're doing?" Sarah crossed her arms over her chest and looked outside at the growing waves of the Bering Sea.

"I've flown these things before, but for some reason, I didn't feel like telling Saenko that."

"I don't really trust her either. She's setting you up to vent that pipe. You can't do it, Sam. It's a kamikaze mission."

"Let's just get this bird in the air and worry about that later."

The rotor began to whirl and pulse like a heartbeat through the cockpit. It grew faster and faster and Sarah felt the deck underneath begin to sway.

"Sam, the storm's coming and the boat's not steady, can we take off?"

"That's the beauty of a chopper, Sarah. Don't need a runway, just need to lift off." Sam pulled the collective stick and hit the throttle, forcing the helicopter off the supertanker and into the air.

The higher the aircraft rose in the air, the more daunting the Bering Sea looked. Sarah felt the chopper push forward while stiff waves toyed with the supertanker below. Beneath the ship and pointing south, a bright white arrow seemed to point underneath the water.

"Is that the pipeline Saenko was talking about?" Sarah pressed her forehead against the cold window and let it ease her throbbing head.

Sam craned his neck over her. "No, oh my God, no."

"What, Sam? What is it?"

Sarah's head suddenly thumped into the window as the helicopter jerked to one side.

"That white streak is methane…the methyl hydrate could be breaking."

"But isn't that catastrophic? Won't we get caught in tsunamis and volcanoes and earthquakes and…"

"Saenko is right, but we're not screwed yet. If it's bubbling up so badly that we can see it from the air, we have to get to that pipe and vent it—we only have seconds. Releasing the pressure could be the only way to…"

"Sam, look," Sarah shouted, jabbing her finger into the glass of the window. "The *Asgard*, I think it's…"

"That's exactly how the other one went." Sam leaned on the cyclic stick and punched the helicopter forward. "We have to get to the *Adrienne Anne.*"

Sarah watched in silence as the waves grew larger than the *Asgard*. They rose over the ship like a jagged mountain range with crests of white foam on the tips that looked like snow.

"Brian's still out there? The crew could be dead by now."

"It's just Ian and Simon with him, and if they took my strong suggestion to get the hell out of there, they could be far enough away."

Sam raced through winds that pushed the helicopter and Sarah listened for the rotor, praying that it would not skip a beat. The sea below seemed to calm as they passed the sweep of white foam that crept from the seabed.

Embedded in choppy waves, Sarah spotted a tiny toy boat.

The *Adrienne Anne* fought to stay upright in the torrent, but it had escaped the path of the methane gas.

"Hang on, Sarah."

She felt the helicopter descend toward the ship. "Sam, we're not gonna land on Brian's ship, there's no room."

"We can do it, assuming those crab pots stay put."

The helicopter wavered in a surge of heavy winds until the left skid scraped against the top layer of metal crab pots stacked several pots high.

"I don't know about this, Sam." Sarah scrunched her eyelids closed and held on to the seat.

Sam toyed with the torque pedals and quieted the throttle until the helicopter balanced firmly on the top row of crab pots. Sarah opened one eye to the figure of Simon Watson in the wind. His fist wrapped on the door to the chopper until she pulled it open against the wind.

"Get out, quick before these pots fall over," he yelled through the whirr of the rotor.

"Go ahead Sarah."

Sam helped her ease out of the seat and Watson immediately cinched a thick boat rope to her waist. She followed the rope with her eyes into the ship's spotlight. Chips of ice cracked off the cable, but it remained securely tied to the ship's crane.

"Come on, Sam," Sarah called into the helicopter. "You have to get out fast."

"No, Sarah. I have to find that pipe and vent it."

"Sam, that's crazy, you're in a helicopter and the valve is fifty feet under water."

Sam leaned toward Sarah who stood in the doorway. He took her hand and looked into her eyes for several seconds.

"Sam, get out of the chopper."

"Sarah, you know we have to turn the release lever and vent the pipe. I can find the pipe from the air."

"And then what?"

"Tell Brian to listen for me on the radio. And don't worry so much."

Sam gave her a slight shove into Watson's arms and swung the helicopter door shut. Sarah pulled at Watson to free herself, but was forced to kneel and cover herself as the chopper took off, whipping a tornado of frigid air overhead.

Chapter Twenty-Nine

Sarah pushed the wheelhouse door open with her elbows. She cradled a hot mug of watery coffee in her hands and bowed her face into the steam. She lifted her eyes to see Brian and a Coast Guard officer hovering over a pile of Sam's maps. His helicopter passed overhead and disappeared to the north.

"He'll follow the trade route to China, that's where the first fissure is marked on this map," Brian said.

"Your guy is amazing, I'll give you that, but none of this research and recovery was sanctioned, so even if you do find him and this fissure, there's not much we can do for you. We weren't expecting a man-made disaster, and we certainly weren't expecting our boat to be stolen."

"Sam knows what he's doing without your help," Sarah said. She walked closer to the men and looked at the map. After a short pause, she set her mug down and turned the map at an angle, folding the upper right corner. "Along the fold—that's where the pipeline runs. It took another of Odin's supertankers closer to China. Odin was on it. He's dead. Sunken."

The two men stared at Sarah, who spoke as if she was in a trance.

"Sam's going to find the exhaust valve. There's a manual release lever 50 feet down the main collection pipe, underwater. If he releases the pressure, a cloud of deadly gas will vent in the air and probably kill a couple birds, but if he doesn't vent it, the whole pipe network will explode and we'll all be dead."

"Nice to have you back, Sar," Brian said. He squinted his eyes and bowed toward the corner of the map, close enough to kiss it.

"Kiho can't get to that valve in a chopper, and we didn't bring dive gear. The sea's getting rougher down there and if there's really methane gas spewing out at will, our divers wouldn't survive the trip anyway. I'm Lieutenant Haber." The Coast Guard officer extended his hand to Sarah.

"Odin's ship had three submersibles onboard. That's how they worked on the pipe," Sarah said.

Brian stared at the map for several seconds and tapped his index finger at it with increasing force. With one final bang, his eyes met Sarah's. She opened her mouth to talk to him, but instead he shoved her aside and skirted his way to the sonar console.

"Captain Eriksson, what are you looking for?"

"Submersibles."

Sarah felt a giddy chill run through her stomach and she looked at Brian as if he had grown ten feet tall. "Bri, are we doing what I think we are?"

"Sarah, get a coat on and tell Watson to start securing those crab pots on board. He can use the cord inside the pots to tie them together. Tell Ian to help him…and tell them to get the crane ready. Lieutenant, with your permission, or without, we're going fishing for submersibles."

The lieutenant's mouth hung open and his body stuttered to react.

"Aye Capt'n," Sarah said.

Sarah leaned against the rear windows of the wheelhouse, watching Ian and Watson fight the wind to balance atop a host of frozen crab pots. Her heart jumped with every slide of the men's feet across the three-story metal structure. But it was easier to watch Ian and Watson than it was to keep an eye over Brian's shoulder and search for Sam's helicopter.

The *Adrienne Anne* huffed against increasing winds, a good sport sailing into the storm. Pencils, coffee mugs and papers slid to the floor and rolled along it as the ship shifted from left to right, and Sarah held tightly to the railing along the window.

"I don't think we can do this," The lieutenant said. "We're still a few miles away and this ship's not going to hold up against the storm.

"Don't worry about the ship, Lieutenant, my girl can hold her own. We are gonna need a few extra deck hands though, if you wouldn't mind getting your crew out of my galley and up on deck."

"You've already broken enough laws to get your license revoked, Eriksson. Endangering my men onboard this tub will only get you into more trouble."

"Well, sir, that attitude isn't gonna get your name on my Nobel Peace prize. And as for your men, sitting their asses down in my galley instead of helping to man this ship isn't exactly a safety measure. Did you train this crew personally?"

"Is that the chopper?" The lieutenant pointed to a blip on the screen.

"That's Sam. See? We're closer than you thought."

Sarah turned toward the men's conversation. "If the Coast Guard won't help, I'm getting down to the deck. That stream of white bubbles down there is methane, which means this is close to where the first ship sank, and the submersibles can't be far."

Brian stared at the lieutenant, then turned to face Sarah. "Okay, kid, it's been a few years, so I hope you remember how to be a deckhand. Cover your face with extra immersion gear and get your ass down there. I'll signal when I see the sub. Ian and Watson will help you with the crane."

"You're letting that girl go down there alone? She's obviously exhausted and probably injured."

"She's a good deckhand—worked on the *Westender* for years."

Sarah pulled on a huge immersion suit that flopped over her body. She tucked reams of the thick fabric into her work boots and secured her laces around her ankles. She tightened the shoulder straps as far as they would go, then crossed them over her head to the opposite shoulders, giving herself a little less room inside the suit. She grabbed the heavy coat Sam had given her and pulled it over her shoulders. It reached down to her knees. She scanned the wheelhouse until her eyes landed on a pair of rubber-coated work gloves. Sarah placed Brian's large glove over her nose and mouth and tied it in place with the lanyard that held the wheelhouse keys.

"How do I look?" she mumbled through the layers of fabric, then strode out of the wheelhouse.

The *Adrienne Anne* tossed more than she expected, and she pulled up her sleeves to clamp the railing with her gloved hands.

Sarah's final step from the staircase slid her to the port side of the ship, then tossed her on her knees to the starboard side. She pulled herself up and dusted her knees, reminding her feet to stop toward the deck winch on the starboard side. Once her hands were secure on the handle of the deck winch, she waved to the tower of crab pots on deck, signaling Watson and Ian in the light. She knew their hearts were pounding to watch her on deck alone.

In the pitch darkness and five-degree wind chill, Sarah warmed herself with the thought of Brian in the wheelhouse directly above her, watching the same water through the sonar screen. She began to recognize debris from the *Asgard* with her naked eyes. Pieces of metal piping banged into the hull of the *Adrienne Anne* and Sarah tried to pretend they couldn't rip through. She hoped the bodies on board were sinkers—she didn't need to see a dead hand float by.

The crab ship tried to push Sarah off her feet and she tried to keep her eyes on the water. The few free strands of hair that blew in front of her forehead caught the night air and froze against her face. They crackled when she moved.

"All done," Ian said from behind.

Sarah spun in shock that he had made it to the deck without her noticing. "Keep an eye on Brian then, will ya? And cover your face." She pulled a glove from her hand and smashed it into Ian's nose and mouth.

Ian let out a muffled grunt and pulled his shirt collar over the glove. The two exchanged an uncomfortable glance until their eyes turned on cue to see Brian waving like a drowning man through the windows of the wheelhouse.

"How long's he been doing that?"

"Quick Ian, signal Simon and help me get the ice off this winch. I think Brian's found the sub."

A pulse of freezing wind began to smack the back of Sarah's head and she turned to Ian who flinched to the beat.

"I think your boyfriend's here," he said. He pointed to an almost invisible chopper overhead.

Ian wrapped his body over Sarah's and she squirmed underneath him while she knelt to the ground under the wind of the descending helicopter.

"You secured those pots, right?" She spoke into Ian's chest.

"Jesus, Sarah, of course we did. Now keep your head down before your eyeballs freeze."

A hurricane gusted from the stack of crab pots and pushed into Sarah's ribcage. She jabbed Ian with her elbow, but he would not release his hold around her body until the wind began to slow and the beat of the rotor turned into a steady chop.

"Get off me," Sarah said. She pushed her back against Ian and found her footing on deck. In the ship's spotlight, she could barely make out Simon. Her eyes began to tear in the light.

"You're gonna break your hand doing that." Sarah didn't have to turn to know Ian was pounding at the deck winch with the heel of his hand, trying to break the ice.

"I don't see any subs, Sarah."

She turned to face the water and scanned the waves with Ian. The squealing sound of metal scraping against metal ripped through the dark night sky and Sarah could feel Watson positioning the crane.

"There's gotta be something if Simon's getting the crane ready."

Sarah watched more fragments of metal piping brush against the hull of the ship. They were more intact than she had expected, which told her that the supertanker went down easily, not tearing apart very much at all. Her tired eyes sent the illusion of sparks flying in front of her face, and the waves made her head spin. She rocked to their motion until the pang of thick work boots strumming the wire crab pots saved her from her stupor.

"Sam, you're back." She whirled around and gave him a squeeze.

"Where's the sub, Hawaii?" Ian brushed up behind Sarah, who inched forward, toward Sam.

"So, you guys figured out my plan. I was just about to ask you if you've found the damn thing."

"Brian was waving like an idiot a few seconds ago."

The three looked up toward the wheelhouse and simultaneously began hailing Brian, who stared back through the windows. Within seconds, he came bounding down the stairs clad in highway-cone orange with a neoprene scarf wrapped around his face.

"We found the sub with the sonar, but it's down there—possibly still attached to the supertanker."

Sarah paused to translate the muffled statement and squinted as if that would help her hear. "Can we get it?"

"Hell, we caught that sunken pot that held the *Westender's* crew, didn't we?"

"What, Ian?" Sarah's shoulders slumped. "Brian, what's he talking about?"

Sam met Sarah's gaze, then nodded to Brian, who looked stumped. "We'll explain it later, Sarah."

"You found the crew? Jack? Nate?"

"Later, Sarah. We have to find a submersible now...in a pile of *Asgard.*"

"Listen, I'll stick on the sonar like glue and send directions down through the intercom. Ian, signal Watson with the crane, and Sarah, you're in charge of the grappling hook. Sam, help her with the deck winch once she catches that sub."

"There's no tow line, Brian. It'll be near impossible to hook that sub," Sam said.

Sarah shifted her hips, aware that her clothing muffled the movement, and shot Sam a glare.

"She's the best fishermen I've ever worked with," Ian said.

"Well then, Sarah, work your magic and fast. From my bird's eye view, I'm estimating we have minutes before the entire network starts to collapse under the seabed. And we still have to pull that sub onboard and figure out a way to get it to that pipeline in this wind storm."

Ian kept an ear bent toward the intercom and flailed his arms periodically to Simon who had tied himself to the controls on the crane. Meanwhile Sarah planted her left foot through a half-inch of sleet on the deck of the ship and her right foot slightly behind it. She rested her weight in her quads and clutched a thick section of boat rope in her hands. A large metal hook dangled from the end. The wind whipped through free locks of hair and her eyes remained fixed over the ocean. Waves began to move, revealing larger chunks of the supertanker. Sarah guessed they were positioned right over the ship, and she placed a hand across her neoprene scarf, pressing it to her face.

"Now, Sarah," Ian yelled.

Sarah caught a glimpse of yellow underneath the churning waves and grabbed the rope, giving it a fierce whip. She thrust the hook into the water and a muted clank told her she'd landed her catch on the first try. Sarah's cracked lips formed a smug grin that she hadn't felt since her last fishing trip ten years earlier. She pulled at the hook and began to feed the rope through the winch.

"Sam, help me get this winch going—this thing's gonna be heavy, so keep an eye on the rope." The line was second nature to her.

Sam skidded into place and Sarah watched over him, still looking at Ian through the corner of her eye. Behind him, the long arm of the ship's crane began to move. She hailed Watson and Ian caught the crane's hook. Like clockwork, as the sub began to surface, Ian jabbed it with the line from the crane and Watson ordered the crane to pull it from the water.

After several minutes of sheer tugging, the submersible plopped on deck with a loud thud. With just a tiny slit to look out of, the sub looked more like a tomb than a means of transportation.

"Well, there's our ride," Ian said. "Who wants to christen her?"

"Can a human even fit in there? Where are the controls?" Sarah wrapped her hands around the hatch at the top, trying to pry it open.

Sam stepped up to the sub and pulled a release latch that sprung the hatch. "I believe this is my area of expertise."

Sarah had barely shot Sam an incredulous glare before Brian appeared on deck from the shadow of the ship's spotlight.

"Alright, Kiho, we got the sub, now what's the plan?"

"Unfortunately, we have to kick this ship into high gear and get in the middle of that pipe network." He pointed off-deck to a giant metal spider that weaved into the sea. "The collection pipe is in the center of that metal mess, and the waves are getting worse. I can work this sub, but the navigational system and the jets look busted. Without propulsion, I have no way to steer this sucker. The mechanical arm off the front of the sub is what they use to collect samples and work maintenance on the pipeline, so if I can get to the pipe, I can shut off the valve."

"Does the arm work?" Brian said.

Sam poked his head into the submersible and plunged his left arm inside shortly after. Sarah tried to listen for telltale sounds inside the craft but the whipping wind drowned it out.

"It should work. The insides don't look damaged," Sam said from inside the sub.

"But we still have a huge problem here, Hawaii. You just suggested that we hightail it into an aquatic war zone so you can play kamikaze in a sub with no navigation. How the hell are you going to get to the pipe? Or were you planning to paddle with that mechanical arm?"

"Ian's got a point, Sam," Sarah said.

Brian squinted into the ship's spotlight for several seconds and Sarah followed his gaze, trying to read the lines of experience in his face.

"You do have some kind of propulsion left, don't you?" Brian said.

Sam poked his head out. "Enough to scoot her left or right, but not enough power to drive it."

"Perfect, then. We keep this thing hooked up to the ship's crane. We'll use the GPS and the sonar to find the pipe and guide you to the valve with the line from the crane."

"Brian that's crazy," Ian said.

"Ian, get Watson down here for a briefing with Dr. Kiho. I've got a Coast Guard Lieutenant to baby sit and a ship to ride into a hell of a storm. And everyone, keep your mouths covered."

Brian nearly skipped to the wheelhouse. His lively gait passed an inexplicable calm over Sarah and she gave Ian a quick shove toward the crane, motioning with her head for him to hurry.

By late night, a yellow moon replaced what was left of the sun, and the only light that shone in the sea came from the *Adrienne Anne's* bridge. The air temperature had cooled to a frigid five degrees and the wind chill made that five degrees seem balmy in comparison.

Sarah hung over the railing of the ship's starboard side and scanned for the trace of yellow that came from Sam's submersible. The yellow line from the ship's crane pointed to it like an arrow, but the sea had swallowed most of the small craft.

"Sarah, get your ass up to the wheelhouse and help Brian. You're the only one who knows that supertanker and the pipeline as well as Sam," Ian said.

"I can't Ian. I'm worried. If that pipeline is even half as fragile as Sam says it is, won't the *Asgard* break it once it hits the bottom of the sea? I mean, the waves are pitching like crazy, but there's still not enough of a surge down there to keep the *Asgard* from hitting bottom."

"We're beyond worry now, Sarah. We have to put our faith in Sam and hope he vents that pipe."

"You're telling me to trust Sam? Wow, I guess we're in some

sort of a role reversal. While I'm being skeptical, what happens when that pipe vents noxious gas directly into the air where we stand?"

"According to Sam, our boat won't get swallowed like the others. We'll just have to cover up and get below deck. We'll leave the sub attached to the crane and cross our fingers that he's still there when we get back."

"How much air do you think he has in that sub?"

"Sarah, just get to the bridge."

Sarah stood up and stretched her back. She turned toward the wheelhouse and forced her tired legs to take her up the stairs. Once inside, the rush of propane heat washed her face in a prickly wave and she pulled the neoprene from her nose and mouth.

Brian sat at the sonar screen with his finger attached to a blip that wavered toward a giant blob that could only represent the *Asgard*.

"I hope your buddy can see better than we can down there," Brian said.

"Where's your Coast Guard buddy?"

"He's actually making himself useful. They got two guys up at the crane, keeping Watson steady, and the others helped tap me into some weather info. They've called back to home base to try and get some choppers in here, but they can't come near this area until the wind calms down and we vent that pipe."

"Sounds reasonable. Is that Sam?" Sarah sat next to Brian, well aware that it was Sam on the screen.

"I hate to say it, but I'm beginning to worry about this mission," Brian said.

As the last word rolled of his lips, a series of rogue waves pounded the *Adrienne Anne*. Sarah stumbled to the ground and Brian hugged the computer monitor.

"Dammit, Sarah. Another attack like that and we'll go offline again." He braced himself through the fierce rocking and steadied the monitor when it calmed.

"Those waves just mean we're getting closer. How's Simon?"

The two looked through the windows at a pile of men who scrambled toward the crane's controls.

"Sarah, this just doesn't look good."

Sam pulled the hot neoprene mask from his face and used it to wipe the sweat from his forehead. His watch told him that he had spent close to an hour and a half in the small sub and the overabundance of carbon dioxide in the cockpit confirmed it. He smeared a fresh coat of spit across the tiny window to keep his breath from obscuring his view. Ahead he could see the pipeline responsible for the destruction of two supertankers. He had spent the last hour and a half face-to-face with the pipe, unable to inch close enough to its valve.

"Send me down just three more feet," he said through the two-way radio the Coast Guard had let them use. His voice had trailed off to a sigh in order to conserve oxygen.

The radio crackled in response and Sam guessed that meant compliance. He hadn't heard an actual voice since he found the pipe.

Sam still studied the pipe. The outside of it was made up of copper, which he found peculiar. Bits of algae and paint peeled from the outer layer, revealing its golden color. He used his dive watch to tell he had sunk to 47 feet, but could not stop his eyes from trying to look up and down the pipeline. With only a snorkel-mask's worth of viewing space, looking up and down only awarded him the view of the submersible.

The sub lurched and shook, and Sam knew that the *Adrienne Anne* had received his command. He sunk inches at a time and the knot in his stomach grew. Sam tried once more to slide to a better sitting position, but the cramped sub wouldn't let him move. The muscles in his legs burned and he felt his broad shoulders bruise against the back of the craft.

Sam scanned the pipeline inch-by-inch as he sank downward, and he couldn't help but sing the theme to *2001: A Space Odyssey* in his head as he went. Every few seconds, the ocean elbowed his craft with a heavy surge, swinging it left and right, and out of position. He could only imagine what those waves looked like on the surface. *Trust Sarah and the crew,* he reminded himself.

After minutes of intense staring and praying through heavy turbulence, Sam caught sight of a long piece of metal that jetted out from the pipe—the venting valve. He wanted to jump for joy, but settled for an internal cartwheel instead.

"I found it," he radioed. "Hold me as steady as you can."

Sam forced his arm forward through the sub and grabbed the controls to the mechanical arm. With barely enough room to move in the sub, he operated the arm using the side of his right hand, limiting his dexterity. He gave the controls a measured tap and the arm wobbled to life. It reached for the valve and sweat formed again on Sam's forehead. The theme to *2001* played louder in his head.

Several attempts later, the arm finally brushed against the lever. Sam instantly clamped the metal hand over the lever and surveyed his accomplishment. The metal fingers barely closed over the end of the lever, promising that they would easily slip out of position as soon as Sam moved the arm. *Do I try for a better grip?* He knew a second attempt could mean losing any hope at grabbing the lever at all.

Sam took a moment to breathe, but in that moment, a loud metal roar woke his senses. *What the...* Sam immediately began swinging his head from left to right with his vision still obstructed in the sub. The scraping sound played again and Sam listened. He looked out the window at the metal hand that daintily held the lever and ate a deep breath out of the submersible's waning supply. He knew the *Asgard* was sinking on top of him.

"Brian, for Christ's sake, pull him out of there," Sarah screamed in Brian's ear. "The computers are saying the supertanker's moving downward. It'll break the sub free from the crane and we'll never get him back."

"I know, Sarah, but giving up now won't save us either. If we can't vent that pipe and release its pressure before the supertanker hits the seabed, the whole network will explode. And then we'll all be dead."

Sarah pounded her fist into the ship's console. "I can't watch from in here." She turned toward the door.

"Stop right there, Sarah Reid." Brian rose to his feet and stormed toward Sarah. "You're just like Kiho. Put your damn immersion gear on and cover your face."

"Right." Her voice shook.

Sarah slipped down the stairs, hitting her knees at the bottom. She sprang to her feet and leaned over the railing of the ship to look at the mess below sea level.

"What the hell are you doing here?" Ian said.

"The tanker's sinking. It's sinking on top of Sam. I don't know why, but I feel like if I keep my eyes on him, it'll help."

Ian stopped looking for Simon's signal and joined Sarah at the railing. "We don't have much time left to get this right, you know. I've been watching that debris too, and calculating how long Kiho's been down there and how much air he must have left. It was a crazy idea, Sarah. But I'm playing it to the end just like everyone else around here. There's no quitting this time—not for either of us."

Sarah looked into Ian's eyes, confirming that he wasn't just talking about Sam and the exhaust valve.

"Who said anything about quitting?" She bit back.

The two stared into the sea, accepting the occasional wet slap that came from the mist of the waves. They enjoyed a brief calm spot until the waves began to creep higher and soak the rags on their faces, instantly freezing them against the skin. At that, they stepped three feet backwards. Sarah slid to her ass and skated across the ship's deck and Ian was next to follow.

"Remember when these five-footers used to be big?" He brushed off his butt and steadied his body on his knees, motioning for Sarah to follow.

"They still are." She let her body flop backwards and stared into the ship's crane above her head.

"That one, um, that one looks like a ten-footer." Ian's voice rose to a scream and he pulled on Sarah's wrists, forcing her to her feet.

"Holy shit, Ian, it's a twenty at least."

The two clasped hands and ran toward the steps that led below deck, but the wave beat them to it. A rush of freezing water separated Sarah and Ian, washing them to either end of the ship. Overhead, Sarah could catch quick glimpses of the spotlight and she prayed that Simon still kept his footing.

The *Adrienne Anne* tilted to the left and right, and Sarah reached for anything to grab on deck. She settled for one of the crab pots and wound her numbed fingers around the steel cage. Encased in ice, she began to shiver like crazy. Her arms and legs flailed and she huffed a thick cloud of breath into the night air.

"Stop it, Sarah. Don't panic." Ian's voice wasn't far behind her.

"Another one," she said through a gasp.

A second wave crashed on deck, breaking just shy of Sarah and Ian. A pool of freezing water rushed at them, sending an icy blast up Sarah's legs that tore at her skin.

"I can't take much more of this Sarah. Is your mask still on?" Ian's voice rattled through his chattering teeth.

Ian, what's happening? Sarah asked in her head, aware that she hadn't said anything out loud. Hypothermia began to set in and Sarah's body started to warm to the cold water and air around her. Her eyelids dropped, but she forced them to stay open just enough to keep an eye on the sea. Wave after wave crashed into the *Adrienne Anne*. Some of them smacked her and stole her breath, while others just teased her, falling at her feet. Wind froze her mask to her face and Sarah could feel the icy outline that sealed it over her nose and mouth.

The waves persisted until they became so prominent that Sarah could no longer even hear them. They blended into her subconscious like white noise. She kept her eyes fixed on the sea until each wave blended into the next, and she no longer could see when another approached. Beneath her, the *Adrienne Anne* rocked, swinging her hands into and away from the crab pot. She felt warm blood rush across them, then freeze.

We didn't make it, Sarah thought to herself. Just as she relaxed her eyes from the sea, unable to see the waves anymore, a white ghost appeared to her. At first, it appeared as foam on top of the ocean's surface, but as she stared at it longer, it grew in height, until it appeared as tall as a giant geyser.

"Sarah, get the hell off your ass," Brian's voice finally turned her gaze and her eyes jumped to his face, bathed in the light of the ship's spot. "He did it, now get below deck."

Brian pulled Sarah from the crab pot to her feet and gave her a firm shake that woke her vision enough to see not a ghost, but a steady stream of white gas shooting toward the sky.

"Sam vented the pipe. And we're all gonna be gassed to death if we don't make it below."

Sarah's feet raced, kicked into motion by Brian, who shoved her from behind. Her brain awoke to dozens of questions, but her mouth was unable to form them.

"It's a damn good thing that mask froze to your face, girlie. Otherwise that gas would have killed you on the spot."

Sarah blinked to find herself already in the galley. A Coast Guard officer leaked warm water from a coffee mug over her nose and mouth. The ice around her face began to loosen and the raw burn of her skin brought her senses to life.

"Ow," she said through pursed lips.

"Well, you're lucky you're alive. Now stay awake with the others so we don't lose you to hypothermia."

Sarah looked at the officer, asking him with her eyes if everyone had survived. She asked if her body was still intact and if her legs had frozen off. She asked if they were still on the *Adrienne Anne* and if the boat was still functional. Then she asked about Sam, and her dry eyes tried to cry.

"Good, don't try to talk yet, you're frozen." The man laughed in response to all of her questions. "We got choppers on hold. They'll come in as soon as that gas disperses and we're closer to a safe zone."

We're headed away from the Asgard, Sarah told herself. Her eyes dropped and she breathed a weak breath into her freezing hands.

Chapter Thirty

"…and so based on the aforementioned data HALO retrieved from the supertanker, Asgard I, prior to it's sinking, it is clearly evident that Odin Energy had been using the guise of research to develop novel technology for extracting methane from the methyl hydrate crust on the Bering Sea floor. A network of tunnels below the crust had been filled with superheated carbon dioxide, which served as a heat source to allow the methyl hydrates in the crust to turn from ice crystals to a liquid/gas state, which was collected through an adjacent network and pumped to the surface vessel.

The data supports the theory that under pressure to increase supply, Odin Energy far exceeded the initial safety limits engineered into the technology. This overheated the carbon dioxide to sufficient measures which caused excessive decomposition of the crust. The increased extraction of methane caused the creation of cavernous pockets within the network. Recent seabed mapping shows that the collapse of one of these pockets led to the methane release which suffocated the crew of the Westender *in mid October. Further mapping at the site indicates that successive collapses of major portions of the methane network also caused the sinking of both Asgard tankers in the following weeks. And while large in scale in comparison to the first release, these larger collapses still affected only five percent of the total methane network.*

Unfortunately, these collapses created additional pressure on the remaining network, and all computer models indicated that without a major release of the methane within the network to equilibrate the system, that the entire network would collapse with little or no further provocation. Because the Bering Sea is located in a region of high seismic and volcanic activity, the consequences of such collapses would have been catastrophic. The amount of water displaced to fill the cavern resulting from the collapse would have been sufficient to create a moderate tsunami within all regions of the Bering Sea, and the seismic activity that would have been caused by the collapse is estimated to have been sufficient to create a tsunami within the Northern Pacific Ocean. Several models also indicate that such activity could have triggered volcanic activity at several of the more active sites along the "Ring of Fire."

Therefore, the crew of the Adrienne Anne, *along with the US Coast Guard and Dr. Kamuela Kihomi of HALO took it upon themselves to open the main methane release valve using a salvaged submersible from the* Asgard. *Dr. Kihomi and the crew of the* Adrienne Anne *returned with Coast Guard escorts, successful in their mission. Continued measurements at the site show that the pressures within the crust have been stabilized, and that some of the methane remaining in the network has begun to transition back into methyl hydrate. It is our hope that this process will continue until the crust in this region heals itself. Until further notice, the area has been government sanctioned for research only through HALO and its subsidiaries.*

As for the impact of the release of a large portion of methane gas into the atmosphere, Odin Energy has been required by federal regulators to forfeit all profits from future energy sales toward investment into the capture and sequestration of an equivalent amount of greenhouse gases from current processes.

Sam steadied the papers of his lab report in the crisp winds of Dutch Harbor and looked through his explanation of the *Asgard* project one more time before sealing it into a Tyvek envelope bound for Washington, D.C.

In the distance, a 130-foot house-aft crab ship sailed in front of the setting sun and glided to the dock. Sam squinted in the sunlight to see a figure emerge from the wheelhouse and saunter down its steps to the ship's deck.

"Ahoy there, Captain Reid. Did you manage to fill the crab tank this season?" Sam called to the ship. He placed his hand over his eyes as a salute, but more as a means to block the sun from his view.

"Dr. Kiho, do you dare doubt the *Westender*?" Sarah strolled closer to the stern of the ship while her deck hands guided it to the pier. "I told you I'd fill her with red kings. I think even Jack would be proud."

"Well, I have heard that you are the best fisherman on this sea."

Sarah tilted her head toward the pier, telling Sam to follow her. He watched her shed a thick orange jumpsuit, revealing her slender frame in a tight thermal T-shirt and a snug pair of jeans. She threw one leg over the ship's railing and climbed backward down the emergency rope ladder. Sam moved closer as she reached the pier, grabbing for her hand to guide her solid ground.

"Thanks, Sam." Sarah stood inches from him and leaned closer, but stopped just short of his body. "Your bags are here. You're leaving?"

Sam stepped back. "Well, now that we've secured the area out there in the sea, HALO needs me back home to save some other chunk of the world, I'm sure. I just finished my report and packed up my lab stuff. My flight leaves in three hours, so I came to say goodbye…and invite you one more time to come back to Oahu with me."

"What, and leave all this?" Sarah turned toward a cloud of thick, freezing mist that sat on the sea like an itchy wool blanket. "Really though, Sam, this is my home forever and always. Besides, Ian's due back with the *Adrienne Anne* in a few days. Don't you want to stay and see the look on his face when he gets beaten by a girl for biggest catch?"

"You certainly are a catch," Sam said with a laugh to let her know it was a bad line.

"Is the car picking you up at the Grand Aleutian?"

"Yeah, I'm going back to my nice, warm suite to wait for it. The GA has been great about hosting my guys from the islands. But I just had a hunch that you'd be back today." He closed the space between their bodies. "I'm glad I was right."

Sarah pulled off her gloves and placed an icy cold hand on Sam's cheek, forcing him to shiver against her. "So that hotel room of yours is pretty warm, huh?"

"It's downright tropical." Sam took her hands in his.

"And you have it for how long? Three more hours?"

Sam squeezed Sarah's hands and let a boyish grin creep over his face. "Sarah, for last time, would you care to come to the tropics with me?"

Sarah gave a quick glance to her ship and looked over Sam's shoulder at the Grand Aleutian hotel in the distance. "I think I can swing that, Dr. Kihomi."

The End